TWO FOR THE SHOW

Also by Jonathan Stone

The Teller
Moving Day
The Cold Truth
The Heat of Lies
Breakthrough
Parting Shot

JONATHAN STONE

TWO FOR THE SHOW

A THRILLER

THOMAS & MERCER

Text copyright © 2016 by Jonathan Stone

Published by Thomas & Mercer, Seattle

www.apub.com

Amazon, the Amazon logo, and Thomas & Mercer are trademarks of Amazon.com, Inc., or its affiliates.

ISBN-13: 9781503934856

ISBN-10: 1503934853

Cover design by Brian Zimmerman

Printed in the United States of America

*To my brothers Harlan and Mike, who couldn't believe I'd never been
to Vegas, and rectified the situation in memorable style.
Both are still avid fiction readers, I'm happy to say.*

*And to our mother, Judy, who always read little Jonny's poems, plays,
and stories with genuine delight and encouragement.*

Thanks all. And keep reading.

Any sufficiently advanced technology is indistinguishable from magic.

—*Arthur C. Clarke*

ONE

It's the strangest job you've ever heard of.

Stranger still, it's mine.

I've been doing it over twenty years. Which makes it a career, I guess.

Technically, I'm a detective. A private investigator. But not the kind you're thinking of. One client. Ongoing investigation. The case never closes. The job never ends.

I'm in the entertainment business. But not in the way you're used to thinking.

I work for a mentalist. A famous magician and stage personality who astounds members of his audience by knowing everything about them—who they are and where they work and who they share an office with and what cars they drive and *used* to drive and *want* to drive and what they just ate for lunch and who taught them in kindergarten and sixth grade and how much cash is in their wallets and what labels are on their shirts and skirts and where they were last night and who they were with, and most impressive of all, even what they're thinking about. Knowing their life situations and communicating with their dead relatives and relating uncanny details. Supernatural powers. Extraordinary ESP. Conversing with the Other Side. All of that.

We've worked Atlantic City. The Mohegan Sun. Branson, Missouri. Royal Caribbean cruises. Mississippi riverboats. Tours, television appearances, even a TV series loosely based on his life. It's been a lot of time on the road over the past twenty years. But for the last few of them, I'm glad to say, we've had our own exclusive venue here in Vegas. For that peculiarly American combination of miracle tent-show theatrics, slick overproduction, and celebrity, Vegas is true north.

Of course, there's nothing supernatural about it. I supply him with all the information. I get it for him with each show. I start with the credit card information from the advance ticket purchases—get the names, the addresses, their pictures, their basic life facts. But that's just a start. I dig in. Hacking new Internet databases, my job gets easier every month. And of course, I follow up with traditional detective work. Tailing. Snooping. Shadowing . . .

What my boss *does* have is an extraordinary memory. A memory that he trains, works out with every morning, and exercises onstage every night. Seeing the face triggers the facts for him. Triggers the account numbers in the mark's pocket. Triggers the names of the kids and the dog and the cat and the recently deceased uncle and the homebound aunt, all of which I've provided him with. He takes it from there. Inserts the theatrics, the lighting, the shock and awe.

So yes, I'm kind of a detective . . . and kind of in the entertainment business . . . and I'm also kind of a biographer. I supply biographies—quickly, efficiently, digging out family secrets by the quick shovelful, looking around in the darkness to make sure no one will see. I get the information to him nightly. We have a smooth, untraceable mechanism for that, which has evolved considerably over the past twenty years. Today, it comes to him disguised as an online brokerage or bank statement. He has his private "account" password, of course, like any online bank or brokerage customer.

His "statement" comes from a website only he and I know, which I nevertheless change frequently for added security. No one questions his right to the privacy of his finances—or his mildly neurotic habit of checking them daily. Not his wife, not his children. My employer, after all, is in the magic business to make money (the best magic of all), and no one questions his daily assurance to himself that he is in fact doing so. As the years have passed, where others in our position might naturally have become less cautious, we've only gotten more so; included in his "statement" will be the information directing him to where his next "statement" will be.

I never see him in person. I can't risk being seen in the same room with him. I spend my life avoiding him—professionally. I have no contact, no intersection with him, except for the information I provide him in this secure, circuitous way. I could never risk attending his show, although of course I watch him on television. My anonymity, my invisibility, is obviously essential to the enterprise.

And obviously, I work alone. (Never has that statement been so profound. It probably explains this need to communicate, to reach out, that you are witnessing here.) Presumably there are people doing a similar job for other "mentalists" and "magicians," guys just like me, but I don't know that for sure, and of course we can never know each other. These possible, theoretical colleagues—who are not really competitors, who would be wonderful to commiserate with, swap war stories with—I can never know them.

In twenty years, my employer and I have been face-to-face only twice.

And have spoken only once.

On the morning he hired me.

I was a kid—still in college, going for a degree in computer science and forensic research. This was the one time *he* was the detective. He'd done his homework. I was an only child and my parents had both passed away—my mom recently from lung cancer and my dad in a highway accident when I was very young—but I was independent and self-sufficient and inner-directed even when they were alive. The perfect candidate. The perfect background. He looked at me, made crystal clear how this was a one-time, all-or-nothing, for-life decision. His look said that he meant it. That he knew what he was talking about. And he did; he was right.

And as he has grown more popular, the prospect of our *ever* meeting again—exchanging greetings, sharing a drink or a meal—has grown more remote. Has become impossible, merely a fantasy, an idle dream. But we need each other. We care about each other. We respect each other. And that need, care, and respect have only deepened over the years. Something I can only sense on his part—because we've never actually spoken since that first meeting.

It's the ultimate symbiotic relationship, but one that takes place at a distance. Does it end only when one of us dies? Not even then. He can't risk showing up at my funeral and revealing any possible connection between us. As I can't risk showing up at his, only for some inquisitive type to realize it was not magic and mentalism but computer hacking and fraud—probably ending his estate's ability to generate income, which wouldn't be right for his heirs or mine (if I someday have any, that is).

We are partners in the truest sense—each unable to proceed or succeed without the other. And despite his fame and my anonymity, we hold enormous power over each other. He is nothing without me. I am nothing without him. We are each other's secret. Each other's best friend, each other's lurking nightmare. A secret shared with no one else. We are brothers who never share a story or a beer, but who are nevertheless everything to one another.

Secrecy, silence, discretion—they're obviously a way of life for me. For twenty years now, I've known nothing else. I'm a professional ghost. And because I have not yet decided, as I write this, exactly what I will be doing with this document, what its ultimate use will be—and in light of a professional habit of protective silence and secrecy and shadow that I am already, somewhat uncomfortably, jeopardizing here—I'll refer to my employer, for the moment any-way, for the purposes of this record, as . . . oh, I don't know, let's call him Wallace the Amazing.

I live nicely. He pays me well. I have a simple but beautiful three-bedroom condominium on a golf course here in the desert. Few have ever seen it. (I've seen Wallace the Amazing's home, of course. Every room of it. On TV specials. Behind him in interviews.) My neighbors rarely ask me what I do. For those few who tentatively inquire, I answer proudly, cheerfully, honestly, "Computers." They look terrified that I'll elaborate, that I'll lose them in technology, so I'm quiet, and they seem happy to leave it at that. There are so many ways to make a buck, after all, and my Las Vegas neighbors seem to intuitively and readily accept that. Las Vegas, interestingly, is a place where the lines are very fluid between work and retire-ment, between full time and part time, between employed and unemployed, between flush with cash and tapped out. People here readily accept all kinds of unusual financial angles and ways of mak-ing money. Which makes it an easier place to avoid discussing or revealing what I do to pay my bills.

And what do my neighbors see, in their lightning glances and assessments, if they notice me at all? Someone trim, compact, neatly groomed, unremarkable. A bland second-tier type, not instantly desirable or attention-getting, perhaps, until my generation begins to age and the big, charismatic alpha males grow bellies and jowls and limp from old athletic injuries and I start to look pretty good in comparison. A beta male of lean muscle and unflashy efficiency and steadiness, built for the long haul. A beta male who earns a second look, a subtle appraisal and approval from alert women who catch my warm eyes, my hospitable smile. So for the sake of my profes-sion and our cautious secrecy, I must look down, turn away, try my best not to draw that approval, try to suppress my smile.

Not always successfully. Debbie saw it, after all. Debbie, my sometime companion. A television-commercial actress who people sometimes think they've met at a party or seen in a department store, but in fact they only know her—vaguely, unidentifiably—from the television screen. Her gift is looking like anyone, and being no one. Filling out a crowd. Fitting into generalized fantasies and thirty-second tableaux of beauty, outdoor health, youthful fun. With her knack for seamlessly fitting in, the perfect accompaniment to my own inconspicuous existence.

She doesn't know what I do for a living. I explained early on that I couldn't tell her, that I'll never be able to tell her, that she'll have to simply accept that fact if she wants us to continue to see each other. But I assured her it is legal and causes no pain or harm—in fact, quite the opposite: it creates considerable nightly charm and joy in the world—and she knows me well enough now to know I'm telling the truth, and so she accepts it. Accepts my terms, sensing it's the truth.

(I know the time bomb that ticks within our intimacy, that dooms us. I know that this enforced, insistent privacy of mine will eventually be the wedge between us, driving ever deeper, forcing us inevitably apart. Her effort to get close to me—to fully know me, to understand me—will eventually, paradoxically, push her away. My necessary secrets hang between us, and those same secrets, I know, keep me from feeling closer to her. I know how easily I can be returned to the occupational loner existence I previously inhabited and mastered—trolling the supermarket aisles by yourself, a drink or two in a sports bar where you are asked nothing about your profession. A mode of existence I know too well.)

We've been seeing each other almost a year now. Our life is quiet, unobtrusive, insular—of necessity. A small, rotating circle of merely casual friends. The two of us running laps together in the morning around my housing complex or swimming them together afternoons in the complex pool. Drinks in the red desert sunset. And always my work—obsessive, necessary, anxious, utterly unknown.

The second time I saw him face-to-face—well, the second time will give you a little more of a taste of Vegas itself, a little more about the tone and texture of our existence here. And a little more about that moment of belief that I see on many of your faces as the television camera pans the audience—thinking it's a sixth sense or special power or tapping a primitive portion of the brain, or assuming it's a trick but still shelling out eighty-five bucks a head to experience the spectacle and joyous mystification at how he does it—and how that belief extends well beyond our packed theater to encompass and characterize a whole city and way of life. People think of Vegas as a godless place—as the epitome, the ultimate expression, of godlessness—but it is in fact a desert brimming over with belief. Belief in good luck, faith in good fortune or a turn of fortune, belief in your flush destiny or just your destiny of a flush, and blind faith and trust in such demigods as Wallace the Amazing. (All the gaudy marriage chapels—that's pure faith. Faith that it will work this time.)

Vegas, in its impersonal nature, its majestic blandeur, its happy democratic night blindness, is also a particularly welcoming town. Send me your perverts, your lunatic fringe, your miscreants yearning to breathe free.

So in Vegas, mobsters like Big Eddie are an accepted part of the desert landscape, well known for their brightly blooming local color—Eddie in his lime-green, cherry-red, or mauve leisure suit, massive jowls pendulating below the wide, starched collar. A bright desert flower giving off a stifling scent of aftershave if you get close enough to smell its petals. A desert flower whose thick stalks end in meat-hook hands whose previous activities you don't want to ponder too closely.

For the several years we'd been in Vegas, Eddie had been a regular at Wallace's show. Regularly brought an entourage, and it was hard to say whether he did it primarily for the entertainment and pleasure of his guests or as a clever method of disguising his own obsession with Wallace the Amazing. Because it can become an obsession. Imagine that you're a nun-educated Catholic boy before getting swallowed up in street life; think how easily you'd get caught up in the thrill, the Lord-like prospect, of actually being able to read someone's mind. And you brood about it, this godly ability, and the mobster mentality, as always, posits, *How can I convert that, how can I use that, what's in it for me?* Wallace honored and rewarded Eddie's obsessive commitment by not calling on him, not exposing him, and I'll bet Eddie figured it was because the Amazing could see into his soul and his past and would of course not want to embarrass him by going there onstage. We did, however, call on a guest or two of Eddie's every so often, and their amazement only ramped up Eddie's obsession.

We should have known or guessed that his obsession was leading somewhere. But we didn't. We're not psychic. So after a show, when a little contingent of Eddie's henchmen grabbed Wallace in the parking lot, it caught me—and Wallace, of course—unaware.

Normally in Vegas, you'd have cameras everywhere—mounted by the dozen throughout a venue, in the hallways and restrooms, canvassing the parking lot. But cameras would make our audience suspicious. They would assume the cameras were spying on them, revealing details, helping with the act, and therefore undercutting it, so part of the appeal of our show is "No Cameras," no surveillance, no extra eyes. Wallace and I had debated putting a transmitter in the toe of his Topsider, or using a micro-camera disguised as one of the white buttons of his purposely conservative everyman button-down shirt, but that had risks too great, could bring all the wonder to a crashing halt, if someone—anyone—caught on. (The municipality insisted on cameras; Wallace insisted on none. Wallace, the super-tax-paying, high-revenue-generating Wallace, won.)

Even from my quiet remove on the fifteenth fairway, I suspected almost immediately it was Eddie behind it. Eddie, who had purchased tickets for that night's show, as I discovered when I searched my databases, but had not shown up for it, which indicated last-minute indecision, maybe a shifting, conflicted abduction plan of some sort. *Should I be there for the show? Should I not be?* I had researched Eddie and his henchmen previously, knew their names and addresses. I started to check credit card purchase patterns for Eddie and his henchmen, and they turned out to be highly irregular in the hours preceding Wallace's disappearance. (How do I access their credit card records? More on that later.) A stop for gas at a station not on their regular route. A similarly irregular purchase at a hardware store none of them had ever been in before—rope, tape, locks, and a chain, the receipt said. (Hmm. Gee.) But the big giveaway was the fast food—tacos, Chinese food, pasta, chicken marsala. Probably would have paid cash normally, but there were four entrées—which told me four people and that, however I chose to proceed, I'd have to be four times as careful.

Of course, the fact that no one can know I have any connection to Wallace, the fact that I must remain a ghost, means I can't call up his friends, can't make investigative calls to hotels or restaurants, can't trace his whereabouts like a traditional detective—but it puts me at a great advantage for actually helping. No one knows I'm there.

Which let me get fairly close to the house where they had him stowed—stowed to do Eddie's bidding, presumably. To read the minds of poker players at a high-stakes table or of a jewelry store owner with a combination safe, to place some big bets, help them pull off a heist; to answer Eddie's questions about horse race or football game outcomes; or all of the above. To be the infallible criminal asset that Eddie had probably dreamed of since boyhood. Eddie was living in a *Superman* episode. Thinking, *This is all I need to become a criminal mastermind.*

Looking in the house's generous bay window with a high-powered nightscope (I have the toys—but just the scope, no weapon attached), I watched. Just the thugs—talking, watching television—and no Wallace, from which I concluded that he was locked away somewhere else in the house. I watched until one of the thugs knocked on a closed door, and I could see him mouth some words at it and cock his head next to it for a response. I smiled with a quick satisfaction. Wallace the Amazing: found.

I waited, patiently. With the patience, the altered sense of time of a man who passes unmarked, unnoticed, undifferentiated hours in front of a computer screen.

I waited until all the lights in the house went out, and I waited some more.

Then, moving around the far side of the house, I could see a small, high window that, given the simple layout and dimensions of a desert house like this, must be to the room behind that closed door. The window was too small to fit through. But I could approach it pretty safely in the cloudless night. (Don't get me wrong, though— my heart was pounding; I was terrified. You never know what thugs will get it in their heads to do; unpredictability is part of their charm.) In a moment, I was looking through that small window at Wallace the Amazing, and he was looking at me, face-to-face for the first time in years. I knew of course what he looked like. It took him a moment to know it was me, because he hadn't seen me since I was twenty. We both looked at the small window grimly. The window between us. That we couldn't risk raising our voices to talk through.

It was one of those desert houses thrown up by the hundreds in the fifties and early sixties—the very start of the booming, blooming desert, the first wave of settlement. Its indistinguishability, its sameness and invisibility, made it a perfect hideout. It also made it vulnerable. Because it was one of those classic pre-slab, pre-condo Western desert houses with stucco walls but a wooden floor—meaning it was raised up a few feet off the sand (so the varmints and bugs don't get in), and you can crawl past the flimsy wooden trelliswork and underneath it pretty easily.

Wallace pointed to the floor. I nodded. But I was way ahead of him.

I'd brought the tool bag I keep in the car with me. Some screwdrivers, some wire, some lock-picking pins and punches and pliers, and the most primitive tool in it, a crowbar. Quietly, carefully, now crouched beneath the house, I jimmied the crowbar between the floor joist and a wide, soft, aged plank of fifties flooring. As I levered the crowbar down, I watched the plank begin to lift up, cooperatively, with only a low, unsuspicious squeak that could merely be the old house's inveterate protests in the desert wind. As I began to loosen the second plank, the first one began to lift up above me, as if magically (Wallace assisting silently from above), and with the second plank loosened, Wallace now slipped lithely through the opening—a nimble seal, like it was a trick he had rehearsed a thousand times. A magic act's trapdoor.

I tried to settle the two planks of wood roughly back into place but didn't spend long at it. The whole operation took less than a minute.

I motioned him silently to follow me. With four thugs only a few feet above us, we could not risk the sound or the time of even a quick exchange of greeting. We could be heard. We could be trapped. Twenty years, and here I am inches from Wallace in the darkness, but I could not risk even a few words. I put my finger over my lips to assure the silence, to protect him.

He looked at me, studied me for a moment, nodded his head affirmatively—with understanding *and* regret? Both, I choose to think.

And once we were out from beneath the house, standing in the yard for a fraught, suspended moment, enveloped in night and cool desert air and the mild fresh scent of the bougainvillea that gripped every nearby wall and fence, the sliver of desert moon above us waning cooperatively, leaving us in shadow, Wallace surprised me when he turned abruptly and took off. Striding almost arrogantly away from the front of the house. Where there was a good chance they would see him. Which, I realized later, is what he wanted. For them to see him, striding out—floating out—across the desert alone. Amazing.

"Hey!" two of the thugs yelled. Because they *did* see him. I cringed, expected to hear warning shots, see them running toward him—but the desert was pitch-black, and he was already too far away for them to catch. Too far away for them to stumble out into the darkness, then hustle back inside for their Escalade keys, hurry back out, rev it up, spin it around, and find him in a sweep of headlights. He disappeared around a hillock, into the darkness. He would undoubtedly get a ride from the next car. Maybe from a shocked fan, gratified to help. Who would, it occurred to me, as Wallace knew, more than likely spread the story, tell the tale.

He would become known for pulling off the miraculous, immaculate escape himself. The word would spread. The myth would grow.

Indeed, the whole episode only added to the Amazing's allure. Now he was not only a mentalist but an escape artist as well. A *real* escape, from gangsters with guns. He now added that skill to the magician's résumé, to round him out, to make him complete. The inexplicable, amazing escape only burnished Wallace's image, even for Eddie himself. It was proof positive to Eddie—who was jailed, of course, if only briefly, as a gesture, but interviewed ceaselessly in jail, his local celebrity revived, in telling the tale. Eddie didn't seem to mind, loved the attention, and here was proof he could wave in the face of the doubters that there was something otherworldly, not of this planet, in Wallace's abilities.

I watched Wallace go, just as the thugs did. I had expected to guide him out, of course, lead him through the dark to my hidden waiting car, to drop him somewhere civilized, somewhere safe. But he had turned away abruptly, silently. Even amid my rescue, maintaining our distance. With his silent turn, making a statement about preserving our arrangement. Not risking or jeopardizing or altering it—no matter what.

So instead, I watched him glide across the desert, before I turned and crouched in a run to my car. Still unseen. Still unknown.

TWO

The immense black-velvet curtain parts, *and he walks out unassuming, inattentive, lost in thought, as if unaware of where he is. He stands in the middle of the stage. A single spotlight bathes him in a fierce brightness, as if he were a medical specimen under examination. For ninety minutes, he doesn't move. Doesn't take a step. It's the antithesis of a stage show, of glitz and glimmer, and that's the point. That it is nevertheless—and all the more—riveting.*

"What you're about to see isn't really a show," he says. (Always the same opening: ritualistic, the call to worship, the opening prayer.) "It's a partnership. A meeting of the minds, a conversation that we are all a part of. It is a connection between us. A connection between us all that is close, and real, and precortical, and in fact the most powerful thing in our lives. A degree of human connection that is entirely unconscious for the fortunate majority of us, but alas, not for me. A connection that I can demonstrate but cannot explain. Every night I come out here with the same wish to explain it, and the same inability to explain it. It is weird, and odd, so weird and odd and inexplicable that it will trouble your sleep tonight, stay with you the rest of your life, but there is nothing I can do about that. I stand here in khakis and a blue button-down shirt and conventional shoes and a conventional haircut to try to make

it all less odd, more comfortable, which doesn't work, but at least I try. Is it a kind of dream state? Some kind of access to our common DNA?"

And then he simply starts. Scans along the front row and says, "Hi, Eleanor. Have we ever met?" A white-haired matron shakes her head eagerly, no. Already looks faint with anticipation. "So it may surprise you to know that I remember when you were a redhead." She smiles, and a murmuring tide of appreciation washes over the audience. "Clairol Shade 251"—her eyes widen—"and I remember when you were a blonde, Revlon Color Wheel 950." And her eyes widen even more, and now there is a rolling wave of laughter at Eleanor's mutable vanity so blithely revealed. "And did you know that sitting in row twenty-four tonight is a man named Rex Sterrett, who picked you up when you were a redhead, at a bar called the Hearty Seaman"—Wallace's eyebrow arching comically at the lewd potential of the bar's name, a responsive fresh wave of laughter, in on the joke—"in Red Hook—I kid you not, folks—Red Hook, New York, on Saturday, March 24th, in 2001. Stand up over there, Rex, look at each other, see if you remember each other. Be honest, now . . ."

And the audience by now is of course going crazy, going crazy because of what they have just seen, and going crazy because they know it is just beginning . . .

"You remember that redhead, don't you, Rex? And I'll remind you both, in case you do this one-night-stand thing a lot, which I know neither of you does, I'll remind you that it was snowing that night, accumulations of six inches, and you talked about, let's see . . ." He pauses. "*Rain Man*, the Cubs, Springsteen, but the snow gave you both the excuse of taking Rex's 1985 F-150 green pickup—remember that truck, Rex?—to your apartment, remember the hole in the leather driver's seat where you burned it with your lighter, Rex? And maybe we'll come back to you two later in the evening to hear what happened later in your evening, but I'm not going to do that to you now . . ."

The audience is roaring.

". . . because do you realize that on your way there you passed a house with toile curtains? The toile is a French barnyard pattern, by the way. Well, that house belongs to Elma Antonella, who's here tonight with her husband celebrating their fiftieth anniversary this weekend. Stand up, Elma." And an astonished older woman screams and obediently stands as if in her pew and the priest or Jesus or God himself has commanded it. "You know the curtains I mean, Elma?"

"Of course! Yes!"

"And Elma, that same barnyard toile is in two other houses of audience members here; it's the bedspread of"—he points—"Anna Durkin."

A blonde woman in a group of blonde women stands and screams, "Yes!"

"And it's the living room curtains of the Arthur Golds . . ." He looks across the room at Arthur and Bev Gold, whom he motions to stand, who do stand, shakily, stunned. "You see, we're all connected, we're all so close, we're intertwined, and we just don't know it; we pass one another unaware, but we have no degrees of separation, none . . ." His theme is connection, and he will go on like this for ninety minutes, connecting classmates, neighbors across fences, couples at adjacent restaurant tables, at the supermarket, on vacations, and it's stunning. "Amelia, you're wearing a brooch inherited from your grandmother, but it was made by the grandfather of Allan Wolf, in the fiftieth row. Look at the back, Amelia, look closely and you'll see the A. W. of Allan's grandfather, emigrated from Minsk, right, Alan?" Gasps, breathlessness, eruptions, paroxysms, an orgy of excitement and credulity and disbelief and belief.

As you can see, I do a pretty damn good job.

But so does he.

"Connection, it is all connection, incredible connection, it's a lesson to us, isn't it, the profundity of our connection to one another, whereas I am only a medium for it . . ."

And then, toward the end of the show, as always, his aw-shucks, I'm-just-like-you shrug. His earnest attempt to share the gift. To take everyone into it. To demystify it in a way that only mystifies it all the more. "That little coincidence that you notice, smile at, half dismiss, maybe mention to your wife or friend. The person you were just thinking about, calling you out of the blue on the phone, suddenly there in line at the checkout, brought up by a friend in conversation. An unusual word you just said to someone, suddenly there on the page in front of you. Your hotel room number is the same as your ATM PIN number. Your golf partner has the same birthday as your wife. Your gym locker number turns out to be your zip code. Someone you were just thinking about, suddenly coming toward you on the sidewalk, suddenly driving by the other way in her new convertible. The kind of little coincidence that makes even the practical, the pragmatic, the faithless, wonder for a moment about the inner clockworks of the world. I work inward or outward from the little coincidence. The little feeling in passing you get from that, a mild, free-floating anxiety or a frisson of fear or excitement—that's what I'm working from, curling in or expanding out from it like a nautilus shell. You wonder: Is there something? Something more to it? Something more you're not aware of, you're not seeing? Yes, there is. And I decided, from an early age, to pay attention. I sensed there was something there.

"It's those little synapses of connection, of one thing leaping inside you to be part of another, that are what I do, what I note, what I have learned to observe. Those coincidences are connection, the poor cousin, the poor relation, of deeper connection, but it's the same thing. Let me be clear: I am not reading minds. I am reading the coincidence, the surprising relationships of the human mind. What we dismiss as coincidence is connection, gently disguised so modern man can accept it, can handle it . . ."

And his closing—always the same. As the lights go down, the spotlight remains on him. "I'm glad you've come. I hope you've had a good time. But to really understand, to truly feel the full effect of the magic of this connection, well, you have to experience it personally . . ." And a second spotlight materializes out of his own, breaks away and skims suddenly across the crowd to land on a startled audience member, and after a moment of focusing, he continues. ". . . like Emily Baines. Thirty-three? Wirehaired terrier and Doberman? Planning a renovation? Still debating the Corian versus the marble, although your sister Anna says marble." And Emily is screaming, wide-eyed, and the audience is whistling, and Wallace says, "Connection. Good night." And the two spotlights, his and Emily's, go black.

Tent show, rock concert, maestro standing humbly by his instrument and taking a bow, all in one.

Wallace the Amazing.

His biography is well known. Easily accessible. Familiar without even knowing how you know it. Legendary. Archer Wallace. Poor boy of the American South. Nothing but sky, dirt, fields—nothing to distract him. Nothing to interrupt the development of his gift. No one to tell him he had a unique ability and frighten him or socialize him out of it. A simple but amazing past. One that I closely manage and monitor at all its Internet sources. Part of my job is to continually buff and shine and embellish this public biography—of simplicity, of giftedness, of springing astonishing and whole from the American landscape.

How does he do it? Rational people are challenged by him, to the point where it makes them uncomfortable, works on their assumptions, turns them anew to contemplations of a sixth sense, of faith, of an unseen universe, of ghosts, of alternate forms of knowledge like intuition, of brain structure, the continuing unknowns of neural pathways, all things that they haven't thought about since high school or college bull sessions. *How does he do it?* He's allowed reporters into his world, to follow him, to spend time with him and his family, and the resulting story, in which the reporter finds nothing, therefore ends up speculating about faith and the supernatural and the ancient capacities of the brain and man's sixth sense and unexplained strands and coils of DNA. And the longer they find nothing, no trail, no hint or trace of me, the more the press puzzles in a magazine profile or a broadcast news segment, the better for Wallace the Amazing.

How does he do it? The simple, rich, reverberating theme of Wallace's life.

How does he do it? Here's a little more on how:

Government databases, IRS databases, credit bureau databases, credit card company databases. For those I can't hack myself, I call on my Internet "friends"—online hacker acquaintanceships of long standing—all of us protected by screen names, and we swap tips and secrets and techniques, and labor under the banners of freedom and the free flow of information. Sometimes I pay for the information. My Internet friends have no idea what I'm doing with the information. They assume, I'm sure, it's for something more conventionally illicit. And I've had contacts, friends, in many of these offices and companies since well before their computer systems were secure. Contacts, friends, who *built* those systems. Friends in their respective IT departments since before there *were* systems.

Plus, there's an entire subculture that thrives, gets an adrenaline rush, from accessing computer systems—not necessarily to profit from them, just for the pure accomplishment of it—and I am tapped into that subculture.

Think of my computer mouse as a real one, skittering around desks at night, finding morsels and scraps sloppily left out, there for the taking. Munch, munch. Click, click. Funny, isn't it, that what appears onstage as the triumph of intuition, is in fact the triumph of its opposite—data. So that night after night, I observe the odd standoff of science and faith. The pure juggernaut power of data versus the ineffable power of blind belief. It's a conundrum, and a nightly showdown: mankind's historic yearning for explanation versus an equally historic enchantment with the unexplained.

He lives in a compound out in the high desert. A bright, shimmering, white-and-pink sandstone fortress of domes and turrets, rising like a mirage, a sensual Arabian fantasy, set up on a bluff, proffering an extra half hour of essentially private and personal afternoon light. Protected by massive gates with fanciful filigree. Among the believers, among the credulous and the converted, the theory is that he chose this spot because it is removed from the mental waves and pulses that relentlessly surround him, that he cannot quiet or avoid except far out in the pristine desert. I know better. That he was simply looking for privacy and quiet for himself and his family, to replicate and preserve the intense control that he is used to maintaining onstage and backstage in his professional life and that he wants, demands, cherishes, in his personal life as well.

And eventually, Vegas's endless supply of rock supergroup reunion shows, the titillating dance and sex reviews, the elaborate choreography in water or midair, the spectacle, the visual assault, all wear thin, no longer fascinate, and there is one show left: Wallace the Amazing, entering minds, invading the last realm, bringing nightly, reliably, a note from the beyond. A show that sends its audience in on itself, that summons everyone's past, that frightens, that exhilarates with the unexplained, that burrows into your consciousness, into all your questions about omniscience and thought and mind and life. A show that is intimate, dangerously intimate, for each audience member, because it is about us as individuals, special, unique. A show that makes magic not out of spectacle but out of our daily world, our daily connections, our daily lives. It is, quite understandably, quite unassailably, the ultimate Vegas hit.

THREE

So what happened? Obviously, I would not be writing this—"outing" myself, setting it down, risking its exposure to the world (and in truth, I still haven't decided what to ultimately do with this account), memorializing it here for you to judge me and what follows as either truthful or mendacious—if something hadn't happened. Of *course* something happened. You don't have to be a mentalist to sense that.

Something that went above and beyond, under and beneath, the facts and data that I supply each night.

Something that overwhelmed the smooth, seamless duo that wordlessly handled Big Eddie and his henchmen.

Something that made Big Eddie look like child's play.

• • •

I'm making a late-night snack, only half watching the show. Dave Stewartson of Cedar Rapids, Iowa, is standing in the aisle, dumbstruck, shaking his head in disbelief, as Wallace the Amazing is talking about Dave's childhood dog, Reddi. "A chocolate Labrador?" "Yes, a chocolate Labrador!" "I see him running around a blue-shuttered house." "Yes, yes, that's right . . . a blue-shuttered house!" "And now he's running by a red bush, and I see money for some reason . . . coins." "Yes, when I was a kid," Dave admits, flushed, stunned, "I buried my treasure under that bush!" Dave, clearly for physical balance and support in the face of these shocks, puts his hand on the shoulder of his wife, Sandi, standing by his side. (Maiden name Parker; grew up at 21 Owens Trail, Lansing, Michigan; certificate in primary education from Michigan State; second grade teacher, Alwin Elementary; sixteen kids in class, Arnold, Sarah, Cal . . . It's all more than passingly familiar to me, of course. I've just done all the research.)

I recognize the litany of facts, admire as always Wallace's artful arrangement and delivery of them, weaving a narrative that will dive deeper and deeper, for the audience's awed entertainment, but something isn't right, and I can't tell what it is, but I have a feeling. I'm a mentalist's assistant, after all—so I'm particularly, professionally qualified to have such a feeling.

I drop the snack fixings, fairly leap over to my laptop, call up the file. I confirm immediately that Wallace the Amazing has all his facts exactly right.

The only problem is, that's not Dave Stewartson he's talking to.

The Internet is showing me a photograph of a different guy.

And what's obvious to me immediately, unless something untoward and unprecedented has happened to Wallace the Amazing, is that Wallace must *know* it's not the right guy. This is what he does, after all, this is the skill he works from, his remarkable visual memory. Unless he's had some kind of stroke, or short-term memory event or disruption, his visual memory has been infallible.

Not the right guy—and yet the guy is acting happily amazed.

I keystroke madly, cross-checking. There is no mistaking. I am looking at the photo of the real David Stewartson. Or at least, *my* Dave Stewartson. A guy whose photo is there on the Internet in front of me. And the guy now on television, in the Vegas audience of our show, is someone else—someone, for whatever reason, who is *saying* he's Dave Stewartson.

I hit keys in a blur, checking now on wife Sandi. And there is Sandi Stewartson online (second-grade teacher Sandi, Michigan State teaching certificate Sandi, maiden name Parker, etc., etc.), but the mousy Sandi seen in online photos does not match the bob-haired and somewhat brassy-looking blonde on my television screen. So . . . double trouble. Tending to move whatever is going on from the arena of mere error to the arena of malign purpose.

The plot thickens almost immediately. Because as I keystroke back to Dave, cross-checking, scurrying site to site, *this* Dave Stewartson—the one still on my TV screen, hugging his wife, lit up, virtually atremble with Wallace the Amazing's abilities—is now making several cameo Internet appearances before me. Here he is on a social networking site. Here he is on an archived computer dating site. Here he is on a job-search site. Here he is on someone's blog. Here he is in someone's group photo, his name in the caption. Yet racing back now to the sites I rely on—"unhackable" police databases, protected governmental and encrypted military-service identification sites with no consumer access—there is the original Dave. *My* Dave. Serious, smileless, guileless. A mild frown. A straight-ahead, no-nonsense guy. A *different* guy.

I am, of course, struggling instantly—panicky, heart racing—with a couple of obvious questions. Which one is the real Dave, which is the Dave Stewartson imposter? Although I'm pretty sure I know already—that somber old photo from the official sites, versus the charmer, the smiler, on the consumer and social networking sites—Facebook, Twitter, LinkedIn—so susceptible to misrepresentation.

Have I not been thorough enough? Clearly not. And now my shoddiness, my not double-checking, my small moment of laxness, could topple us. Bring it all down.

And still the bigger, simultaneous, and more confusing question: Why has Wallace called on him? If this Dave didn't match the visual description, didn't click with Wallace's prodigious visual memory, why did he choose him?

Maybe it was a momentary slip on Wallace's part—just a momentary lapse, and now he'll have to dig out of it. But this strikes me as off, somehow. The whole enterprise, his life, *our* life, is built on not making a slip like that. In having *never* made a slip like that.

And the big accompanying question: Why is this fake Dave (if this is the fake Dave) playing along like this? Is he going to turn at any moment and reveal—prove with his driver's license and birth certificate, waving them around, offering them to the TV camera for a close-up, for instance—that he's not Dave Stewartson at all. Showing that Wallace is merely a smooth charlatan, a high-level, supremely accomplished card counter of some sort (which arguably is exactly what he is), backed into an error that pulls aside the curtain, unveils the utterly conventional rods and levers and pulleys and strings.

I check my official data again. It's as if I can't believe, can't accept, what I already know. The online picture is Dave Stewartson—Dave of the blue shutters and the chocolate Lab and the buried treasure, I'm certain—and this guy on television is *not* him.

I check another file, one always at the ready on my laptop—my file of "frequent fliers," crazy acolytes, stalkers, and nut jobs known to me and Wallace. I'm familiar with, on the lookout for, all of them. I thought for a moment I'd forgotten one, but no. No one like him there in the file.

Another possibility: this guy has been given—or else has stolen—the real Dave Stewartson's tickets, and is a legitimate, or illegitimate, guest of the real, somber, frowning, official Dave. This we've had happen before—but it was the visual ID that always prevented this brand of trouble. Wallace knew what appearance went with what set of personal data before he set foot onstage. So how did Wallace, the unerring Wallace, stumble into this?

And with this imposter playing along like this—so entranced, so receptive, so amazed—does Wallace even realize his mistake? Or does he know exactly what he's doing—and I don't?

My heart is pounding. I am riveted, transfixed, as if watching an oncoming train wreck. I am now in front of the TV screen, jumpy, coiled, ready to scream, to strike at it, like a Giants fan when the Eagles score, like an ardent liberal when the conservative invokes God or intelligent design. Ready to enter the television, administer swift, blind, unthinking physical justice to the babbling figure, who in reality is only projected light, only pixels, akin to throttling a ghost.

"So . . ." Wallace continues confidently, the ersatz Dave Stewartson and wife still amazed, the audience of a thousand still appreciative. "As you have seen, I have connected to Dave's old dog, and his old blue-shuttered house, and a few other things, and as you know about this show, we are dealing with the otherworldly, the phenomenological, the unexplained, and in keeping with that tradition, pay attention to what happens here. Because the problem is"—he turns boldly, broadly back to Dave—"the problem here is you don't have that dog, you didn't have that house, you didn't grow up in that town. I don't think you're really Dave Stewartson at all, are you?"

Gasps.

Including—needless to add—my own.

But even here, at this moment of confusion, of panic, of crunching anxiety, I doff my hat, I bow down to Wallace's flair and instinct for drama, for upping the ante.

"The question is, why are you playing at it? What's going on here?" asks Wallace the Amazing grandly, and it is a dramatic moment in the show, not least because Wallace never asks the questions, never risks appearing at a loss or at sea.

What's going on here, indeed?

But now I see, at least, that Wallace *does* know. Knows this isn't the researched, vetted Dave. And I see—anxiously—that he is utterly trusting my research. The infallibility, the perfect record of twenty years of my research.

So trusting, he is making a bold move with it. I feel my heart stuttering . . . like a drumroll of anticipation.

Why would he risk it? Why would he play with fire like this?

Did he sense something was off, out of the ordinary, even *before* he called on him?

And if this *is* an imposter, if it's some kind of identity theft—which would make sense, given "Dave's" credulousness, "Dave's" playing along with the amazement—is Wallace expecting imposter Dave to stumble and mumble and crumble in the glare of lights, shuffle uncomfortably, maybe make a run for it? In which case Wallace will be a hero, and a fraud will be unmasked on national television—great news for Wallace's show and ratings.

But Dave stands his ground. He is all innocent confusion and stiff resolve. "But I *am* Dave Stewartson. That was my dog Reddi who slept by my bed when I was growing up. Those were the blue shutters on our house. This is my wife. I promise you." Big smile. But clearly a little insulted by the mentalist's implication.

The wife dutifully nods. Sandi.

Twinkling eyes. Middle-aged body, but sculpted and tight. Just past bombshell, but the bomb still ticking. And although from one angle the two of them are typical out-of-towners—at least by their now doubtful bios and addresses and buoyant, smiling mid-western style—I sense something ineffably Vegas about them too. Something slick. A weird angularity to both their faces. And I sense a voltage running strongly between them.

I want to look again online at the real Sandi. But I can't stop right now, can't distract myself from the TV screen.

I figure Wallace is about to have the imposter show his driver's license, hold it up to the camera, but he might figure the license—which may, after all, say Dave Stewartson—would only back the man up. It's too risky. He takes a less risky tack. And shows, once again, his mastery.

"So you're saying I'm right. I'm right about your past . . ."

"Yes." Emphatic.

"I'm right about your name . . ."

"Yes, amazingly, yes."

Wallace frowns. "There's something in the way here. Something isn't right." And this covers Wallace brilliantly, because whatever the aftermath of this moment turns out to be, it will explain Wallace's extrasensory stumble. It will reaffirm his direct if not always perfectly straightforward contact with the mysteries of the universe. And who, anyway, expects the universe's mysteries to be straightforward?

"So Reddi or not . . ." Wallace says now, referring once more to "Dave's" childhood dog and to his own moment of confusion, and now his eyes squinting, as if suddenly seeing into something, realizing something. "It's turning out I was . . . more Reddi than I thought." Wallace smiles, recovering, commanding, smooth. "Because there is more than one Reddi here tonight. Pamela Ardsdale?" And Pamela and her girlfriends scream, and the spotlight moves from "Dave" to Pamela, and Wallace says, "You worked at Reddi-Cut Carpet, didn't you?" and Pamela and her girlfriends scream again, and the audience laughs, and the show moves on.

And it's all a message to me really—this whole moment in the show is a directive to me, as direct and telegraphic and immediate as Wallace can get, which says, *Chas, get on this and see if you can figure out what the hell's going on.*

I *am* on it. All over it. Alert, checking, toggling my attention between the television and computer screen. Looking at the weak chin, the pasty skin, the drooping eyes of the Dave Stewartson in the online photo from secure Internet sites, and at the tanned, full-chinned, muscular, twinkle-eyed, charming, chiseled Dave Stewartson standing in the audience.

I open a little software program of my own devising, which instantly gathers all the Dave Stewartsons in the United States into one database, all 3,864 of them (it's a big country, 320 million of us, and it's a common name—damn) with any photos available (driver's licenses, passports, medical records, posted photos) arranged by birthday, and I scan through them and find both my Dave Stewartsons, next to each other, as it happens, since they are sharing not only a birthday but a driver's license number, a passport number, and a Social Security number. The real Dave Stewartson and the smiling, concocted one, who has neatly, efficiently, and outrageously wrested the real Dave's life away from him—and in the best-case scenario, is only temporarily sharing it in the televised spotlight, no doubt without express permission.

And worst-case scenario? This fake Dave wants to somehow test, somehow complete, his inhabitation of the life and soul and memories of the poor real Dave Stewartson, wherever he is. (And where *is* he?) Or he has some other reason for wanting to be seen on national television in this assumed identity—to send a message, to be known, to be discovered.

And most likely scenario? The most logical, but still stunning, explanation? Staring me in the face. Slapping me in the forehead. The outright lie that, I'm suddenly sure, will turn out to be the truth.

"Dave" is simply cornered. He has stolen someone's identity—hook, line, and sinker—and here he is at this show, probably figuring he would never be called on. One of two thousand audience members, what are the odds? He probably figured it's all fake and canned and staged anyway and he'd never be at risk—and suddenly he's in the spotlight, and he puts on a great impromptu performance—as good as Wallace's, as good as it gets.

He says it is his dog, his shutters, his past, because now it *is*. Because now it *has to be*. If it wasn't his dog before Wallace recounted the story, it is now.

But this is national television. And someone else besides me has to know the real Dave, someone else has to recognize the blue-shuttered house and the Labrador named Reddi. Someone is going to recognize these stories and find out what happened and come after this guy . . . meaning, if Wallace can negotiate past this moment (and it looks now like he will), it will pass for us, and fighting identity theft isn't our job.

Meaning, I don't really care about this guy stealing someone's identity. It doesn't surprise me—there are all kinds of scams percolating across criminal America. Logic, and the fluent and continuing success of our own, says we are hardly the only ones out there . . .

What bothers me is that "Dave" could *expose* our scam. Catch the interest of some vigilant cop, who was enjoying Wallace the Amazing with the rest of America. Is "Dave" holding that over Wallace? Does he even realize it?

In which case, I might have to help keep this "Dave" from getting caught. I might have to make sure he preserves his fake identity, to minimize that risk.

Another charlatan that I'd need to support behind the scenes.

FOUR

Identity theft. Setting aside, for the moment, forged signatures and siphoned bank accounts, it's arguably the world's most metaphysical crime, isn't it? Because you're not actually stealing someone's identity—they are they, and you are you. In an absolute sense, it's not possible to steal someone's identity—unless the crime comes to involve DNA or plastic surgery, appropriating someone's unique appearance or genetic code.

Their *actual* identity is never in jeopardy. It's the world's version of their identity, and the *proof* of that identity, that is in jeopardy. So on its surface, it's a crime in only a very vague sense. If you say you're someone else but never steal a dollar, apply for a job, or profit in any way from saying you're someone else, has there even been a crime?

And, whether in the metaphysical version or narrow legalistic version of "identity," can you steal someone's identity completely? Is anyone that disconnected, that severed from life, from their present and their past, that someone else can come in and scoop it up?

Well, yes.

Me, for instance. I'm cut off from life. No one would know if someone took over my life; they'd only be filling a void, after all. Someone could do it to me. In a way, someone *has* done it to me. Wallace the Amazing, my employer. Reducing and virtually eliminating—carefully, professionally—my presence in the world. Giving me, at the same time, in exchange, a unique and lucrative way to earn a living. But I'm a cipher. A professional ghost. For good, sensible reasons, I have little identity of my own.

To me, identity theft is exactly the reverse of what people think it is. In the kinds of scams and frauds I was crediting to the fake "Dave," you're stripped of everything *but* your identity. That's all you have left, after your credit cards and your possessions and everything else is gone. Your identity is the one thing they *can't* make off with.

But it turns out, of course, you're not very comfortable with just your identity. You feel naked, exposed. It's everything *but* your identity that you've lost, but you feel your most vulnerable when reduced to, relying on, identity only.

I recognized for the first time—explicitly, acutely—my fear that I would be cut off from life. My fear that my one attachment, my umbilical cord, would be severed. My identity was so tenuous, so connected to Wallace's.

Could someone do it to me?

Very soon, the world's most unconventional detective—the geeky Internet gumshoe—is fulfilling the world's most conventional detective role. I am tailing them—"Dave Stewartson" and "Sandi," his "wife," if that's what she is. And even though they are looking alertly, I'd say professionally, behind them, around them, walking into and out of Vegas hotels and restaurants and even shops and an all-night supermarket—in one door and out another—it's easy to follow them. Because I am invisible. No one knows me. I don't exist. A great advantage in tailing someone.

I follow them, never getting too close. Keeping them too far ahead of me to see them in much detail—or for them to see me very clearly either. But I'm close enough to observe them spending money with vigor and determination and élan, enamored of its power, which suggests to me it's new, which suggests to me it's not theirs. Which leads me to suspect that Dave Stewartson—the *real* Dave Stewartson—is rich, confirming the inadequacy of my original research, or indicating that it was cleverly, purposefully misdirected. The real Dave Stewartson, it seems, was an excellent find. And the more I observe, the more I sense that these are scam artists—but not killers. They would not kill the real Dave Stewartson, I don't think.

. . .

I was pleased to see them turning, looking behind them. It confirmed their duplicity. Something was clearly up. I followed their rented red Mustang, distinctive enough to pick out from a quarter mile back in Vegas Strip traffic—why, I could drop the tail, stop for a snack or a restroom, and find their car again fifteen minutes later. I waited in the supermarket lot while they brought out enough bags of groceries to indicate an open-ended stay. I waited in the drugstore lot, while they brought out a bagful of over-the-counter medications. I accompanied them—unbeknownst, well behind them, like a porter or guard they're not even aware is in their employ, always in the next throng of people—into the lobby of their hotel, the preening, pompous Bellagio, its famous fountains like colorful arteries and veins of a massive soulless beast, ceaselessly nourishing its soaring pretension. It took no great detective work to realize that the bags of canned groceries and the fancy hotel room did not necessarily go neatly together. Which is perhaps why they had shifted the groceries to other bags, so the hotel staff would not see them bringing so many groceries in.

It was easiest to tail them in the casinos, where they played some high-stakes hands of poker and blackjack, enjoyed some elaborate meals accompanied by top-shelf liquor, left generous tips. One place I couldn't accompany them was to their high-roller suite. But that told me something useful too. That they were spending money like there was no tomorrow. (In celebration, or in anticipation?) That night, a call girl went up to their suite about an hour and a half after them. I was pleased to see that—it gave my imagination something to occupy it. They were clearly intent on enjoying the fruits of Vegas while they were here. I was close enough at one point to hear a clerk ask them, quite reasonably amid all the convention-eers filling the lobby around us, if they were here for "business or pleasure?" Their backs were to me, but I could see them glance at each other—clearly unsure how to answer. The pleasure was apparent. What exactly was the business?

I waited. Vegas stakeouts are easy. Hotel lobbies, casinos, are truly all night, truly without time, so there are no dead hours, and there is action, movement, to occupy your time and your attention, to keep you awake, and you are neither noticeable nor alone while you wait. In Vegas, in fact, it's practically a legitimate occupation to sit observing in a busy hotel lobby. Your presence, your amused observation, isn't questioned in the least.

I'm glad I waited. At two in the morning, an hour after the hooker's exit, "Dave" and "Sandi" came down lugging the grocer-ies, got into their red Mustang rental, and headed out, with their careful, curious entourage—me—a cautious distance behind them.

The chain motel where they finally stopped (chain motel—I would soon become aware of the appropriateness of that term) is about ten miles from the Strip, in what some call the real Vegas, the working man's Vegas. The Vegas that was here before and, part of me suspects, will be all that is here at some point, again.

Here, I'd be too obvious following them in, so I watched from outside the tiny motel lobby's (fortunately) big plate glass window, looking in past the classic pink-and-blue neon VACANCY sign. The "Stewartsons" didn't stop at the registration desk. They headed down the narrow hallway, and I slipped quickly, silently along the motel's side lot in the dark, watching for a light to go on in one of the rooms.

. . .

There. A light pops on. I move quickly, carefully, closer to the window. In time to see them turn the television on—a confirming shift of light through the window—though they never actually watch it, I notice.

I see Dave and Sandi unpacking some groceries, putting them on the counter, talking back and forth with one another, each going into the bathroom briefly, emerging a minute later. This is as close as I dare to get for now.

They aren't in the motel room for long. Dave looks around it one last time, checking, before closing the door. He turns off the light but leaves the television on.

From the dark side lot, I watch them get back into the red Mustang and pull away. And for the first time in twenty-four hours, I don't follow the Stewartsons.

Maybe it takes someone steeped in scam to recognize it. Or maybe with the clues—the "Dave" at the show, the free spending, the extra motel room—anyone would. But I know what they've done. It's simple. First they took a guy's Social Security number and credit cards, like any and every two-bit ID thief. But then it turned into something bigger, better—a much better thing than they had first thought. Because it turned out the guy was rich. Endlessly rich. And the guy was alone. And when they saw how much money he had and how alone he was, they took the next step after taking his Social Security number and credit cards—to keep a good thing going, they took him. They were already pretending to be him. They were already reestablishing purchase patterns. Perhaps they had already become him, assumed his identity entirely. It wasn't such a very big step.

I know exactly how they did it, of course. How they found out all they did about him. Because I do the same thing. I work the same way. I utilize the same data, the same channels of information.

I'm just like them.

And I understand how alone the victim can be. How cut off and isolated. How he could have lived that way for years perhaps, could have adjusted to it, made his peace with it. Because I do that too. I've accepted that too. No one knows I exist. I can never be too close to anyone else; no one else can be too close to me.

I'm just like him.

So I identify with both of them, the perpetrators and the victim; I recognize them both.

And how do they know so much about him? How can they know these little details if they have erased him, buried him, if he is gone?

Because he is *not* erased or buried. He is not gone. He is being kept. He is alive. And no one is better suited to find him, to rescue him, to draw him out of his predicament and his loneliness, than the one person who knows what has happened *and* the one person who most profoundly empathizes, identifies. It is in effect, after all, rescuing myself. My doppelganger. My instant, automatic friend.

I don't know exactly what I will find in that motel room, but I will find something—or someone. I had watched the Stewartsons head down the road, melt into the horizon, and although the prudent thing would have been to follow them, wait till they were ensconced at a restaurant or blackjack table before racing back, I had the sense they would not return too quickly. And though I operate professionally on evidence, none of us can afford to ignore the evidence of one's gut instinct.

My need to preserve my invisibility means I have some reconnaissance, some extra steps to take, during the next few hours. I watch and wait as the motel shift changes. As the early morning manager comes on, as he chats with the desk clerk for a few minutes and circles the property once distractedly, while the relieved clerk leaves for more congenial environs. I watch as the migrant busboys and dishwashers and janitors stumble in exhausted from their late shifts to their long-term rental, shower one after another, and collapse into exhausted sleep. So that in just a couple of hours, I can map out fairly completely what rooms are occupied with whom, what rooms have me in their sight line, what rooms don't. I know it well enough to be fairly certain I won't even be seen, and certainly not thought about, when the desk clerk takes a bathroom break and I stride into the lobby and down the hall to the door of Room 103 with my universal keycard, the same one housekeeping and motel management use. (From the laptop in my car, I had gotten the name of the motel's key maker through its purchase records, and the correct serial number and activation codes from the manufacturing company—then after fishing an old key out of the motel trash and networking my laptop to a portable keycard magnetizer that I bought online a couple of years ago, I activated the card pretty much the same way the desk clerk does it.) Press into the slot. Pull up. Blinking green light. It works . . .

I push open the door to Room 103.

At first blush, nothing unusual, nothing amiss. But what's amiss is that there *is* nothing amiss. Beds still made. A closed suitcase on the end of one bed. A motel room occupied, but not occupied. I poke around in the cheap bureau drawers, slide open the flimsy closet door—nothing. I am about to leave, disappointed, mystified, when I open the bathroom door wider, only as a final, unthinking gesture before I go.

• • •

Shrunken, white-skulled, dangerously emaciated, curled in the empty bathtub, covered, at least, with a thin blanket, he blinked in the sudden light. His whiteness, the sheer, translucent skin—he obviously hadn't been in the sun in months, maybe years. Fragile, brittle, a late-stage cancer patient appearance. Skin hanging off bones. My gasp of surprise and his own gasp—a duet of shock and communion. He was doubly chained—to the base of the toilet and the base of the sink—though it looked like he hadn't muscle enough to even lift the chain, much less break it free from either fixture. Sunken black eyes. Only stray tufts of hair at wild angles on his otherwise bare skull—as if seeking their escape from so inhospitable and alien a surface. He was a living ghost. Barely living at that.

He was hardly recognizable. But he hardly had to be. I had obviously just met the real Dave Stewartson.

Dave Stewartson kept alive so that he could continually provide the details of his life, no doubt, so the big, healthy, suntanned, gym-buffed, new improved Dave and sidekick Sandi could inhabit that life all the more convincingly and continually. Dave Stewartson kept alive for signatures on documents, for easier access to bank accounts, brokerage accounts, retirement savings, for the store of his knowledge. Dave Stewartson kept alive so that there would be no homicide investigation, so it would be at most a missing persons case, if that, because maybe no one had reported him missing. Maybe these scam artists were that artful in choosing a wealthy, cut-off, perfect victim; maybe he was that alone. All this was running through my head as I carefully isolated and snipped one link from each chain with the lock cutter from the tool bag always in the trunk of my car, as I lifted him carefully out of the tub—so strangely light-weight as to be hardly human, hardly a man anymore—as I half led, half carried him out to my car, laid him in the passenger seat like a just-released patient, and slipped out of the motel lot, accelerated away from the shock and the misery, nevertheless having shock and misery secured, strapped in, in the seat beside me.

He said nothing. I said nothing. Weak, head against the headrest, he stared out the window. Though at one point he turned toward me, and in the slant of Vegas night light—thin and un-neon out here, far from the Strip, the stars and moonlight more vivid out here, as if asserting their reality amid the panoptic challenge of thickly manufactured illumination a few miles away—I thought I could see his eyes swimming in tears of gratitude. He was barely alive, and we both knew it, and the recognition of that kept the conversation to a minimum. I spoke as you would to a patient—only the essentials.

"I'm taking you somewhere safe."

He nodded acknowledgment.

Somewhere safe—where hardly anyone knows me. Hardly anyone sees me. A few neighbors to nod a friendly hello, my girlfriend, Debbie, that's it. As I said, I'm a ghost. So it is unextraordinary, hardly merits mention, to bring a second ghost—a real ghost—into what is already a ghost's residence. He'll feel right at home.

• • •

He sleeps on the single bed in my small immaculate guest bedroom, where no one has ever slept before. Soup. Crackers. A loose-fitting shirt and pajamas from my closet. A little walking—to the john, back—and then a little more walking, around the condo. I see him looking in the mirror. The atrophy of his muscles is as strange, as remarkable to him as to me.

"Here you go, Dave," I say to him, handing him soup and crackers on the patio.

He looks at me, eyebrows raised, momentarily startled, it seems, confused and amazed, at hearing his name spoken aloud. Maybe surprised that I know him. Maybe just the suddenness of the simple humanity. His identity suddenly returning to him—in so simple a way. They had probably never called him Dave. Would not acknowledge it, had not said it aloud. Maybe they had called him anything and everything else, taunting him with the theft of his identity, working the psychologies of imprisonment and torture, trying to make the lost identity a fact in his mind. But here is his name spoken in a calm, soothing, friendly tone of voice that he has not heard for a long time. He looks at me—examines me—doesn't know, after all, who I am, what my motives are, what my connection to all this is.

He spoons the soup, nods in gratitude, manages a small smile, while he tentatively swallows a spoonful.

He sets down the spoon. Looks out at the warm desert morning. Closes his eyes in the sunshine, lets the sun wash over him like a bath.

"My life was stolen from me," he says.

"I know."

He turns to look at me. Still white, fragile, but piercing eyes. "How *do* you know?"

I don't answer. I can't tell him who I am, of course. I feel nothing but sympathy for his aloneness, for his isolation, and I may have saved his life, but I can't tell him exactly who I am (well, my name, sure, but nothing more) or what I do or how I know.

"Who *are* you? *What* are you?" he asks.

"I can tell you my name. I can't tell you anything else."

"Meaning, how you knew I was there," he says.

"Yes, meaning that."

"Can you tell me what happens now?"

"What happens now is whatever you want. My suggestion— you go to the police, and put an end to the other Dave Stewartson and his companion."

He looks at me, smiles a little. "They seem pretty evil to you, don't they?"

I am stunned. *They don't to you?* (Is this some kind of Stockholm syndrome, Patty Hearst–ish, identification with the oppressor?)

He takes another sip of soup, savors it.

"Then I'll go to the police for you."

"Oh, don't do that," he says.

"Why not? Don't you want your identity back? Your money back? Your life back?"

"If you go to the police, you'll get drawn in yourself. I'm sure you'll live to regret it."

It is a mysterious, oblique, strange statement from him. But of course, he's right. I can't go to the police. I can't risk exposing myself, or how I make my living, or any of it. But how could he know that? Or does he only suspect it, from the manner in which I retrieved him. From the spare, carefully impersonal surroundings of my home. An educated guess on his part—an incisive one. Amid the carnal wreckage, his mind is sharp.

Of course, my indecision, my confusion about what to do with him, shares a space in my mind with the fear of fake Dave and wife/companion managing to find us—coming after us, knowing that we're going to expose them—ready to take pretty substantial action, knowing what's at stake for them.

When Debbie shows up that night, I open the door and tell her she can't come in.

She's been away on a TV shoot in Minneapolis and then St. Louis, and amid my ministering to the real Dave, and still attending to my daily data duties to Wallace, I've lost track of her trip a little, and suddenly here she is.

And as I am saying it to her, attempting to explain without explaining, she is looking at the sickly, shriveled, pale, clean-skulled, skin-and-bones figure behind me, who has wandered into the living room despite my explicit directions to stay out of view. She looks back at me—horrified, mystified, confused—a look that indicates she has no idea who he is but, more significantly than that, who *I* am.

"Debbie, I should have called. I got preoccupied here. I'm asking you to understand . . ."

But she has apparently reached her limit. And this moment of my "unwelcoming" her in, and the sight of the strange creature behind me, unleashes a flood of reaction that has obviously been dammed up for months. The flow of outrage and confusion and hurt is so out of character to her customary warmth and calm.

"Understand?!" She is again looking past me to Dave, squinting at him, trying to process what she sees in any reasonable or feasible way. "You can't tell me anything about your business. I accept that. Like an idiot, I accept that. Your odd hours—I accept that. And now, this . . . person . . . is in your home, the home we practically share, share in the most significant and physical way, and I am not allowed in! And you won't tell me why. You don't trust me enough to tell me why."

"I do trust you. I would trust you. But this is information that would be dangerous for anyone to have. I wouldn't even trust myself with it. It would be wrong for me—"

"Don't color it, don't spin it." She cuts me off. "You don't trust me." She looks at me, with finality, with a change in her. "Well, I don't trust you." She looks up at the condominium, at the door, at the entrance, as if taking it all in one last time, readying to say good-bye, as if wondering what she is even doing here, what she was ever doing here in the first place. "No one could have been more understanding, Chas. No one else would have gone along for so long. You had a good thing. *We* had a good thing. And you blew it." Her eyes are wet. "You blew it for both of us."

"Debbie . . ."

But she is already down the porch steps.

"You'll know it soon enough," she calls back behind her.

I know it already.

My doppelganger.

I lie in bed, unable to sleep, staring up at the ceiling, obsessively thinking of him lying a few feet from me, in the next room. My doppelganger. Cut off, isolated, unknown by the world, a world unaware, unseeing. I can't hide it from myself. It was like seeing myself, a truer, stripped-down, abandoned version of myself, lying there in the tub. A metaphor of my aloneness. Should I have left him there? For one part of me, the appropriate action was to leave him, to not touch anything, to have no one know I was there. The other part of me, though, couldn't leave him, had no choice but to take him. It was like rescuing myself. But rescuing myself entails action, and action creates visibility, and visibility creates consequences. It produces evidence, it leaves a trail, it risks traceability. I lie there thinking about that precipice—that fine edge between action and inaction, that line between subject and object, between observer and observed—that I have traversed today. That fine edge that can cut you, slice you deep.

To find someone chained to a tub in a motel. It is shocking, and yet it is Vegas. It is the expected perverseness of Vegas, and the half-expected perverseness of a desert motel. It is a tableau of utter foreignness, yet has the shock of recognition, as if a vision toward which my whole life has been leading. The naked, withered form chained in the bathtub. Unknown, alone. Mine to pass by—to close the door quietly, to leave to whatever crime is underway. Or mine to save.

So much sympathy for my withered doppelganger. Is my own soul that withered, that isolated? My own tetherless, transient motel soul?

There in the dark, my mind churns: the vision of Debbie turning away, looking across the desert at the familiar emptiness—literal and metaphoric—ahead of her once again. The same desert that I look across now, from my bedroom window, the same vision of emptiness. That's the thing about Vegas—once you're beyond the lights and noise and panoply of merry distractions—there's the communion of the desert. The measureless sameness of scrub and sand that you all look out on, equally. Lying there, I watch her walk out into that desert again, over and over.

Vegas is so simple—Manichaean, elemental. Blinding bright light, surrounded by unforgiving blackness. Noise and sound, surrounded by high silence.

After a few days, Dave gains a little weight. Dave puts on a little muscle. Dave's hair begins to grow back in. I am nursing him back to health.

"What do you want to do? What do you want to do with your freedom? Go after them, or start over? Those, it seems, are the only two choices, and I'll support you either way."

He looks at me. "I have a third choice," he says.

"What's that?"

"To stay here." He smiles.

"That's not a choice," I say.

He nods. He knows.

Of course, my work goes on during all this. I must work without Dave—shriveled, slowly recovering Dave—knowing what I'm doing. Though I'm tempted to share the secret of it with him—that's how special his status is. My computers are in my office, their contents accessible only by passwords and codes, so I have no worry about Dave looking around.

The first night, as Dave lay stretched out on the couch in front of the television, drifting in and out of sleep, I took a small risk. I flipped through the channels, and stopped, as if by chance, on Wallace's show. I had to watch anyway, professionally, especially now, and I could do so in another room of the condo, but it was easier to keep an eye on Dave if I could watch him and the show at the same time.

I watched Dave drifting in and out, glassy-eyed, trying to focus on the screen.

But he was more attentive and alert than I thought.

"He *is* amazing," Dave whispered at one point. Apparently taken with the performance. "You wonder how he does it," said Dave. "You really do."

The next night, as if purely to be polite, I asked if he'd like to watch Wallace the Amazing again. He nodded that he would.

On the third night, I tune it in without asking. It seems to have become part of our routine. A routine significantly disrupted by a simple question.

"You work for him, don't you?"

My mind seizes. My blood pulses. "Work for who?"

"For him. Wallace."

"What are you talking about?" I am struggling to remain calm.

"You didn't think I was watching that first night. But I was watching, and watching *you* watching. Watching you watching intensely. Not the watching of a man who had casually been flipping the channels a minute before. Or pretending to casually flip them.

"You see," says Dave, "I heard the two of them talking about going to Wallace's show. Dave and his companion. Going to catch the famous act. That must be where you saw them. And then you followed them to get to me. Why would you risk being so involved? You're a decent guy, but no humanitarian. For you, there was something more to it. I could sense that. So yes, I think you work for him. You may even be what makes the Amazing amazing."

And then I sense something too. I pick up on something, just as my shriveled recovering guest has.

That his insight is a little too insightful. A little too knowledgeable from him.

I leap up, run to my computer, slamming my office door behind me, bring up onto the computer screen and look again, more closely now, at the official passport and driver's license photos of the real Dave Stewartson.

And the poor, shriveled-up, unrecognizable wraith I have rescued from the bathtub? Who I have nursed back to health?

I see it's not him.

Blowing up the photos to full screen. Letting a retouching program fill in missing pixels for a close-up, hyperrealistic look.

Goddamn it! It's not him.

"Who *are* you?" he asks once more, calmly, as I emerge furious from the office.

"No," I say, grabbing him by the arm, by the shocking skin and bones that my grip closes around, the end of frustration, the edge of violence. "Who are *you*?"

He looks at me—blank, unblinking.

"Archer Wallace," he says.

Archer Wallace.

The real Archer Wallace?

Wallace the Amazing, indeed.

(Remembering, of course, that I'm not using, can't risk using, real names here. Maybe I will ultimately. But not yet.)

I am reeling.

Everything changes.

FIVE

"That little coincidence that you notice, *smile at, half dismiss . . . the person you were just thinking about, calling you out of the blue . . . an unusual word you just said to someone, suddenly there on the page in front of you . . . someone you were just thinking about, suddenly driving by in his new convertible . . . The kind of little coincidence that makes even the practical, the pragmatic, the faithless, wonder for a moment about the inner clockworks of the world . . ."*

I am a half step, a full step, two steps ahead as he tells it. After being for the past week a half step, a full step, two steps behind. It's so painfully clear how I had assumed amid the shock of it that the shriveled, bare-skulled, shrunken form in the tub was the real Dave Stewartson, but now it is Wallace—the real Archer Wallace— who had been stumbled onto serendipitously or, more likely, discovered by the careful sleuthing of this couple (in which case they are detectives of a sort, with skill sets a mirror of my own), who saw the opportunity to kidnap this hidden Wallace, and then to blackmail Wallace the Amazing with the discovery. To threaten the rich Wallace, the Wallace who stole for *some* reason (convenience? revenge? to avoid a scandal? to cause one?) the identity of this cut-off, shriveled, strange, isolated, *actual* Wallace.

I would now bet there'd been contact beforehand between Wallace the Amazing and the "Stewartsons," leading up to the night of the performance. Threats, counterthreats, phone calls, e-mails. The inevitable escalation to an extremely public forum—national television. But neither party backing down or giving in.

That's what "Dave Stewartson" was doing standing up in the theater. *We're here. We'll do whatever it takes to get your money, to make you pay. We know you're a fake. We're not afraid. We assume your act is fake. But we* know *you are.*

That's what Wallace was doing, calling on him. *I know you're here. I'm not afraid. You'll never get me. You'll never bring me down.*

And of course, I had completely misread it. It was a standoff. Both parties aware of it. The "Stewartsons" had pulled off the same kind of identity theft—stolen the real Dave Stewartson's identity (and Sandi's too, from somewhere) as fluently, as deftly, as Wallace the Amazing had apparently, long ago, stolen this Wallace's—as if merely to prove to Wallace the Amazing that they knew exactly what he had done and how he had done it and could even duplicate it. As if to show Wallace the Amazing how much they were onto him, how well they understood his tricks.

Kidnapping. Extortion. The "Stewartsons" risking it because the prize was so big. The mythic Vegas-size success of Wallace the Amazing. His past, current, and future earnings. I knew too well the staggering sum it came to.

And all the corollary questions—starting to swirl around me like a cold wind gathering into a storm—when, where, how had Wallace the Amazing, *my* Wallace (or whoever he truly was), taken on this identity, stolen this man's past?

My employer for my lifetime. My twenty-year partner. Not who he said he was. I am reeling, sorting it through, sick to my stomach, dizzy.

The Wallace at my breakfast table continues explaining. Explains that the Stewartsons (or whoever they actually are) had assured him that they would split the extorted proceeds, the Vegas "winnings" with him. His trust in them was irremediably eroded, of course, when he ended up chained to the bathroom fixtures for safe-keeping. (But I am already alert to other possibilities in that fixed-to-the-fixture treatment beyond a simple brute double-cross of their partner. That, for instance, such treatment might have arisen when the Stewartsons saw Archer Wallace getting ideas of his own. Or realizing, for instance, that he didn't need their partnership to get even with Wallace the Amazing. I presume the professional-seeming Stewartsons had not chained him up for no reason.)

Which is all why the real Wallace has gladly stayed here, quietly recovering.

And why this real Wallace didn't react, stayed silent, when I referred to him as "Dave." He wasn't about to risk giving up such a safe place in which to recover.

So the "real" Dave Stewartson is no longer at my breakfast table. He has disappeared, becoming instead the absent symbol for the cruel potential, the threat, of "Dave" and "Sandi."

"I see how upset you are," Archer says, "how confused and alarmed, to discover I'm Archer Wallace. But I had to tell you, to really know if I was right about you—that you work for Wallace the Amazing, that you're involved with him."

I cannot answer him.

"I know you can't answer me—and that's just confirmation. I have to assume you're part of how he does what he does. But he was performing other tricks, ugly tricks, before he met you, believe me . . ."

Before he met you. History, the past, all being remade . . .

Yes, it was showmanship, that tense televised moment between "Wallace" and "Dave" that I had witnessed, confused and anxious. But not the TV showmanship I had thought. It was the showman-ship of each of them *for* each of them, mano a mano, each show-ing the other how far he'll go, demonstrating his fearlessness, his power—the con artist Dave Stewartson (whoever he really is) versus the con artist Wallace the Amazing (whoever *he* really is). A show for two that millions of others stood by innocently watching, misunderstanding. Including me.

And of course, the biggest question about Wallace, *my* Wallace, is why? Why take on the identity of the real Wallace? For money? Probably. Inevitably. I had little doubt that would turn out to be part of the equation. The bottom line is always the bottom line. But was there something more? Was it the appeal, or necessity, of wearing a new identity, of starting over? Did the new identity provide some kind of protection? And I have to ask, as it occurs to me, was it to protect himself from me? To protect against this unknown kid he had just hired, to whom he was entrusting his secrets and his life? And I realize it wouldn't be all that surprising if he had built in a means of escape. If he constructed a disguise that he could slip out of—sneak offstage—at a moment's notice, knowing the need might someday arise. An always-ready position of retreat. Should anything happen to "Wallace the Amazing." Or to this strange, exclusive, utterly dependent relationship between Wallace the Amazing and me.

And if that faded, pale official photo of Dave Stewartson on the Internet is indeed the real Dave Stewartson, then these "Stewartsons" (whoever they really are) are not grudgingly dragging *him* around. They have efficiently taken care of him, somehow silenced him (with threats? some form of capture or imprisonment? something worse?) and the only way to escape a similar fate might be to reconstruct it, find out what that fate was. These are professionals, and this is their big play, and they are not going to let it—or Archer Wallace, their trump card, their leverage, their proof of the Amazing Wallace's criminal past—slip away so easily.

My choices now: to stay here, wait for them to inevitably find me, and try to defend myself? Or to take the real Wallace, stuff him and a bag or two into my car, and stay perpetually, permanently, ahead of them? Hobson's choice—meaning not much choice at all. And whichever I choose, of course, I must continue, at least in the short term, to deliver the data, do my job, for Wallace the Amazing.

I no longer trust blindly in him. I no longer know who he is. Part of me wants to deliver him a load of misinformation, let him bumble and stumble around onstage, to the confusion, then hoots and derision, of the audience.

Who is he? The only solid thing in my life, the rock, the center, the organizing principle, has now gone liquid, amorphous. A con artist—a potentially ruthless and heartless one, to steal an identity wholesale, and who knows what else he stole along with it. And I can't just call him up and ask. Or wait backstage for him and demand an explanation. Because I can't—still can't—violate our rules. Because whatever else he may or may not have done, he hasn't violated our agreement. So how can I? And maybe he *has* an explanation. One that I'll even believe.

As the shock wears off, the reality sets in, and its attendant risks. If the Stewartsons—by all indications, pretty competent, if entirely unscrupulous researchers—figure out who I am, what I do, what my role is for Wallace, if they figure out how cut off I am, they won't be able to resist the opportunity. To get rid of me. "Handle" me in whatever unthinkable way they handled the original Dave. In my isolation, I am such an easy mark. My aloneness—it can work for me. It can work against me.

But my anxiety is getting ahead of itself. One thing at a time. They only know by now, presumably, that their Wallace has disappeared. They don't know me. Not yet. How much they learn, how quickly they learn it, will depend on their detective work, which is too early to judge, and no other investigation, after all—by journalists, fans, professional debunkers—has discovered me yet. (This is different, of course. A physical trail. And these are, whatever else they may be, professional criminals. A different skill set. Different methods. Different breed.)

But they might realize—or reasonably assume—that I know they're after the real Wallace, based on my rescue of their charge, their quarry, their missing prize. If they even figure out it's me—or someone like me—behind it. If they even discover there's a "me" at all.

• • •

"Dave," "Sandi," and now "Wallace," *my* "Wallace": What does it mean, really, to take on a new identity? Las Vegas is arguably America's ground zero for that. People pouring into the city to begin a new life, to start a marriage or end one—to say nothing of those flowing in by the thousands to "lose themselves," to simply be someone else, someone more glamorous, more carefree, for a few hours, for a few days. (For years and years, Vegas was America's fastest-growing city. And no wonder—its transitory nature makes it the perfect place to hide or start anew.) It's a place where people come to remake themselves, for slithering snakes to slough their old skin in the desert and grow a glistening new one. But what happens when people come here to remake themselves and discover that they're still the same? That it's not so easy to remake oneself? That the past, the truth, leaks out? What do you do when you discover that you are stuck with who you are? Is it an occasion for acceptance, for a desert-lit moment of truth and self-discovery? Hah. It is almost certainly instead a moment to wrap yourself in some new layer of crust and coating like a quick desert tan, or else to finally lash out, to scream your frustration to the merciless, unresponsive, empty desert, or to take it out on whoever or whatever is closest. Maybe some can slough that skin, start over in the hot, dry cleansing desert, but surely some discover they cannot. And no one can do it entirely.

At first, I'm furious enough at "Wallace" to consider taking Archer Wallace and his story to the police. Let them investigate, get to the bottom of it. Certainly it's one way to save myself from the Stewartsons. Escort into downtown Vegas the still shockingly white, bony, broken Archer Wallace. Of course, it would all come quickly tumbling down—the act, the show, the income, the partnership, this life. But would the police immediately doubt it, not be up to it, screw up the handling of the truth, merely because of its complexity? The Stewartsons taking on someone else's identity, then blackmailing "Wallace" because he had done the same thing, and "Wallace" running what might previously be classified as entertainment by the police but would now be seen primarily as a scam, given his false identity, given his theft of assets, etc. There would be newspapers, testimony, drawn-out trials and appeals, given Wallace the Amazing's deep pockets. I would spend the next few years in close proximity to the Stewartsons, to *both* Wallaces, in the same hearing rooms, waiting rooms, and courtrooms. My privacy, my quiet, would be gone forever. Could someone like me handle that? Someone so private?

"Your condition," I say to Archer Wallace now, continuing to adjust, to newly understand. "That didn't happen to you over a few weeks. You were like this when the Stewartsons found you. Did . . . did Wallace . . . keep you locked up like this?" Or were you a bum, living on the street, financially wiped out, ill-equipped from a previous life of privilege to deal with street life or the hardships of reality?

He looks at me, doesn't answer. At first. And then it comes in a flood.

. . .

His parents had died in a boating accident in the Gulf of Mexico during his junior year of high school, and all their money went to him, their only child, with no instructions and no guardianship attached, and no close living relatives, and he dropped out, dismissed the live-in help, and rattled around in their big antebellum mansion for a few weeks, before hitting the road with a pocketful of hundreds. In those few rushed, chaotic, otherworldly weeks of death and inheritance, it became apparent to Archer Wallace that he hadn't a true friend in the world, that everyone was angling for a payout, so he cut all his ties and took off, to start over.

I asked him if his parents' accident had been covered in any of the local papers at the time. He shrugged, had no idea. But I had the strong suspicion it must have been, and I was right. (For old newspapers, you used to have to rely on libraries, descend into their bowels to their outdated, rarely consulted microfiche machines and collections—old newspapers were just about the last thing left that you couldn't access online. It really made you feel like a detective, sitting hunched over in a dusty carrel, scrolling through ancient headlines. But now, of course, there are online sites for old newspapers too.) I wanted to check for the story in the local papers for a couple of reasons. First, to see how closely Archer Wallace's version of events matched or strayed from that of a local reporter or two. And second, and more importantly, I figured someone else had come across the story, might have discovered it this way too, from the local papers. Maybe heard about it, maybe read about it, maybe both, but became somehow infinitely and intimately aware of it.

Someone who had grown up, as it happened, pretty close to Archer Wallace's little one-horse southern town (according to the few, spare details of the "official" myth-soaked "biography"). Close enough, I realized, to read the story in the papers, or hear about it, the facts of the tragedy passed casually, offhand, high school kid to high school kid.

Local folks were dripping with sympathy, I'm sure. But I could see how it would look to a certain ambitious, impatient, cynical, brilliant, fame-hungry boy. *This kid Archer Wallace—this dumb-luck kid in the newspaper—has now got everything. Endless money, no responsibility. He can do anything. Go anywhere. Be anyone. While I have nothing. Well, not nothing—suffocating parents, both working three jobs, a family that struggles to eat, living hand to mouth and meal to meal, sharing beds and sharing baths (not bathrooms, baths), breathing on one another, no space, no place, no privacy. I want to be that kid. That Archer Wallace.* And with the boldness, cunning, and ambition of youth, he didn't see why he couldn't be.

The real Archer Wallace had no real plan, of course, so he kept a significant portion of his money—initially at least—in little mounds and rolls of cash hidden around the immense house whose secret corners and tucked-in places he knew so well. He soon saw the risks of that—yes, he was completely adrift, but not completely stupid, he tells me. So before taking off on his extended travels, he opened an account in another town, an anonymous bank, where people didn't know him. He chose the anonymity, somewhere far enough away, where he presumed the story hadn't followed him. Where there would be no pointing, no special treatment, no deference, no whispering. Where he was only a nameless, faceless, unremarkable account holder. With a plain-vanilla checking account.

And someone—someone ambitious, brilliant, cynical, someone following closely but not too closely—opened an accompanying, linked *savings* account, and began to transfer funds. Copied Wallace's signature. The high school experience everywhere involves fake IDs for buying beer and getting into bars. Someone used the same simple techniques to produce a license with "Archer Wallace's" new photo and his name beneath it. Usually at stake—a few six-packs and enhanced chances of meeting girls. At stake in this case— a fortune. But it was the fortune of a high school kid, and no one thought in terms other than high school, and it was the simplest thing in the world to pull off in a sleepy, trusting, casual, small southern town. It aroused no suspicion, and he was able to test both his ID and his technique when he simply shifted the money from checking to savings. And with Archer Wallace out somewhere on the open road, this shrewd, enterprising boy, wandering into this new bank, could even begin to experience what it *felt* like to occupy the identity of Archer Wallace. He could come make his transfers, flirt innocently with the tellers; he could *try it on*. With the real

Archer Wallace unknown and far away, he could safely *become* Archer Wallace a little. Maybe more than a little.

Once all the money was in savings, he could transfer it in one sum to another institution where he'd opened an account, then take out the money and take off to another life. Before Archer Wallace even returned. And when and if the real Archer Wallace did return and realized he was the victim of an ingenious theft, he'd have no idea who the thief was or where he had gone. I think of our first years on the road—unknown entertainers, always on the move, no broad reputation yet. When we finally began to earn one, when Archer Wallace might have first heard of us, it would have been too late—Wallace the Amazing already established, with bank accounts, multiple identifications, credit, home ownership, a family. Much more of an Archer Wallace than some wandering, orphaned country boy suddenly claiming to be the famous magician. The real Archer Wallace—well-off, carefree, coddled since childhood—suddenly without parents or resources or even much of an official identity, spirals downward into a life of penury, struggle, disconnection, who knows what else.

Something along those lines. I could see it so clearly.

You don't have to work very hard to imagine what the Stewartsons saw when they walked back into Room 103 of that motel. To feel what they felt. Whether or not they are actually killers, they have a record of—a capacity for—decisive, possibly violent action. Because they have somewhere, somehow, eliminated the real Stewartson or Stewartsons—buried them in a field, tossed them overboard, rolled them into a carpet, left them in a dumpster, disposed of them somehow. So you can imagine the need for retribution, for retaliation, working its way up in the fake Stewartsons—free-floating anger, because they have no idea yet who seized their quarry or else turned him loose. But they know the weak, debilitated Archer Wallace didn't pull it off himself. They know someone helped.

You don't have to work very hard to see the simmering, threatening questioning they put the motel clerks and the Central American maids through, the implied threat behind their questions, the rage standing by, like an accomplice, tapping a lead pipe in a palm, ready to step forward and swing at the slightest provocation, maybe even doing so, here or there, just to stay in practice, just to stay in shape.

And did a maid or clerk see something? Did they see my car sitting across the street? See me stride through the motel lobby? Help a sick guest out to the parking lot? I don't know if the Stewartsons will be able to find me, but I don't know that they won't.

And all this time, I am working. Doing the research, providing, as always, the necessary data for the show. Does Wallace trust what I am delivering him? Why not? He doesn't know that I know any of this about him, about his thievery of someone's life, about who he really is or isn't. Although he might realize that I was watching the quick kerfuffle—the stumble and smooth cover-up—between him and Dave Stewartson. And might realize that his star researcher—rattled, startled, confused—might research what he had just observed a little more deeply.

• • •

And then, a turn of events I might have predicted—if only I had realized who I was actually rescuing from the motel. Who I was actually saving.

"Take me back to the Stewartsons," Archer Wallace says suddenly.

"What!"

"I want to go back. I want to continue with our plan, split the proceeds with them, honor the deal they offered me. But I won't let them chain me to the tub this time."

He sees my startled look, regarding him as if he is delusional, so he tries to explain. "Look, they were afraid I was going to get scared.

Back out on them, run away. They saw me as only a pawn in the plan. And I started to see myself that way too." He pauses, considers the logic of that for a moment. "But I'm stronger now. After this, they'll realize they can't mess with me like that anymore. I won't tell them how I got away, but they'll see I have the power to escape. And I still want my portion of the deal. Because I still want to get even with Wallace the Amazing, and this is the best way to do it. And they still need me, after all. I'm still the proof of his criminal past that would destroy him, that will give us all leverage . . . and cash."

I'm stronger now. Thanks to me. Thanks to my cutting the chain links in the bathroom. Thanks to my care and feeding.

I thought I was saving the real Dave Stewartson. If I had thought I was saving the Stewartsons' fellow blackmailer—and plunging my quiet, orderly life into question, confusion, anxiety, by discovering the real Archer Wallace—I would not have acted so heroically, so instinctively. I would have left him in that bathroom.

He pauses, considering again. Sits up taller, adjusts his shoulders back. "Come to think of it . . . why do I even need them?"

You need them because they are the pros, I'm thinking. *Because they're threatening. They're scary. They generate consequences. You need them, because you think you don't. Because you don't understand the seriousness of the game you're about to play.*

"Are you going to tell them about me?" I ask.

"You're part of the cash machine. You're part of the goose and golden egg. You won't confirm it, but I know. It's obvious. So I'd be crazy to give you up. To risk unplugging the cash machine. I guess you'll have to trust me not to tell. It's in my own self-interest, all our self-interest really, to keep Wallace the Amazing generating income. Remaining successful. Plus, if I give you up, then *you* become the leverage; they don't need me anymore—you take my place as the one to bring him down. So I won't be doing that. No, you need to stay on his payroll." He smiles. "A payroll that's about to expand, that's all."

"And you think they're just gonna let you waltz back in and rejoin them? Like nothing happened? Like you never left? They'll trust you less than ever. These are not nice people, Archer."

He shrugs. Is quiet. Is thinking about that, I hope.

I try once again to find out more about Dave Stewartson—the ghostly original one, *my* Dave Stewartson—but these new Stewartsons have done a good job of obliterating him. I stumble across more and more of the new Dave all over the Internet—licenses, IDs, tax filings, applications, more social media. All of it has digitally consumed the original Dave Stewartson, swallowed up his memory and his evidence, so that all I have is that one original picture, which presumably the new Dave has attempted to take down if he knows about it. I stare at the old Dave again—official, somber, expressionless. I didn't search deeply enough, carefully enough. I made an amateurish error. I am staring at my own failure. The old Dave is in some government files, in someone's old photo albums, but whose? Where? What broken family? What fleeting friendship? The picture says, in a small scratchy voice, like a thin, struggling radio transmission: It's me. Don't forget. It's me. I'm still here. Find me.

Carefully casing the motel for hours, rescuing Wallace just before dawn, I hadn't slept at all. And since then, not surprisingly, I had continued to lay awake at night, restless, unable to sleep, thinking about both Wallaces, and myself, and my awkward painful last encounter with Debbie—Debbie now gone. A kind of strange, dizzying, intimate dance, the four of us, a discordant music swirling around us. I eventually gave in to complete exhaustion, curling into my mattress in a dizzy haze, my hyperwakefulness suddenly overwhelmed, collapsing into slumber. Done in by the events of the past few days.

Which is why it still seems dreamlike, nightmarish, caught initially in some state between dreaming and wakefulness, when I wake to find Sandi Stewartson on top of me.

A blonde on top of you as you wake—this is of course a Vegas dream. But I awaken, in fact, a few stumbling seconds later, to the click of handcuffs (which could still be part of a Vegas dream, of course, but in this case are not), and I am hustled in my underwear out of my dark bedroom into my living room, where Archer Wallace my houseguest is attached to one of my dining room chairs, his arms, legs, and mouth duct-taped, and his eyes wide, staring at me and at the scene. I am shoved into the chair next to him. All the lights are off. The Stewartsons check the windows, where I drew the shades and curtains earlier, and once they see they are all closed (my own thoroughness of privacy, suddenly working against me), they turn on a low kitchen light that still keeps us all in shadow.

"What did you think?" says Dave Stewartson snidely, leaning down into my face. "Did you think that when we turned around to check behind us, we didn't see you? Did you really think that going in and out of the Bellagio, we didn't see you waiting in the lobby? That we didn't see you in the market? That we didn't see your nondescript piece of shit car in our mirror? Why'd we keep turning around, you moron? To make sure you were still there." He seems irritated, somehow insulted at my amateurism. "We could see how incompetent you were. We were afraid we'd lose you. And we had no way to know anything about you—who you were, what you knew. Hell, we couldn't very well just turn around and ask you, God knows you weren't going to tell us anything, and we figured threatening you might not accomplish anything either. So we had to wait until we could see where you live, get you at home, and the only way to do that was to offer you our prize here." He gestures to Wallace. "We figured you'd just come in and look horrified and not touch, and when you left, we'd follow you home. But we also knew you might want to be a hero, and rescue the prize from us, which worked just as well, still told us where you live, and at least a little of who you are and how you see yourself." He grabs another of my dining room chairs, spins it to face us, sits. His irritation seems to ebb a little. "We would have been here earlier, but we wanted you to get comfortable, start to feel safe, drop your guard a little, while we were checking other things. Making sure nobody else lives here with you. Making sure the girlfriend is out of the picture. It all took a while, and none of it's as complete as we usually like, because as you know, Chas, you're pretty well scrubbed from the world. You're practically a spy. A spy here in Vegas. A nonentity. A ghost. Now what exactly would you be doing out here with a background like that?"

I am obviously dealing with a certain level, or at least a certain kind, of professionalism. I've always known that the highly democratic Internet—its databases, sites, passwords and codes to be cracked by hackers—is a boon to law enforcement, and the same boon to scam artists. I see now that I'm not the only technologist in Vegas.

Stewartson, I notice (my eyes adjusting to the low light), is holding an orange from my fruit bowl. Now he peels it. Detaches and sucks slowly on a section. "And this actually works out better. Because while you may not respond to the threat of harm to yourself, now there's our pal Archer here, and we're sure you'll respond appropriately to the threat of harming him, fragile as we both know he is . . ."

• • •

They were settling in, I saw. Stewartson and his babe, Sandi. Curtains drawn. In the low light, something in the angles of their faces, their noses and cheeks, catches me. Their features project a kind of unnerving strength and aggressiveness, which they both seem to share. An assertive tightness around their mouths, eyes puffy and bulging. Like some subtle deformity portending criminality—a predictive trait discovered by university researchers. Weird and undefined in the muted light.

I wasn't so concerned with my own safety. I wasn't even that concerned with Wallace's. They needed him—he was what made their blackmail work—so what could they really do to him, beyond terrify him or pretend they didn't care what happened to him. No, my big concern (as Sandi duct-taped me to the chair, working silently, expressionlessly, clearly with plenty of practice) was how I was going to do my job. How was I going to give Wallace the next show's information? What would he do if I couldn't get it to him? Suddenly cancel the show? Say it was a sudden illness? A family emergency? (In a way, *yes*, a family emergency.) My computers, in the next room, showed nothing—I was always careful, even in the house alone, not to leave revealing screens or information up there if I wasn't sitting there—but I still could not figure out how or when I was going to be able to send him what he needed.

"You've got a lot in common, you two, don't you?" said Stewartson, checking the duct tape on Wallace and on me. "Both under the radar, both pretty much alone. Have you discovered that about each other, your brotherly bond?"

If Wallace didn't get the information he needed, he would know there was something wrong. The absence of communication was really the only way for me to signal that something was wrong, and after twenty years, it would be a strong message. He would realize, I hoped, that he now had to rescue me, as I had rescued him. The Wallace that I no longer knew, no longer trusted—now, for the first time, I really needed him.

With both of us tied up tight, my doppelganger brother and me, the Stewartsons did a little reconnaissance around the condo. Stewartson soon confronted the locked door to my office. He returned, looked inquisitively at me. "You lock a door in your own condominium?" Ripping the piece of tape off my mouth—the sudden sharp sting on both cheeks made my eyes water—he waited for an answer.

"There's lots of valuable computer equipment in there. I've been robbed before."

"And a locked office door is going to discourage a thief? You kidding? It's going to do just the opposite." He pressed the same strip of duct tape back over my mouth.

He went out to my garage, returned a minute later, crossed the living room with an armful of the tools from the bag in my car's trunk, and in a moment I heard some pounding, scraping, a sharp sound of wood cracking, and then silence—obviously while he looked around inside the office after breaking open the door. He didn't bother to ask me where the key was, or demand that I open the office for him. Maybe he figured I'd try something, or find some way to stall. Maybe it was less risky to leave me tied up. Maybe the destruction was mostly to make a point.

He returned to eye me. "That is a lot of computer equipment."

"I'm a consultant."

"What kind of consulting?"

"Information consulting."

"What kinds of clients?"

Only one. "You name it," I said. "I'll work for anyone."

"See, I don't think that's true," said Stewartson, sitting down again, settling into a spot on the beige couch this time. "The way I see it, I stood up at that Wallace the Amazing show, and suddenly you're trailing us, and then you take Archer Wallace from us, suddenly willing to be involved, to take a risk. I'm seeing a little cause and effect here. I think maybe you and the Amazing Wallace are connected. Connected through those computers, I'd venture to say."

A professional. An artist of the criminal kind. No dummy. "Like I say, turns out you hardly exist. I doubt that's an accident. So here's a guy who doesn't exist, except for his impressive roomful of computers. And the nice condo, the food in the fridge, it comes from somewhere. So I wonder what it means, if you can't get to those computers of yours," he said, as if with an offhand curiosity, a mere comment in passing, but looking at me closely, to gauge my reaction.

• • •

With the curtains drawn against any sense of day or night and the cheap kitchen wall clock invisible from the living room, you lose all track of time. With your elbows and knees and ankles pinned into place by duct tape and plastic ties, your muscles have no choice but to give in, relax into the resistance of your vertical bed, your upright home. The duct tape tight around your wrists and ankles, the forced immobility—both factors constrict your normal blood flow, creating a lethargy paradoxical to the situation. I find myself drifting in and out, moments of an exhausted semi-sleep. Seconds? Minutes? I see that Archer Wallace, next to me, is at moments sleeping upright too. Time collapses. Time deforms. Expands and contracts. Like waiting for a delayed flight in a featureless airport lounge. Sitting for hours in a bland bureaucratic hallway. The purgatories of modernity—and this is one more new form. Sandi and Dave drift in and out of the living room only occasionally. I hear them cobble together meals from my thinly stocked refrigerator; they peel the tape off my mouth, stuff a few bites of sandwich into me, pour a little juice down my throat, then do the same with Archer Wallace. I wonder if the goal here is to return him to his previous state of abject fear and docility, and take me along for the ride. They say little to each other, nothing to us.

And in this drifting, this drifting of unknown intention toward unknown outcome, I can't help but notice that this imprisonment in my own home, oddly, isn't so different from my regular working life. In quality, in texture, yes—the terror, the lack of control. But in *actuality*, in what is literally happening—and not happening—it's much the same. I am strapped in a chair, immobilized, silent, for hours on end. What's any different about that? Only that there are no computer screens in front of me. Only that my confusion, terror, anticipation, and dread are what's in front of me. But when I quell those, when I let those dull and die down, it's not so different at all.

And then, finally, Sandi turns on my big living room television. And suddenly the four of us—two of us bound—are watching a Vegas channel to which I subscribe. As if we are simply another strange Vegas family, no stranger than most.

Care to guess what show we are gathered around?

Though I try to hide it, to act nonchalant, only half-interested, I've never been more anxious to see a Wallace performance.

"You seem a little nervous," says Dave Stewartson, archly, smug. "Why would that be?"

I don't answer. I watch the screen. I had expected that Wallace would cancel. That he would alter the act, do some different tricks. That he would perform a different kind of show.

• • •

But Wallace the Amazing came onstage as confidently as ever. Made his graceful small talk. Took questions. Went into his mild trance, as always. I could sense that something was different about him, though, and of course it was. He would have to come up with some tactics, conjure up something, some misdirection, some other kind of magic. I felt hollowed-out, defeated. At last, I had failed him.

He began to call on members of the audience, and called out specifics. The names of their dogs. The colors of their curtains. Their first girlfriends. Their latest girlfriends. Weaving them into narratives. Showing relationships between audience members, where they had no idea there were any.

In short, doing the same show as always.

The Stewartsons were more than mildly disappointed. Sandi looked at Dave with an annoyed I-told-you-so expression. Dave must have revealed his hunches about me and promised her fireworks, and yet there was nothing. The anger was simmering in Dave; you could see it. I had the sense he would take it out on me.

As for me, I was in shock. A state of awe. Watching him, listening to him—everything about the show the same, everything about it profoundly different—I felt a shift in the universe, an almost physical realignment. A sudden new understanding of the unique, wildly ambitious kid who'd grown into the man on television in front of me, who knew how different he was, knew he deserved more, so saw it and seized it, compelled by something akin to a sense of mission, perhaps, to escape that backwater southern town. I realized that he had humored me all these years, hired me only to confirm and support his abilities, so that he could fact-check himself. I was the safety net beneath his high-wire act of mentalism, and tonight he simply walked the high wire without the net, because in a pinch, in a tight spot like tonight, if he had to, he could do it.

Wallace the Amazing, most amazingly, it seemed, *was* psychic. Or whatever more scientific, accurate, or sophisticated terminology than "psychic" existed for his brand and degree of prescient abilities. I felt, finally, at last, after all these years, what thousands, millions, felt in the presence of Wallace the Amazing, witnessing his show— felt at last that shift in my understanding, that shift in the universe. The recognition of, if not a world beyond, at least some separate dimension to this one. I finally accepted the notion of a capacity beyond myself. This was, I realized, a moment of religious conversion. A moment of religious experience. I was born again—or born, anyway—into something primal, substantial. I *knew* it, was *gratified* to know it and feel it authentically and thoroughly. If only briefly.

The weight of evidence still said no. The science said no. But something was nevertheless revealed. Until I realized the truth— and the realization hit me hard. No psychic ability. No sixth sense or paranormal fluency. Somewhere, squirreled away, holed up somewhere in circumstances and conditions that would be immediately recognizable to me right down to every mundane detail— bank of computer screens, empty closets, refrigerator full of takeout leftovers—there was someone else just like me. Someone else delivering the information to him as well, maybe so he could cross-check it, check us against each other to make sure we were both doing our work and neither of us was getting sloppy or slipshod or suddenly pulling a fast one on him. But mostly, mainly, it was to protect him from, to handle, a situation just like this. To let the show go on. Somewhere, there was someone, for all these years, all this time—someone else cut off, isolated, in Wallace's employ—someone just like me.

Yes, Wallace the Amazing *was* amazing.

And I realized the corollary. That he was covered. He didn't *need* to rescue me. Arguably couldn't *risk* rescuing me, couldn't risk the connection between us being known or seen.

I am on my own.

Alone, with the fragile, unstable, real Archer Wallace.

Meaning, I am alone.

"So what *do* you do for him?" Stewartson asked me, proffering a wedge of orange teasingly in front of me, then taking it back, biting into it himself. Still annoyed at my evident superfluousness, my apparent lack of immediate value or connection to the show—but still curious.

I still wasn't going to tell them, because that would have meant the end of it. The end of the act. The end of everything. Wallace the Amazing had been my surrogate family. For now, at least, I had to protect him. For now, I knew no other way, no other choice. Whatever his real name, his real identity, turned out to be.

But now I also knew he could go on without me. That he *would* go on without me. That he already had. So what harm was there in telling the Stewartsons what I did for him? Maybe there were more of us "detectives," more of us suppliers—three, four, a dozen, all unknown to one another. Maybe he added more of us as he grew more successful.

I was angry, hurt by what was now a series of lies—his name, his past, the actual size and nature of the staff that surrounded him—piling up, and who knew how high the pile would grow? The pile of lies atop which I looked out now, my perspective skewed, angled, false, the lies still shifting beneath me. Who he implied he was versus who he actually was. My bedrock understanding that I was his lifeline—and then, suddenly, I wasn't. I was angry, hurt, but of course, he had never explicitly said or promised otherwise.

So why not join the Stewartsons? Help them pull off the blackmail? God knows I could be helpful to them. No one knew him like I did—his whereabouts, his inclinations, his judgments, his relationships, his very thoughts. Why not get even for his misrepresentation? There was every reason to save myself from the infliction of pain, the torture, that undoubtedly would ensue if I continued to resist the Stewartsons' questions. Why continue to be loyal? Jesus, what was my crazy loyalty about?

• • •

Soon enough, I understand why we are still tied up. Why the Stewartsons are settling in. Because my condo provides a perfect way for them to keep an eye on both Archer and me, as well as a useful, serendipitous base of operations. My grabbing Archer, holing up here—it now looks practically like an invitation to them.

They e-mail Wallace the Amazing. I have never e-mailed him, of course; it is too direct, too easily traceable. But for them, it is simple. They send a short, pointed piece of fan mail to his website. They sign the e-mail "Dave Stewartson." You know, that strange fan from a few nights ago? That will get his attention. An e-mail, a communication, he's undoubtedly been watching for anyway.

It does get his attention. He writes back as cryptically but purposefully. You can see the purpose, the focus, the anger, the comprehension, arcing behind his response to one more rabid fan.

We're with Archer. He says hello.

says the Stewartsons' e-mail. Innocent, but telegraphic.

Who's Archer?

says the e-mail back. In its entirety. Implication: I'm not admitting to any understanding of what you're talking about or even who you are. Implication: I'm not giving this bull crap the time of day. Implication: Come and get me. Go ahead. Just try.

Who's Archer? Is that a message to them or to me? Everything tempts me to abandon Wallace, or whoever he is. Everything tempts me to, but for whatever crazy reason I remain a dutiful employee.

Hands and legs bound, mouths taped, we are side by side in the dark, Archer and I. (He is no longer who I originally thought—the invisible, absent Dave Stewartson—and yet, in his disconnection and isolation, he is still my doppelganger.) We are held identically captive, literally composing each other's shadow in the light from the blaring television, in case there was ever any doubt. We look at each other, eyes to eyes, incommunicative, merely factual, the rest of our means of expression—oral and facial—taped over. It's a late-night blizzard of infomercials: abdominal machines, weight loss programs, miracle face creams, vitamin regimens, all of it cast out broadly like an electronic fishing net across America. I watch the screen's color, blinking and flashing in the face of Archer Wallace—cragged, white, a recipient over whom the messages wash like the light, a distant blur, not for him. The blasting of the television is hardly intended to entertain us. It is, I'm sure, to mask the antics in my master bedroom, where the athletic Dave and Sandi are unwinding, amped up by the excitement of their criminal escapade, by recovering their Archer Wallace prize, by making e-mail contact—acknowledgment, a response—and thus being a step closer to hitting the jackpot. But the TV's blare doesn't mask the bedroom noise.

I am still thinking about my misplaced loyalty. The bedroom noise is an irritant—but it's about to be a blessing, and a signal, I realize in a moment.

Connection, connection. We are more connected than we know.

And he is right. Because here she is.

Tiptoeing in the front door as if merely coming in late from work, as if being careful not to wake me asleep on the couch in front of the television.

Debbie.

My Debbie, now standing over Archer and me.

Debbie—as if drawn to me, from somewhere out of the desert, in my hour of need.

Debbie, who still has her keys to my condo, of course, and could lurk outside, waiting for the perfect moment to enter, which doesn't come any more perfect than the current animated primal bedroom antics.

She stands for a moment, taking in the two of us tied here. A vindication at least of her decision to help. I presume that she was watching the house, trying to decide whether to come in, to forgive, to try again with me, when she saw a couple breaking in. Or else she was just swinging by, uncommitted, curious, unsure what she would feel or do as she passed, and saw the unfamiliar car, and all the drawn shades, and managed somewhere, given this house she knows so well, to peek in to see what was going on. But either way, waiting cautiously, until the right moment to enter, to assess, to help.

And as she stands over me, looking at me tied up and taped, we both listen to, can't help but hear, the spirited grunting and groaning in the next room. Even here, amid the extreme tension of the moment, or maybe because of it, an unmistakable sexual charge passes between us. For a short moment, here in the television's shadow, there is no mistaking the rush of desire mixing with the flood of my gratitude. It's bound only by the ropes and tape, obvious in my eyes above my taped mouth.

Quickly, silently, catlike, she moves to the kitchen, returns with a serrated knife from my hardly used butcher-block set, slices through the tape on my wrists. I seize the knife from her, cut down and through the tape on my ankles, and go to work on Archer

Wallace. Though we can't discuss it, can't risk making a sound, it is obvious that we are listening for either Dave or his girlfriend to climax; we know we have until then.

I look at Debbie; I look at Archer; I look around the living room. I realize I might be seeing my own home, my safe house and sanctuary, for the last time. I can't return here; they'd know where to find me. Debbie, the real Archer Wallace, my home—a triumvirate of meaning for me, a triumvirate of my connection to the world, and in seconds I am taking in all three and facing some fundamental shift that I can't yet define.

I quietly rush into my office, grab my laptop, slap it shut as I tuck it under my arm, like a little black dog I'm rescuing from a fire, and we hustle together—me, Debbie, and the fragile but improving Archer Wallace—out into the darkness.

As we scurry for Debbie's car—mine they know, hers they don't—I am dealt one more surprise, this one not as welcome as Debbie.

Archer Wallace, fragile Archer Wallace, just behind us, without warning, limps off to the right and into the desert blackness.

Away from my rescue. Away from my heroism. Away from me.

Just like Wallace the Amazing, when I rescued him from Big Eddie's thugs. The same trot off into the desert. As if to return me to my previous nonexistence, to ghostliness. As if what had just occurred had never occurred at all.

Debbie—surprised and confused, but sensing that he is somehow on our side, is one of us, that he *needs* us—wants to call out to him, stop him, but I brusquely cover her mouth, stifle her. We're still just outside the condo's bedroom window, and if the Stewartsons hear anything, they'll be off each other and out here in a flash, armed. No, the first sound they hear needs to be Debbie's car pulling away, only taillights visible—if they hear or see anything at all.

The real Archer Wallace—emboldened? possessed? not thinking clearly after the physical and mental strain of a day and night taped to a chair? or thinking extremely clearly?—disappears into the desert darkness.

Debbie fires up her old Triumph, and we slip away, down the bland desert street into the night, into the unknown, into a new world.

SIX

Debbie's place is cozy, lived-in, quaint, a comfortable cottage she has rented for years. I've never been here before. Not because of some arrogant she-comes-to-me-I-don't-go-to-her reason, and not for some if-I-stay-there-it-escalates-the-relationship, fear-of-commitment reason, but simply because my work for Wallace has generally required me to be at my own house, with my computers. Now I'll have to figure out an abbreviated way to do it, to deliver off my laptop only—of course, I know now that he has a backup system and may not need me anyway.

My first real visit to Debbie's house is as a fugitive from my own, a man on the run. On the night I say a furtive good-bye to my own home, with not even time for a glance back, I am finally saying hello to hers. Noting the contrasts between the two, noting the striking similarities—the same cutlery, the same glasses from the same Sam's Club sale—telltale signs of adults living alone.

Of course, two things have happened to alter the dynamic between us: the strangeness of my occupation has intruded, coming alive in the person of the emaciated real Wallace; and Debbie has rescued me. To say nothing of the fact that I can't go home right now, which leaves me to stay here or at a motel, which we both know is riskier. Holed up at Debbie's, I am—in the short term at least—effectively lost. In this case, a very good thing.

"I won't ask you who he is," she says. "I know you're not going to tell me. But can you tell me where he's going? Does he *have* somewhere to go?"

I shake my head. "He's got no money. He knows no one. He's got nowhere to go or hide. They're going to find him . . ."

"Who *are* they, anyway? Who *are* these people?"

I look at her. I can tell her honestly. "They use the name Stewartson. Dave and Sandi. But who are they really? I have no idea."

The Stewartsons standing up in the audience that first night, to make themselves known. I think about it. (It's the one kind of stage entertainment where there's such an intimate interaction between performer and audience, isn't it? Singers, rock stars, dancers, tumblers, and illusionists, staging spectacles, take no such risks. They have no such intimacy. And of course, Wallace's "act" is more intimate than even another magician's. It is, ironically, an "act" that is all about intimacy, and honesty, and exposure.) The Stewartsons' behavior after the show led me to an erroneous judgment about their amateurism. Their ability to follow me as I was following them, to uncover and hold Wallace, to so efficiently find and trap me, indicated something far more than the enthusiastic amateur Vegas grifter. (Vegas is of course rife with grifters. And I have to accept the fact that, behind all the technology and sophisticated data management, I am in truth only a grifter myself.)

So at three in the morning, after Debbie and I have held each other, wrapped ourselves chest to chest, alive, relieved, together—after we've found our connection again and felt that connection drift naturally, powerfully, familiarly yet freshly too, from our hearts to our loins—I get up out of bed, tiptoe out to the breakfast nook, and power up my trusty laptop. I turn to my sources that I have nurtured, to my databases that I have cultivated like plants, to my special network. For twenty-four hours, I've been reactive. It's time to be proactive. I've been playing defense. It's time to grab the ball back and march down the cyber-field into enemy territory.

Fake Dave Stewartson. That smiling quintessentially American visage. Let's dig a little deeper.

At first I can find nothing. Which backfires on Dave. The fact that he is able to manage his Internet presence—or absence—so well, only confirms my suspicion that I am dealing with someone who is no amateur. I dig deeper. Deeper still. I tap into my reliable government and police and military sites. I use a graphic interface that allows me to do identification from a photo portrait only. I'm in full research mode. I'm awake. I'm alert.

And in an hour, Dave is a different dude. Though not a very surprising one. First of all, it's Stewart Davidson—of course. Practically mocking me. Navy Seal, segueing to highly trained servant of the US intelligence services. Forced retirement on an internal violation in a diplomatically sensitive situation in South America. Pension adjustment reflecting this forced early shift in duties and subsequent forced "retirement"—which I take to be some form of termination (this obvious from Stewart Davidson's pay stubs, tax returns, etc.). Six intensive years of training. Three years of active service. Then, finished. Not a very happy math. One that explains both his bitterness and his footlooseness—if that's a word. Some of the actual dates are unclear, even redacted, but the nature and tone of Stew's bio, of his service to his country, of his life, comes through loud and clear. It's startling to realize how quickly and thoroughly he built an online "Dave Stewartson" (or simply added one to the thousands of existing Dave Stewartsons) to compete with the Dave Stewartson I had found. There is no rich Dave Stewartson in a ditch or dumpster somewhere, I realize. This former US intelligence operative just created him out of whole digital cloth with the click of a few buttons, probably swiping enough details from existing Dave Stewartsons to construct a credible new one. He had then simply intercepted a "real" Dave

Stewartson's show tickets—the easy trick of a forwarded address or mailbox grab—correctly suspecting that with Wallace's incredible visual memory, or whatever system Wallace used, he would know immediately which photo didn't match which live audience member. And maybe too, Wallace recognized Davidson from somewhere, which just confirmed the imposture for him.

My "trusty" Internet—I know it and use it as a place to uncover the truth. But it's even more effective as a place to create lies. Lies I fell for easily and completely.

Perhaps more interesting is his companion, "Sandi Stewartson." Hardly. Sheila Barton. Special Forces. Currently on active duty. *Active duty?* What, keeping an eye on Stew/Dave? Or managing to be in two places at once—not an unimaginable accomplishment, given the suspect organizational skills and record of the huge US military. Do they think she's in Managua or Montevideo, when she's actually in Vegas?

Anyway, it explains a lot—about their tracking of, sniffing out the real Wallace, etc. At least I know who they are. It doesn't, as you can imagine, make me feel much better. They presumably still don't know who I really am, or where I am, or much about me at all, which, considering their training and skills, makes me feel a pinch of pride there in Debbie's breakfast nook. But that pinch of pride is of course overwhelmed by fear and uncertainty—and sympathy for the real Wallace, making his way somewhere in the desert.

It occurs to me that knowing their names and pasts has made the two of them, paradoxically, even more unknown to me, even more foreign and opaque. Because based on their biographies, they have led lives of action, of movement, of exposure, of physicality. They've dropped into and out of cities and countries; into and out of dangerous, fluid, chaotic, dynamic situations; into and out of the line of fire—in utter contrast to my own life spent in front of computer screens, utterly cautious, predictable, and unchanging. Our experiences are antithetical. I have uncovered their identities, but who they truly are, what makes them tick, is still impenetrable to me.

At the same time, I begin some corollary detective work. I start sifting through local public records, to find out who else moved to Vegas the week that I did. To find out which of those thousands of Vegas immigrants was single. And who, of those hundreds of singles, had also moved around Branson, Missouri; and Billings, Montana; and Nashville, Tennessee—living in hotels, motels, or short-term rentals during the same weeks or years that I had. Because if I can narrow it down to one name, then that's the person, my unknown psychic twin, who is doing my work now. My backup. (Or else I was always *their* backup.) Could there really be three or four of us? A half dozen? A dozen? Impractical. Expensive even for Wallace. And way too risky that one of the six or more of us would slip, be a little sloppy, inadvertently reveal him or herself. But there is at least one person other than me. Someone who presumably doesn't know that I exist, who is still working away unaware, just as I would have been, except for the advent of Dave and his action-figure companion babe.

Who is it? Where are they? Would they even begin to believe me, if I find them, if I tell them? Or do they know already? Did they know it all along and thus never mythologized their boss, who has us laboring, after all, on nothing more than a glorified, clandestine factory line.

Research monkeys, in different cages, with blankets hanging between us.

So the Stewartsons (Stewart Davidson and Sheila Barton, yes, but I have gotten to know them and will always think of them as the Stewartsons) now have two roundups to perform. It will be pitifully easy for them to find Archer Wallace, I'm afraid. Cruising the avenues, his lean fragile body lit garishly in the Las Vegas night. He won't be able to disappear into the crowds of tourists—exuberant college kids in shorts and tees and baseball caps and tattoos, midwesterners plump as chickens, waddling short of breath along the Strip from hotel to hotel, as if wandering among sacred ruins. He could blend into the underworld of Vegas bums and vagrants, but would they accept him into their small fraternity? Does he have the strength to live on the streets? They are a particularly and surprisingly hearty and resilient bunch. If the Stewartsons are the pros they seem to be, it will be easy for them to find Archer—and maybe not much harder to find me.

SEVEN

Wallace the Amazing, of course, is the perfect blackmail candidate. A criminal past to hide. Everything to lose. A public that will be merciless. A persona that will be destroyed. In his vulnerability, he is pretty much irresistible. I could see that. Here in Vegas, he is like a walking slot machine, overloaded with coins, ready to pay off. And the real Wallace—he is the found coin, the dusty roadside quarter, ready to be pushed into the slot. Pull the lever and coat yourself in riches.

I could understand it, Wallace suddenly peeling away from me and Debbie, deciding to do it on his own. What did he need any of us for? This was to retrieve his own identity, after all. Yes, to compensate himself for the financial loss, to force financial redress, but also to retrieve and restore his self. I could understand the impulse. But he was a babe in the woods. He had no idea what a high-stakes game he had entered. Blackmail was not blackjack. This was a mirrored casino, and everyone at the table was disguised, and nothing was as it appeared.

Blackmail. You'd think the word's origin would be straightforward: an incriminating or threatening piece of mail, a practice you'd assume arose in the shadows of the spread of literacy. But online, I see it actually comes from the black "mail," the dark coat of armor that a knight wore—a mounted, intimidating form of threat.

It has evolved, of course, with technology. The written missive became the telephone call: furtive, intimate, the insinuating whisper of violation or rape, before the line goes dead with threat, with intent. The twentieth century's most celebrated version, of course, was the cutout letters from various sources, forming words and phrases into a jagged and untraceable message of threat, the letters ironically cheerful and colorful and angled jauntily. The typeface of a clown, if you ignored its content.

Today's blackmail message? It arrives cloaked in the same electronic anonymity as a hundred other daily marketing come-ons, sexual solicitations, unfiltered spam, delivered via Facebook, text message, Twitter, LinkedIn, or conventional e-mail, and its job is to stand out in its anonymity as not anonymous at all—as in fact, more intimate and targeted than any of the messages around it. An old nickname will do it. A small tantalizing piece of a shared long-ago secret. Any concise form of "I know. And you know that I know."

TO: Archer Wallace

FROM: Archer Wallace

SUBJECT: Archer Wallace

Need to settle our account. Let me know if you receive this e-mail. Details for payment to follow.

This was the e-mail that Wallace—the real Archer Wallace—sent to Wallace the Amazing. The e-mail I saw a day after I was settled into Debbie's and went online. And probably the most remarkable and mysterious thing about it was that I was copied on it, put right away into the coiled, tightening loop, a bystander shown the precise twists of the hangman's knot. Archer Wallace must have seen my e-mail address over my shoulder at some point while he was in my apartment. Does he want to impress me with being bold enough to take on the blackmail project himself? Does he want me to be a witness should something happen to him? Does he want Wallace the Amazing to know that he knows about me— although he doesn't know the nature of our relationship exactly— and knows that we're meaningful, important to each other, and he wants to threaten Wallace the Amazing with that, hold it over his head? Does he intend to cut me in? It's mysterious to be included in the communication. And nothing says that Wallace my employer will include me in the response, if he responds at all.

Of course, everyone knows that e-mail can be traced, that it's not ever truly anonymous, that there is a tech-geek subset that knows how to follow its trail, that the digital fumes can be sniffed to their source. But you need experts for that. And you know by now that I am one.

A little research shows me that the e-mail was sent from the Las Vegas public library. (Yes, there is such an entity—a gleaming but sleepy and somber downtown institution whose very existence is steeped in a half century of irony; its existence, in an age of municipal cutbacks and a challenged local economy, is increasingly precarious, but like any other desert creature, it somehow persists and survives.)

So innocently direct, that e-mail. The Stewartsons will eat Archer Wallace alive, swallow him whole.

I can picture the Stewartsons searching the early dawn. Scooping him up off a sidewalk like some wild-eyed, skulking piece of wildlife with the broad swift net of their combined expertise. Unlicensed fishing. An unfair contest. Reaching out of their red Mustang, grabbing his twiglike arm, hustling him off the street . . . but if they've been looking, so far they've missed him. So far he's slipped their net.

I don't say a word to Debbie. She wouldn't understand. She'd never let me go. I slip out to her Triumph. I need to get to Wallace, the real Wallace, before the Stewartsons do. To extort the money from the Amazing Wallace, to threaten his successful present with the reality of his past, they need Archer Wallace alive, yes, but not by much. And not for long.

Presumably, the e-mail gives me a considerable head start in finding him. The public library is one place he might actually blend in—where his bald head, wisps of white hair, translucent skin, and fragile physique might not stand out amid the shut-ins, the blinking bespectacled researchers, the nocturnal, the dispossessed, the pallorous, the vampires caught here in Vegas through some chain of error.

But he is not here. He has not installed himself in a research carrel, as I had assumed. Has not unobtrusively set up shop. He is gone, on the move, stealthy, thinking at least a step ahead, observing and adapting the professionalism of his previous hosts; he will pick up e-mail responses from somewhere else, if he doesn't circle around and retrieve them here later. He'll issue his instructions from elsewhere. I search the periodicals room, double-check every one of the easy chairs where the bums are stretched out, snoring, muttering, off their meds. I slip up the long, silent aisles of books like an explorer heading upriver into deep jungle. But there is no one here except the occasional hunched, bespectacled native. Archer has disappeared into the Vegas ether. Maybe he only cc'd me as a test, to see if I could track him here through e-mail, so he'd know if he needed to be more careful or not, to check how far my technological powers extended, to see if he was safe or not.

And what was I going to do if I found him? Advise him not to go through with it? Tell him how dangerous blackmail is? He already knew all this. It was hardly information. I was only here to somehow protect him from the Stewartsons. And if they weren't here, if they hadn't found him, then perhaps he was protected enough, and there was no reason for me to be here.

Is he looking at me from the window of some standpipe? From behind some air-conditioning or heating vents or machinery?

The Vegas library. I had expected it to be a kind of oasis, but for me it turns out to be more empty desert. I head out of its cool gloom back into the searing sunlight.

I pull Debbie's old Triumph into her driveway, head back inside with a carton of milk, orange juice, a can of coffee, and a loaf of cinnamon raisin bread—sufficient explanation, I thinly hope, for my sudden disappearance with her car.

Crack!

An explosion at the side of my head.

The concussive noise so close.

A spinning room.

A sudden blackness.

In a moment, I find myself surrounded by my own groceries.

Lying on Debbie's bright-green entrance rug and hardwood floor.

I'm staring down into the rug's forest of bright-green fibers, as if I've just tripped.

Which I have. Tripped on my own stupidity and carelessness.

Dave holds the gun to the back of my head as I lie there. "Hey, hero. She ain't here. But you are."

And when I am once again shackled to a chair, when my mouth is once again taped and I am nice and docile and cooperative, I am subjected again to the verbal stylings of Dave Stewartson/Stewart Davidson—as if merely picking up where we left off.

"Now where were we?" he says with a smile. As if mainly to demonstrate how I can be taped back into a chair, easily, anytime, anywhere. That it's nothing for them. To show that I can't escape. Not really. Not ever.

Dave once again pulls a chair up next to mine, once again turns the chair to sit on it backward, like any and every old-movie interrogation. I am looking once again at the strangely angular face, the tautness around his mouth, the fearsome bulge of his eyes. But despite my once more being a "captive audience," the tenor and purpose of this conversation prove entirely different.

"Wallace the Amazing, he fooled you, didn't he? Took you in as much as he took in Archer Wallace. Maybe worse, for all the years it's gone on for you."

He couldn't know that. He was speculating. I didn't say anything.

"I know you grabbed your laptop when you left your place. I don't know the exact nature of your relationship with him, but I'll bet it has to do with that laptop. And the fact that there's so little record of you, so little paper trail or evidence of your existence. And the thing I noticed the night we watched him on TV—whatever you were doing for him, apparently he doesn't need you to do it anymore. Clearly you're more dispensable than you thought." He smiles thinly. "He's abandoned you to the likes of us."

He pauses, examines his hands for a moment, frowning, as if hoping to find a cigarette in one, or a cuticle that needs some work, or another section of an orange. "But *we* want you, Chas. We respect your skills. This is your town, not ours. And we know you can find us Archer Wallace." He flexes and stretches his hands, and I see in them mute experience, the tools of wet work. "Think about what I'm saying. Think about how shocked you are, how disillusioned, how uprooted you feel by what you've learned about your boss. Think about how your world has already been turned upside down. Think about the state you found the real Wallace in. And as you've realized by now, that wasn't something we did. That was something he did to himself." He leans back, exhales (as if releasing frustration in a controlled discharge) into the air above him—and if it were an exhalation of cigarette smoke in a backroom interrogation, the smoke would now hang for a silent moment, dramatically, like a complex question, gray and musing. "Think about what it means to have agreed to a certain existence, to a certain life, and it turns out that whole existence came with false terms. Under false pretenses. See, I think you know a little something about that." Those big hands drum for a few beats on the back of Debbie's chair. (I had her car—so where, how, is she not here?) "We want to propose something. Don't say anything right away. You'll be skeptical at first. Just think about it before you respond. We're willing to cut you in. Substantially. That's how much money there is. Do you have any idea what kind of stake we're talking about? How much Wallace the Amazing has? Your years of service. You can get compensated for it—by your employer, no less—in one lump sum. We're offering a partnership. Something Wallace the Amazing, your former employer, if that's what he was, never did."

It was, of course, everything I'd been thinking. Everything that irked me, that I had been brooding over, that I was bristling about. Wallace suddenly *didn't* seem to need me. This could be my severance package.

"Think of it as your severance package," says Stewartson. I blink at hearing what I've been thinking uttered aloud.

I squirm in Debbie's chair. I don't know how I feel. Stewartson can see that. "Let me give the idea a little shape and substance for you. Your share would be five mil."

The sum has finality, authority, clarity to it. *Five million.*

He rips the tape off my mouth in one motion. I wince from the sharp sting.

I look at him. "Five million." I wanted to hear myself say it. To hear my own voice utter the words into actuality.

"Five million if this works. Five million, or nothing. Nothing in between."

I nod. Understanding? Acceptance? Acquiescence?

Sandi is already freeing my nimble keyboard fingers.

• • •

After a few minutes the Stewartsons took off, leaving me alone to start on my side of the bargain. I watched the red Mustang pull out from behind a truck down the street, where I had never thought to look.

I didn't bother to search the little house for Debbie, I knew the Stewartsons had already looked thoroughly. She had been smarter than me, must have escaped when she saw their car. Her cell phone was on the kitchen counter. She must have left in a hurry. She might not risk coming back so fast. Seeing her cell phone there—that thin last thread of connection, now broken—I felt the pang of separation more than I thought I would, sharp and immediate. A further severing from each other. Her even temper, her straightforwardly upbeat view of things, the familiar comfort of her voice, coming from the darkness in bed beside me or through a tiny phone speaker—all now gone.

I did the only thing I could think of. The only thing that would inch me toward normal. I opened my laptop.

There was the e-mail reply back from Wallace to Wallace. I thought Wallace the Amazing might simply pretend not to have seen it, since acknowledging it would begin to lend credence to it, which would be the wrong tack for him to take. His return e-mail to Archer—all one line of it—was sufficiently cryptic to have no definitive meaning in an investigation or a court of law. But it was a clear enough indication of his stance, of his temperament, and even of a sense of irony.

TO: Archer Wallace

FROM: Archer Wallace

SUBJECT: Who do you think you are?

• • •

A few hours after that—once I'd returned to my own condo, safe again, now that I wasn't trying to hide from the Stewartsons— Wallace the Amazing amazes me once more.

Because Detective Armondy and Detective Hammer of the Las Vegas Police Department are suddenly at my door. Flashing badges in the Vegas sun. Squinting into the cool darkness as they step inside. Just like in the movies—as if they know how they are expected to act. The whole deal. And big boys too, both of them. Meaty as offensive linemen. "Can we sit down?" As in, we're gonna be here a little while.

The LVPD. One of the detectives is studying me. I already have the sense. That Wallace to Wallace e-mail. They must have seen it too.

They settle themselves carefully into the chairs I direct them to. Chairs no one had ever sat in before, I realize. Before I got taped into one.

"What's this about?"

"Somebody is trying to blackmail Wallace the Amazing."

Wow. A preemptive strike. Wallace the Amazing has brought in the Vegas police. Gutsy. Risky. He is going to head this off quickly, fire from both barrels—presumably because he is truly concerned about everything coming undone.

I'm smart enough not to say, "What's that got to do with me?" I know why they're here. My being cc'd on the e-mail is at least as mysterious to them as it is to me. "I know the e-mail you mean," I tell them. "I thought it was sent to me by mistake, or else a joke I didn't get." Wallace the Amazing obviously forwarded the e-mail, as is, to the police. They have not been able to trace it to the sender either. But they have been able to find me, the cc, the e-witness. Is Wallace the Amazing willing to risk connecting the two of us? After all our cautiousness, after all these years? Does this simply prove further he doesn't really need me?

"You know who sent it?"

"No."

"You know Wallace the Amazing?"

"I know *of* him. I've seen him perform. I watch his show. He *is* amazing."

"He said he knows you."

My heart pounds. Did he give me up? Just like that? Turn on me? Over this? My strangled look of fear, of anguish, is maybe taken for anger, irritation.

"He couldn't have said that. Because he doesn't know me."

Hammer smiles. "No, he said he doesn't. We were just . . . asking." A clever little play by the LV detectives, the kind they love—not in the manual, but certainly in the playbook.

"And you don't know who sent it?" I am asked again, seriously. Back to the real question.

"Well, maybe I *do* know them"—I'm establishing a tone of scrupulous honesty—"but the *to* is the same as the *from*, so I can't tell who it is."

"Any guesses?"

I shake my head.

Detective Hammer settles back a little. "See, thing is, this isn't just garden-variety blackmail." He cocks his head, looks around my neat, spare condo, blankly assessing. "Wallace the Amazing is an institution. He generates revenue for this town. Employs lots of people. Gives generously to local organizations. Police. Fire. Children's hospital wings. Cut to the chase: guy is part of the local economy. Big part. Maybe whoever sent this has really got something on Wallace. But personally, I'd rather not know what it is. And Las Vegas doesn't want to know what it is. Because whatever it is, it can't weigh in at nearly what this guy Wallace has done for this town."

He looks at me, making sure I understand. "Okay, so you don't know who sent this." He pauses meaningfully, he's nobody's fool. "But if you figure it out, it might be good to convey this sentiment, this point of view, to whoever sent it. There's an extra level of, uh, local sensitivity that they need to be aware of. There's more at work here, *capisce*?"

Wallace. Impresario and civic supporter. Piling high the chips of goodwill. Of social capital. As if anticipating such a calamity. His high-profile, unsubtle insurance policy against it.

Why *did* Archer Wallace put me on the e-mail? To push me out into the open? Or just to warn me? Or—and as soon as I think of it, I know this is the reason—because any subsequent electronic tampering I might try would now be detected by the police. He was tying up my nimble keyboard fingers.

"Blackmail is illegal, whatever the facts behind it," Hammer says pompously. "Whoever sent this is doing something criminal already, right off the bat, whatever he may or may not be holding over the victim. That's why it's good Wallace came straight to us with this and didn't try to handle it himself. His instincts are good. But even if this blackmailer ultimately wants to come to the police with whatever it is he has, he needs to think about it. You know, whatever it is, if Wallace hid it all these years, the police could hide it too."

He shrugs. He doesn't look at me. He doesn't dare. It is as if the words exist, float independent of him, as if he has nothing to do with them.

Why is he revealing so much to me? Clearly because he knows that I know more than I'm letting on. That I'm connected in some way that he's not forcing me to say. Not yet, anyway.

I promise them that I'll call if I get another suspicious e-mail. I show them out politely. "What line of work are you in?" Hammer asks.

"Computers."

He looks at me. I answer before he can ask.

"I tried to see where that e-mail was coming from," I pretend to confess. "I couldn't trace it any better than your guys could."

He smiles. That seems to satisfy him.

The Vegas police. Preemptive strike from Wallace the Amazing. Upping the stakes. Throwing me over? Or warning me I'd have to swim on my own from here.

I now have to move carefully, I realize. I'm probably now being physically observed. Can't contact either the Stewartsons or the real Wallace. We'll have to stay away from each other. This might be the end of any involvement for me. Have to keep my nose clean.

• • •

It was only later that I realized what the Amazing Wallace was doing.

Local civic booster. Part of the economy.

I'd watched Armondy and Hammer's unmarked car pull out slowly—circle around and pass by again ten minutes later, as if to convey to me explicitly that yes, they would be watching from here on in.

It was all perfectly staged. The ten-dollar haircuts, the leathery too-long-in-Vegas tans, the physical heft of doughnut stakeouts. So it took me a while to realize that those weren't real detectives. That Wallace the Amazing would never alert the police, never risk bringing in the real thing, when he could head everything off with these actors, and there was no risk of the curiosity of the real police, and he'd still be safe. Wallace would never risk it if he didn't have to. Look at his show, the care, the planning, the elimination of variation and risk. No, this was certainly the route he would take. As if confirming, or commenting on, his own permanent impersonation, by siccing a secondary impersonation on us.

That little detective show was intended primarily for the real Wallace—maybe a fake restraining order with it, I'd bet. Probably they couldn't find him, in which case I was the next-best thing, and made an excellent dress rehearsal. And if I did know where the real

Archer Wallace was, I'd pass on the news—the police position on this, the high hurdle that had already been set in front of exposing the truth, so maybe it was better to back off, call it off, etc.

Preemptive strike, indeed. A cleverer one than I'd thought.

And was I just as inauthentic a detective as they were? Since I didn't originally detect their artificiality? Are they inadvertently—or purposely—some sad commentary on my own cut-rate brand of detective?

I had to find the real Wallace. Before they did.

EIGHT

Fortunately, he stands out physically. Shockingly. That extreme emaciation, the thin tufts of hair, the translucent skin. Yet the Stewartsons and the fake detectives haven't seen him, and they have all, I'm sure, cruised the Vegas night, the hooker-dealer-gambler-pimp neon night, and haven't located him.

Which tells me what I need to know. That he has found his way someplace where he is *not* standing out. Where he is blending in. Unobtrusive, unnoticeable. I have spent twenty years blending in like that, learning to go unnoticed; I've learned a thing or two about it.

The unseen Vegas. It is indoors, as artificial and hermetic and self-contained and well air-conditioned as casino Vegas, but there the similarity ends. The unseen Vegas is retirement communities, eldercare facilities, nursing homes, for our failing parents and grandparents. An unseen Vegas population that does not match, that contrasts with, the city's youthful, brazen, bronzed, endless-night culture but is there beside it—white, weak, moving their fragile bodies through the dry, mythically salubrious desert air. The only place Archer Wallace can disappear. The only place his appearance makes him *unnoticeable*. (Here, or a hospital. Not out of the question, but a higher standard for entry—verifiable sickness, after all—and maybe too confining and closely observed once you're in.)

It would probably be a big facility, where his arrival will go mostly unnoticed, unremarked upon. A big facility. With Wi-Fi and free Internet access and computer terminals for the patients/residents lined up in the hall so that they can go online easily, check headlines and box scores and stock quotes and look for the lone stray e-mail from a distant guilt-racked relative. I call the four biggest eldercare facilities, tell each administration I'm looking for my uncle, who, with his failing memory, neglected to tell me which one he was going to be checking into, but let me describe him—lean, bald, white-skinned.

"Sir, we've got dozens of new arrivals who match that description. Just give us his name."

But of course, I know he's not using his own name. It's the one name he won't be using: Archer Wallace.

I tap into each facility's credit card transactions. Looking for the flurry of activity indicating a new arrival. The facilities have everything already—bedding, food—but maybe there's something. Some medication. Anything.

At Golden Care, a clothing purchase. Who shows up without clothing for a terminal stay, a visit until death, except Archer Wallace, who has no clothes? I tap into the inventory control on the computer of the local store where Golden Care made the purchase (Jesus, no security at all) and find the transaction. Three men's medium short-sleeve shirts. Three men's pants. All of it a single purchase. All waist twenty-six. Someone thin. Emaciated. Bingo. A little more investigation of Golden Care, and I see they're at the low end of these facilities—a Medicaid facility, pay weekly, indigent care provider, not much checking on residents. I can see how he could make his way in.

· · ·

I head over to Golden Care at sundown—golden hour—mealtime for the institutional elderly. When I can review all the residents, dining together in their depressing dining area, in various states of alertness. I pull into the lot of Golden Care and take it in: a series of buildings tossed up together sometime in the sixties, I'd say, without apparent benefit of an architect or site plan. (Wide-open, dirt-cheap desert land so who cares, what the hell.) Sidewalks overgrown with high weeds. A deeply cracked entrance fountain that hasn't seen water in decades. Lots of plate glass, so the residents can look out on empty, relentless nothingness, an earthly proxy of the cosmic nothingness they are all headed for. It's easy to locate the dining area—the longest row of windows. I scan carefully from outside the plate glass, observing the white-haired men and women hunched over their meals, slurping, mumbling, or chatting with one another.

Or at a table alone—reading a newspaper.

There he is. Wallace.

Maybe I *am* a detective.

The dining area lets out onto a sorry little patio. I enter the dining area through the unlocked patio door. The few Golden Care staff members I see are all preoccupied with empty dishes, wheelchairs, phone calls.

I sit down opposite him—carefully, slowly, as if he'll dissolve right in front of me. He looks up like he's been expecting me. No smile. Barely an acknowledgment of my being here, of my finding him here, but acknowledgment enough.

"Sorry to run out on you like that," he says. "Bet you figured I wouldn't last an hour."

"Something like that," I confess.

"Obviously I'm a little heartier and more resourceful than I appear," he says.

"And highly motivated."

"My e-mail."

"The only thing that surprised me more than your boldness in taking on Wallace yourself was including me on your e-mail. Copying a third party. That has to be a blackmail first."

He doesn't answer, just smiles.

"I don't know whether you want me as a witness, in case something happens, or you want to drive a wedge between Wallace and me because you suspect some association between us, or you want to prove some connection to me, or all of the above."

He doesn't answer me, as I knew he wouldn't, but he does respond.

"And what *I* don't know," he says, "is whether my old friends the Stewartsons have won you over, or offered you a deal. They can be persuasive . . ."

Now it's my turn to be silent.

"On the other hand, you're here without them. So you haven't shared my whereabouts with them. Not yet, anyway."

He picks at his food for a moment, looks up at me. "He stole my money. He stole my identity. There should be consequences."

"Should be."

"And the fact that there may not be . . ." He shakes his head. "But there are *going* to be." He says it firmly, angrily, resolved. A few of the elderly look around at us.

I lean in conspiratorially. "If he refuses—you must have thought about this—are you really prepared to go to the police?"

"If I have to, yes. Because if I don't, he'll dodge the wheels of justice forever."

"He'll probably dodge them even if you do tell the police."

"That's a chance I'm prepared to take."

"He sent a couple of detectives to see me," I tell him.

"What?" This surprises him. "*He's* gone to the police?"

"They were really looking for you, asked me if I knew where you were—because of my being cc'd on your e-mail, I'm sure. They found me, couldn't find you. But I think they're expecting me to pass the message on to you . . ." I did not tell him the detectives were imposters. The threat of real cops was more likely to deter him from his quixotic mission.

"Did the police follow you here?" he asks. A little panicked.

"Not that I could see." I had looked behind me repeatedly, doubled back on myself, saw nothing. "So the message for you . . ."

"Yes?"

"That Wallace is important to this town. Part of the economy. We don't like things that make us or our citizens look bad . . . That kind of stuff."

"But if I show them the evidence, they'll have to do the right thing. They'll have to investigate. Prosecute . . ."

I shrug. "Not necessarily. And anyway, what evidence exactly?"

He looks off.

That might be the dark and perfect beauty of what Wallace the Amazing had pulled off these many years. That there was scant evidence.

"Where do you stand?" he asks me point-blank.

Where *do* I stand? Help this underdog with his crazy plan, and bring a little justice into the world? Turn Wallace the Amazing in, or ally myself with the Stewartsons for my five million share? Or distance myself from both these blackmailers, and stay loyal and true to my previous life, to my paycheck, to my universe, to my employer, to the myth of him?

"I don't want you to get hurt, Archer." That's all I really know at this point. That's all I really know about where I stand, for now. His vulnerability, his aloneness, in taking on the entertainment juggernaut of Wallace the Amazing, a powerful system that I helped to hold in place, that I helped create, that controlled him—although it now seems the "system" isn't me exclusively.

I look at him—hunched over, hiding out here, life and health gone. This stooped, prematurely aged, and beaten specimen, up against the institution of success and ingenuity and adulation that is Wallace the Amazing. All this man has on his side is the truth. It is literally his only possession. A commodity with little value in this town where the artificial reigned supreme. Where artifice is the founding principle. But truth is probably in equally short supply, of similarly little value, in every other city too. In Cincinnati, Dubuque, Boise, Racine, Saint Paul, Joplin, Iowa City. All the places they might have you believe—with their serious faces, their dark suits, their somber demeanors—that truth is worth something. Arguably Vegas is at least more honest with itself. Part of me wants to see where the truth would lead. Wants to help truth mount up, ride into town, and watch its effect from safely behind the saloon doors. Watch its white horse's hooves circle in the dirt, watch the dust rise up and choke some people and make others cough uncomfortably. Truth, the new kid in town. With uncanny aim. Unrufflable nerves. Whatcha gonna do about it, pardner?

"All you've got is the truth . . ." I say aloud.

He looks at me. Lights up, comes alive at this. "Yes. And in the end, is it everything? Or is it nothing? That's the multi-million-dollar question."

Five million, to be exact, I think to myself. Five million to me, and who knew how much more to the Stewartsons?

"Five million, ten million, fifteen million, give or take," he says. Each figure tossed out with an accompanying twirl of his fork. Guessing, fantasizing. Obviously undecided on what he could or would demand. Uninformed on what was there.

Give or take, indeed.

• • •

Having found Archer Wallace so quickly, so adeptly, you'd think it would be easy for me to find Debbie, who, presumably, was in hiding somewhere, having done a smart little sidestep, probably out her back patio, to avoid the Stewartsons and their head-cracking greeting of me. She had not returned to her neat little home, as far as I could see, as I circled it slowly several times—and she did not come back to my condo either.

Maybe I was, for now, simply someone to avoid. *I* would avoid me. From her point of view, whatever I did for a living exactly, trouble was clearly tracking me now, and she might not end up so lucky the next time she had to save me. Maybe it was simply, understandably, self-preservation on her part. When I looked in the window of her place a day later, her cell phone was no longer on the counter. I assumed she had come back for it, and could reach me if she needed to. That is, if she wanted to.

But the other possibility, of course—the one that I tried to push out of my mind and couldn't—was that the Stewartsons had found her at home the day they burst in looking for me, and they were now "keeping" her (somewhere) to ensure the trustworthiness and usefulness of their new partnership with me. (Pros like them, it must have been easy to find us—talking to neighbors at my condo, getting a description of Debbie, a description of Debbie's Triumph, whatever.) And they clearly liked keeping people. Her cell phone might be in Dave Stewartson's pocket—just out of her reach.

She had saved me from the Stewartsons. Was her reward to be chained to motel fixtures? And if the Stewartsons had her, they would probably have learned a lesson when I scooped up Archer Wallace. They'd undoubtedly be more prudent, more adept, in hiding her from me.

And though the adrenaline rush of her rescuing me had faded, my appreciation had not. I don't know whether in the chaos of inverted identities and perceptions, of my life and beliefs thrown into a maelstrom, I was unconsciously drawn to an anchor, but she was the anchor I yearned for now. Maybe my new sense of closeness, of desire for her, was somehow worth the swirl of events, the uprooted craziness.

Whether she was being held in case I needed more "persuasion" as a partner, or she was just hiding till I had extricated myself from the chaos of my life, it put anxious shadows into my thoughts and dreams, and fresh urgency into my plans.

For now, the anchor was cut away from me; my boat was unmoored in unknown seas, and I was on my own.

• • •

I began to reconstruct my own life—my own movements, my own residences—over the past twenty years (forgotten motels, featureless short-term rentals, temporary domiciles and living situations that ran together so unmemorably, so fluidly one into the next, that it required receipts, calendar datebooks, the Internet's infinite memory to revivify it). Once I had done all this grunt detective work of dates and geography, once I had it charted in front of me, the rest of the task turned out to be still substantial, but at least methodical.

It was a matter of finding, and then eliminating, all those other fellow travelers (right now only addresses, ID numbers, car registrations, tax filings) who had moved from city to city with me. With every new city that I charted from my past, some of the names got crossed off, of course, while some were added, and as I continued—traveling digitally over my route through the fuzzy, foggy years—fewer and fewer names were constant. And once the attrition of geography and facts had narrowed it down to a small handful (by which time, by which small handful, I was fairly trembling), I put names to the numbers and the movements, and sluiced it down finally to one.

Dom Carter.

The one person who has moved along with me, week to week, city to city, close by, likely within a few blocks, for literally the past twenty years. Eerie to think it.

My Internet searches revealed no further information about Dom Carter than the name. Which in and of itself strongly indicated, nearly confirmed outright, that Dom Carter was exactly who I thought.

Dom Carter.

I stared at the name, scribbled on the pad, the silent tournament of elimination finally reduced to this opaque "winner." How does he play? What will his game be like?

How will Dom look, what will Dom say, how will he react if I confront him? It was preoccupying to say the least. And of course, part of the prize of Dom Carter, the nearly painful pleasure, was that he was likely living within a short drive of me. Which turned out to be exactly the case. A firm, final confirmation.

• • •

I pull in across the street from Dom's condominium. A blue Camaro in the driveway. A little bit of personality, in a job that allows none. This little bit acceptable, still invisible enough, in the milieu of Vegas. Wonder how Dom likes Vegas?

I get out of the car, lock the door.

I look at my hands. They are trembling. I rest them on the roof of my car for a moment, try to steady them. It's no wonder. This will be pivotal. This will be a confirmation of a world different from what I have so clearly imagined and inhabited for twenty years. This will rewrite it. This will coat it over in a new color, hide the previous color forever. And this, answering the detective in me, will be evidence of a different Wallace from the one I always thought I knew. Evidence indelible. Irrefutable. Safely out of reach of whim or imagination.

I still don't know if I'm going to go through with it.

I know I'm going to go through with it.

Dom may or may not have imagined the idea of someone else doing what he does, the idea of redundancy, which had only occurred to me after twenty years, and only through an inadvertent revelation. Dom might not even believe me. I'm not sure *I'd* believe me.

A trim nondescript walkway. Hardy plants in the sand that require no care. Utterly self-sufficient. Hardly draws a second glance. Like Dom. Like me.

I ring the bell.

Dom opens the door. And I know it is Dom, instantly, by the sterility that frames Dom. By the condo's unlived-in, unoccupied feeling, by the rented couches. By the side-by-side computers—an easy giveaway.

The obviousness of it centers me. Keeps me upright in my dizziness. Because standing there before me is the first complication. One I somehow should have predicted, but could and would never have, I guess.

Dom is Dominique.

And Dominique is beautiful.

And the smile that I diligently, professionally suppress—the smile that earns me second glances and approving appraisals—escapes from me now, unbidden, authentic, surprised.

"Yes?"

I'm able to process the name thing quickly: Dom from Dominique, not a lie exactly, but not the truth exactly either. Easier for her to move through paperwork, through life, dodge uncomfortable situations and entanglements, with purposeful ambiguity. Going by Dom—maybe a helpful reminder to herself of her own imposture. Helping her to never forget.

"Hi, I'm . . . Jim Isaacson, and, uh . . ." There are about a thousand places to begin, and I can't pick from among them.

"And what?"

I'm too dumbfounded, too off-balance, to find a gentle, polite, oblique way in. I have only utter directness available to me. "We need to talk, Dominique."

She is suspicious but can't help the edge of her own smile. "We do, huh?"

"Yes."

"About what . . . *Jim?*" Her eyes narrow. She has picked up somehow from me already—from my expression, my stance, my unsteadiness?—that it's not my name. Which only confirms for me, this is a detective.

I look at her with import. "We need to talk about Wallace the Amazing."

She furrows her brow mechanically, gives the practiced response. "Wallace the Amazing? What about him?"

I smile. "That's exactly how I've handled it for the past twenty years."

Now her placid beauty goes visibly off-center—unmoored, challenged. She has caught the whiff of something significant.

"Dom—Dominique—I do what you do for a living. You do what I do. We're each other's backup system. Tennessee, Baton Rouge, Phoenix, Chicago. We've shared the same existence for twenty years, a few miles apart. I never would have guessed there was another one, which is why you may be having trouble with the idea . . ."

I find myself spilling it all at once like that. And maybe it makes it seem more credible. I have no idea whether she can handle it, or accept it. Or whether she has long suspected such a thing, or even known for sure, or like me, had not the slightest inkling.

But I have my answer in an instant. Something darkens in her eyes; a light goes out—a light of innocence, clearing room for dark truth.

Silently, perhaps shell-shocked, she opens the door wider, and motions me inside.

Two cups of coffee. I watch the broken understanding cross her face. I watch what happened to me, happening to her. My sympathy goes out to her.

But throughout it, she's breathtaking.

"And why are you telling me this?" Knee-jerk defensiveness. Resentment at having her morning, her life, disrupted, her world rocked. But it's also a good question: Why am I? What's to be gained or derived, exactly? Am I looking for an ally? Do I want to be known at last? At least by someone? And more than that, understood? Appreciated at last? The full answer, I know, is deep and subtle and multifaceted. For now, I cobble together a response.

"We're detectives. We're after the truth. We live for the truth. I thought you deserved this truth."

She looks at me, cocks her head. "Detectives?" She shrugs. "Well, I guess."

How embarrassing. How revealing. How perfectly belittling. Seeing what we do as "detective" work—that was only my eccentric, lonely glorification of it. My grand definition of it, my grand delusion, for twenty years. She's never even thought of the term.

And then, setting down her coffee cup, as if the first step in ushering me out: "Look, you really don't know me . . ."

Oh, but I do know you. You have moved around from city to city, venue to venue, and have therefore not been able to establish a relationship, have therefore remained isolated, cut off, alone. You have filled your time with reading, with daydreaming, with empty projects, with false cheer. You have filled the emotional emptiness with fantasy, with perverse imaginings that drive you crazy, that you have to switch off like a television screen. Your existence has stayed lean, everything about it—from the disposable objects in your rental home (things you don't care about, nothing that lays down roots) to your perennially unsatisfying takeout meals, quick, second-thought calories and nothing more. You look lean, hungry, your arms and abs ripped from constant, empty exercise to fill the void. Even your eyes are hungry-looking, and though this is a fashionable and sexual look, a turn-on to others, it comes out of need, and desperation, and hunger in oneself, which holds little promise for a relationship, if one should stumble into one. And oh, one does—here and there. Briefly. Interrupted, before it can even begin, by secrecy, by insularity, by professional privacy that can't be risked or punctured. Yes, I know you. And you, by the way, know me. You just don't know yet, how well you already know me.

And why be silent? Why not say it aloud? Why pretend, be formal, when the intimacy is automatic? This is me I am looking at. I am looking at a mirror. We talk to our mirrors, after all. "Oh, come on, Dominique. I do know you. And you know me. We've lived the same life for almost a quarter century. Thinking, obsessing, about the same person, about each night's performance."

She smiles gently, resigned. "The same life, with one big exception."

And I hear my own words—*"thinking, obsessing, about the same person"*—and I know it, sense it, moments before she says it, so her saying it merely confirms my stomach-sinking awareness.

"I sleep with him." Looking expressionlessly at me. Adding nothing more for the moment. No further commentary or punctuation needed.

And the moment I saw her, when I saw the sudden and disarming beauty, I should have realized it. I should not have plunged headlong into my own fantasy of the two of us, of my double, my other half, this romantic notion . . . I should have taken a breath, taken a step back.

And the instant question, of course: Where do her loyalties lie? Will I be reported? Has she been leading me on, gathering her own data?

I look at her. She looks at me. And now I see how completely wrong I was. I thought I knew her completely. But I don't know her at all.

"Well, I don't know if I'm glad I learned this, or not," she says quietly, just above a whisper, really. "I'm going to have to think about that. You and I, we deal in the power of information and knowledge every day, but I'm not sure that information and knowledge are always such a good thing." She sips her coffee, and without looking up, says, "Strange, how well we know each other, and how much we don't." And then looks at me, smiling ruefully, mimicking her boss lightly, faintly, profoundly, and in a way she knows I'll recognize. "Connection. Connection. We're all connected."

And it is only in leaving Dominique's kitchen, passing through her sparsely furnished living room, as devoid of artifact and the past as my own, that I see the one exception, a silver-framed faded photograph of an attractive, smiling couple at an amusement park. And something about its place of honor on the shelf, the empty space around it projecting a kind of unspoken holiness to it, inevitably unleashes the detective in me. It is obviously her parents. A single, old photograph, surrounded by no photos more recent. I lift my index finger to point to it, to ask her about it, but she anticipates my question, answering flatly, factually, as if to head off any further discussion.

"My parents. Deceased. Both killed in a train crash, when I was nine."

Any sympathy I might have felt is overwhelmed by my mind's sudden whirring.

Connection. Connection. We're all connected.

NINE

Obviously, the fake detectives, Armondy and Hammer, had not caught up with Archer Wallace, because he delivered his next blackmail message, and it was quite a variation on the oblique, nearly invisible, easily deleted e-mail he had sent earlier. Its cousin. Its opposite. Because this message ran on the news zipper that girdled the New York, New York hotel, sandwiched between national events and sports scores, and was crafted in a way to create mystery and startlement but give away nothing. Cheerful sounding. Revealing nothing, and everything—in that, the message was its own bit of stagecraft.

> A.W.—I'm in town with Dave and Sandi, but working independently. You know I know. Let's get together on it.

An intimate koan, sent out across the zipper. Sitting mysteriously between marriage declarations and buckeye ads for auto dealerships. Now of course, anyone was free to look into the message. To do their own bit of detective work—though "A. W." and "Dave" and "Sandi" probably wouldn't get them very far. Archer sent me a private e-mail—subject line: "NY NY zipper, 2:50 p.m."—just to make sure I didn't miss it.

Jesus. The news zipper, used for blackmail. The world moves forward in unpredictable ways.

Was it a volley intended to drive the Amazing Wallace crazy? After the fake detectives, to show commensurate recklessness? *Anything you can do I can do crazier.* On getting over my initial shock—seeing the note there on the zipper, watching it circle, and then disappear after its allotted few repetitions for the next set of electronic messages—I calmed down and realized that the odds were likely that no one would think twice about it. They would go on uninterrupted with their Vegas lives, assume it was merely the message of an old friend reaching out Vegas style to another old friend, and quickly forget it. But wasn't there the risk that someone would be curious, look into it, begin to insert themselves into the story?

Its second audience, and further intention, was clearly the Stewartsons. To say to them in flashing neon, *Look how far I will go, I'm in charge here, this is mine, back off, don't mess with me . . .*

It also may have been meant to inspire, to formulate in fear, what might be the next step. If Archer leaped like this from message one to message two, what would he do for message three?

• • •

It is a game of chicken, I realize, a tightening circle of move and countermove, poised to spiral upward. Neither side wants to *actually* go to the police—if Archer Wallace does, it exposes and brings down Wallace the Amazing, yes, but then Archer will never get his blackmail money, so both sides lose. And if Wallace the Amazing goes to the police, the blackmail ceases, and yes, Archer is prosecuted, but in the process, there is a closer look, an investigation, of the Amazing Wallace, and when the truth of Archer's claim becomes clear, the Amazing empire eventually crumbles, and—again—both sides lose.

And speaking of money: Why hasn't Archer Wallace made the ask? The zipper indicates that he hasn't. He hasn't assigned an amount, proposed a figure. Hasn't gotten to that. Why? Something in me already knows the answer to that. Because it's actually not *about* money. Because Archer wants something besides, beyond, the money. And if it's something other than money, it may not be payable. There may not be any transaction that will satisfy. No earthly exchange that will suffice.

• • •

In light of those fluently fake detectives, and Dominique's very existence (parallel to mine yet unknown to me), and the shifting identities of the Stewartsons, and ghostly Dave/Archer, and Wallace the Amazing himself—in light of all these inversions of expectation in my previously narrow, orderly, comprehensible life, and, most of all, of that framed photograph of her deceased parents in Dom's condominium, I began to think again about my father's highway accident and my mother's cancer. How Wallace had approached me at my moment of greatest vulnerability. A master of psychology, of human frailty, right from the start. I had left for college just a few weeks before, in the wake of a fierce argument between us. My mother had a locked trunk full of my dad's belongings in the attic, and I had always wanted to see what was in it, and she had always insisted that I was not old enough. I argued that now that I was going off to school, I should be allowed to look through it, and she still refused. Said it was still not the appropriate time. So I left with the angry notion—ironically prescient—of returning only for absolutely necessary appearances: holidays, weddings, deaths.

I came back from college straight to my mother's funeral. She had obviously kept her illness to herself, because it was a complete surprise to her small handful of friends and acquaintances who were there and who, like me, had only just learned of her illness too. They were friends I didn't know—women from her bridge game, clerks from local stores, apparently, people from the church services I had never attended with her (feeling remorseful about that now)—but I was relieved to discover she had all of them in her life, close enough and meaningful enough to be there for her. We had no living relatives. (As you know, that was part of the reason Wallace picked me. Few if any familial obligations or commitments. Relatively free to make *him* my family.) And my mother had largely kept to herself. Had always been an extremely private person, which I attributed to my father's early, sudden death. In its wake, she had drawn inward, enveloping herself in grief, and then, self-sufficiency. Although I was too young to remember, I had probably done so myself in some unconscious way—probably a natural human reaction, a hard-wired defense, to the disruption of my father's sudden death. When I left for college, she must have taken the opportunity of the sudden silence and time on her hands to put some household affairs in order, to be even more organized than she already was. Because there in a desk drawer when I opened it—alongside bank and financial statements organized neatly in a folder—were her instructions and arrangements for a funeral and cremation and disposal of ashes, should anything happen to her. And whether she had done all this before or after the discovery of the aggressive cancer—highly organized, or simply bored and alone, with an eerie sense of approaching fate?—I'd never be able to say.

I did my part, though in a fog, understandably, and without much grace or experience; I was a college kid after all, and only by a few weeks. I hastily organized and administered the funeral, according to her explicit instructions. Followed her sheet of directions precisely. Dialed the numbers of people I didn't know and delivered the news. I contacted the bank officer on the card in her folder, as her folder said to.

Which allowed me to leave the funeral, pack my few remaining possessions into a couple of duffel bags, return to school, and never look back. I didn't even bother opening the locked trunk. At that point in my life, I decided, I didn't want to know. I didn't care.

I wanted to turn my back on all the sorrow of my past. I swore I'd never return to such sadness.

And then, there was Wallace with his offer. He was very frank. He had read about the funeral, and about me. He was looking for someone like me. Here were the advantages. Here were the disadvantages. Take it or leave it. But please—for you *and* me, Chas—take it.

And over the years, of course, the question would nag at me. Should I go back? Should I go back? It was always a question fraught with pain, and morality, and contemplation, and a wash of emotion.

But never with suspicion.

TEN

Of course, I am a fake detective too. I am just as fake as the two who paid me a visit. A real detective solves things. Puts clues together. Places the puzzle pieces reverently on the table, presses them into place with satisfaction. Constructs a chain of logic as secure and unassailable and reinforced and irrefutable as an actual chain. A real detective seeks and finds justice for victims, defends us at the fraying edges of the social contract, is justice's own catcher in the rye. A real detective either doesn't sleep because of an injustice or an unclosed case gnawing at him, or sleeps utterly and soundly in the knowledge that his function is moral and essential. A real detective knows the camaraderie of teamwork, of a common goal, and even the detective who is in style and habit a loner knows the satisfying connection to the common good, to the moral loners before and after him. To something even greater and more vital than camaraderie. To a brotherhood of relevance.

Whereas I am a detective for the sole purpose of entertainment. For the purpose of stagecraft and turning a profit. A vital cog in a powerful and relentless wheel of revenue. I am a detective—but do I share any camaraderie with real detectives? Sure, plenty. Seeker of facts. Seeker of truths. Follower of the trail. A core connection. But then, let's face it, our paths diverge . . .

I am a detective who gets at little truths quickly, but then hides them in the context of a larger lie. I am a rare and oxymoronic creature—a *criminal* detective. Clearly illegal, in my online reach and methods. Though our only purpose is entertainment. We never use the information I find for anything nefarious; we get rid of it, delete it, electronically shred it afterward. Responsible. But still illegal.

• • •

A perfect job for a fake detective is merely *pretending* to look for someone. After finding Wallace at Golden Care, I now have to avoid him—while appearing to be looking for him, since the Stewartsons expect me to locate him. I double back over streets, switch direction, venture into the deepest hidden corners of Las Vegas (ancient, cluttered pawnshops run by big-bearded bikers or yarmulked, trim-bearded Jews; SRO residences stinking of men with stained clothing, broken suitcases, and broken souls; bankrupted half-built developments at the city's outermost edges, like mankind's defeated colonization of a far planet), always making sure that the Stewartsons are never far behind. Or just far enough that it appears as if I have no idea they are there. It occurs to me that it is the inverse, the mirror, of when I was first following them and it turned out they knew. I go into gleaming new markets and filthy beat-up convenience stores, wallpaper-peeling motel entrances and soaring skylighted hotel lobbies, am in them just long enough to ask questions, then come out, catching glimpses of the Stewartsons' car. I want them to see me working, diligently.

But the habitual falseness of my strange occupation—the generalized, overarching lie of it, temporarily exaggerated by my fake investigative movement around the city—is suddenly assailed by the all too real. The actual, the physical, invades the cerebral. Because I'm alone at my computer one minute, and I'm being knocked around my own condominium the next. Roughed up, slapped hard around the ears and the back of the head, shoved hard against my own bare walls. No handcuffs, no duct tape this time—as if to show me they don't need it. As if to show me their control is just as effective, just as total, without them. This time, it's pure intimidation—simmering irritation finally unleashed in my little living room. A minute ago, I was alone, but now it is a very lively, crowded scene in here: me, the Stewartsons, their fury, my fear, my careful answers competing with my dumb terror. I'm still shaking off the last blow to the side of my head, the hardest one yet, the one that has me sliding down my own wall, from which I'm looking up at Dave Stewartson. A post-blow grogginess hangs over me; that's all I can feel or think about, and yet there's a strange contrary sharpness and alertness inside it, a sharpness and alertness to survival, to reality's sudden robustness, its new crisp edges and colors and sights and sounds, despite the groggy throb of the blow.

Stewartson bends down to me. "Where *is* he? Fucking albino, knock-kneed, skin and bones, wandering the street. Where the fuck is he?"

I shrug.

Slap! A reminder slap, meant to jar and stir the memory of the previous blow. It works. "You know! Don't pretend you don't! Don't insult us!"

This is quite a partnership, I'm thinking. An ironic, detached observation that seems to help me bear the pain.

Also helping me bear the pain, handle the crowded scene is the fact that Debbie, at least, does not seem to be part of it. Her continuing absence from the Stewartsons' orbit doesn't guarantee her safety. But she doesn't seem to be available to them to use as leverage against me. A good sign.

"You've checked the hospitals?" I ask innocently, neutrally.

Slap! "We're not idiots. You know where he is."

I feel myself drift out a little—now the pain is all I'm aware of. The room throbs, pulses. Consciousness is becoming a challenge.

Why am I doing this to myself? Why am I allowing this? Why am I protecting Archer Wallace? I should stay out of it, make it between the Stewartsons and him. But I *am* involved. Why do I feel I owe this to the real Wallace? It's ridiculous. But as I'm about to tell them where he is, as I'm about to say "Golden Care," two simple words—slap! Which only slaps me further into awareness—of fear, of reality, but also of anger, resentment, alertness, and commitment. Their violence backfires. Only draws me closer to my doppelganger, makes me identify with him.

"Either you found him and aren't telling us or you haven't found him and aren't holding up your end of the deal." Stewartson shakes his head mournfully, ominously—making clear this deserves another slap, either way.

Jesus. This treatment, and they didn't even *know* if I knew anything.

"Find him!" commands Stewartson. His face contorted with rage. "We're cutting you in. So no more bullshit!"

Nice partner. Nice partnership. Clearly they see their offer of partnership as providing certain physical privileges to them.

Okay. Okay. I'll find him.

And I realize:

They're telling the fake detective to get real.

• • •

An hour later, as I recover from the shock and insult and challenging conditions of my partnership, as I down aspirin for the headache, soak my head in cold water to regain my equilibrium, I have the sense—despite or *because of* their violence—that the Stewartsons, correctly or not, must really feel they need me. They would hardly tolerate my "bullshit," as Dave called it, if they thought they didn't. Which tells me they understand, intuitively if not explicitly, what

I can do at the keyboard. That I am, for them, a kind of maestro there. Their violence would only go so far—was only a stage show of its own. For now, anyway.

And once again, the maestro sits back down to the keyboard. Picking up where I left off, before the rude interruption—back to hacking databases, doing the research, packaging and providing it as always to my employer, nothing amiss, nothing out of order. Because through all this, I still have to deliver the goods to the Amazing Wallace each night—even though I know now, he doesn't seem to *need* my goods. But if I give up the preparation of the show, he'll question my absence. He already suspects my life has intersected with the extortionists—he sent Armondy and Hammer my way, after all—and he doesn't know, has no *way* to know, how much involvement I have with the Stewartsons, how much I've learned about his past, where my loyalties lie. And even if I had a secure way to communicate with him on this, whatever I would say, he wouldn't know if it was the truth or only a cover-up. He wouldn't know where my loyalties lie, for a very good reason. Because *I* don't know. I wish I could just observe. Do what I have done my whole life—stand aside, lean in from the sideline, see what happens, watch the action, watch it play out. But I am under the lights on this. I am onstage. And there is no curtain, no stage wings, no exit.

The Amazing Wallace stole the real Wallace's identity. But he has made the identity worth something, which is why the real Wallace is coming after it, retribution in the form of extortion. So neither one is innocent. Both are criminals—one long established, the other waiting eagerly in the wings. And I need to take a side, place my bet and play the odds. Welcome to Vegas.

The discovery of my professional twin creates an opportunity I never had before. I've had to work every day of my adult life for Wallace the Amazing. Researching the information, digging out the facts. I had to be utterly reliable, always there. But now that I know he doesn't depend solely on me, I can do what I couldn't before: I can look into what I have begun to suspect—if she'll cover for me.

"I need to talk to you, Dominique." Standing once again at her door. Here in person, to emphasize the importance of the request.

"Why?"

"I need a favor."

"Uh-oh."

"Not a big favor. I need you to do your work for Wallace, just like you always do."

"Not much of a favor there."

"But I need you to submit it twice."

"Twice."

"Once from yourself. And once from me."

"You mean, alter it a little, when it comes from you."

"Exactly. I need to go somewhere. Just for a day or two. Will you do it?"

She must recognize the need from her own life, after all. Recognize the professional imprisonment, the same urge and lust for freedom. And I know in asking, as she must know too, that I will owe her one for this. That the next favor will be hers to ask.

And how can I trust that she won't simply tell him? She is his at-least-occasional bedmate, his lover, after all. And she was clearly as surprised and confused to discover my existence as I was to discover hers. So I know she could take this opportunity to make herself numero uno with Wallace the Amazing, even more essential to him, more powerful, unchallenged, supreme. But I had felt her disappointment at the revelation. Her anger at him. Her mental regrouping. There was a bond between us. A bond of profession. A bond of years. And if she is like me, she won't tell him she knows about me, any more than I would tell him I know about her. She'll keep the knowledge to herself, harbor it for some later more useful deployment— why reveal it for no reason? And this is where a detective has to go with his instincts. Instincts are part of the job. For a fake detective like me, just as much as for a real one.

There is one more bond between us, of course. One more bond to bring up here. A bond I don't yet fully understand, but the same detective instincts are whispering its significance.

"Dominique, I have to tell you, when I saw that photo of your parents . . . My parents are both dead too. Don't you see? He *chose* us for that. For our vulnerability. For our isolation. For our instant loyalty." I look at her. "Please . . . cover for me."

I smile once more at her. A smile without flirtation or charm. A smile of need, of desperation, of seriousness. A smile that says only, *I need this, Dominique.*

"I'll do it," she says flatly. No indication of curiosity or resentment or anticipation. Nothing more in her response than simple agreement. And maybe the acknowledgment of our bond. Yes, she'll do it.

ELEVEN

There is magic, and there is magic. There is a stage show—which upends and disrupts your expectations while at the same time fulfilling them—and there is a magic that makes a stage show seem trifling, a magic that can surround and immerse you, that can make you rethink everything, that can turn your mind and memories inside out, that digs into, scratches at, the deepest chambers of your understandings. That attacks your hard wiring. One might argue that's going beyond the realm and province of what we call "magic," but as you'll see, we're only talking degree.

I had sworn I was never going back. I had sworn I would never set foot again in that godforsaken patch of undifferentiated, dusty, arid, rural plain—not properly midwestern, not properly southern, unassigned and unidentified, with little geographic or regional belonging, and not even defined topographically. The place where the little that I knew and loved had died, where every tie had dissolved, where nothing held me, and there was no reason to return and every reason to turn my back.

I flew in late at night. (Strange to think it's been only a short, few hours' flight away all these years and yet has seemed so distant in my imagination—like an unexplored galaxy, light years away.)

Rented a car. Checked into a motel. Tossed and turned and stared up into the blackness above the bed for a few restless hours. The blackness hung outside the thin motel window as well, a remarkable blackness and silence, after the bright, noisy ceaseless, nightless, timeless rhythms of Las Vegas.

• • •

So you can imagine the magic—upon waking up to a clean, calm morning light, dressing quickly, running my head under the cold water in the sink, getting into the rental car—of arriving in, driving through, my old neighborhood, all of it smaller looking, more beaten-down looking, but otherwise unchanged. As if somewhat miniaturized for my convenience, in order to take it in at once.

And perhaps you can imagine the magic as I go up the walk of our old house to our front door . . . the chipped paving stones unchanged, the deep edge of grass still there, memories cascading, a liquid rich wave of memory moistening, fertilizing, the dusty ground around me. Remembering my childhood thoughts and associations on this exact path, from this exact view. Both observing as if from a distance the thoughts of a child, but also thoroughly inhabiting those thoughts, occupying them, because that child is me.

But you certainly cannot imagine the magic of my ringing the bell, hoping and praying for a sympathetic and understanding young owner, and the door being opened by my mother.

My mother.

Standing at the screen door, as always, as if about to call me in for dinner. My long-dead mother. My own expression of utter dizzying confusion and shock and incomprehension is mirrored perfectly in her own. We have never been more powerfully mother and son, never more connected, than at that moment.

I catch her as she collapses into the ladder-back front hall chair, my own rubbery legs about to buckle too . . .

Staring at each other . . . beyond language, beyond the bounds of any emotion we have experienced or even imagined before . . .

"Charles . . . my God . . ." Barely a whisper, as if from beyond the grave.

We simply, mutely, stare some more.

At each other.

And into the cruel, generous, unknowable universe beyond us.

"It's a profound sense of connection. That's the only way I can describe it, and that description is inadequate. That deep sense of awe that you feel occasionally, at a birth or a death close to you, in certain fleeting moments of motherhood or fatherhood, a sudden link to the well and flow of human feeling, to the primal chain, to the basis of humanity that we pay little attention to, that we are detuned from . . . But I pay attention, I am in tune with it . . ."

Sitting on an old unchanged kitchen chair, at the old unchanged breakfast table in the old unchanged kitchen, through the fog of my own confused ecstasy, my wide scatter of feeling, through her stumbling half stutters of her own utter incomprehension, I begin to understand. To process the fake obituary of my accidental roadside death, sent to her, which she shows me now . . .

I see again her memorial service—the respectful, dutiful smattering of bridge friends and local clerks and acquaintances I'd never met, because they didn't exist as bridge friends and clerks and acquaintances, because they'd all been hired for the occasion. The dour solicitous clergyman, saying all the appropriate, explanatory things about the illness she had kept hidden from even her closest friends. The orderly instructions she had left, so orderly and precise because she had not written them, because she'd been away, on a trip with her friends, her *actual* friends, all safely out of the way along with her, to allow her funeral to proceed. And then she'd gotten the news of my accident, my demise—nothing left, tragic—and subsequently received the ashes, on the mantel now . . .

And already I am seeing how the trick was done, and all its attendant ingeniousness. Her death serving as an impetus, a sudden and powerful motivation, to accept Wallace's offer, to drop out of school, start to earn some income, hit the road with him, leaving little time to brood about her, and little point in returning home. Dead of a cancer she never said a word about. Dying alone, never revealing it, never burdening anyone with it, as was her apparent wish. Would I ever have bothered to search my trusted Internet further, my trusted repository of truth? Where I would have found a fake obituary, and nothing more?

(And the fact that she would not have told me about her sickness—*that* would be my mother, classic, 100 percent. Not wanting me to worry, to go on with my all-important college classes, leading toward a career that would allow me to flee our backwater, that would be my ticket out. I knew that was what she wanted for me—escape to something better, to a career that I was committed to, one where I felt important, essential. In Wallace's offer, I knew I had found that. I knew she would be proud.)

• • •

And why had the master magician risked staging the whole funeral? Why had he not found a simpler way of informing me of her "death?" A somber phone call from someone after the "fact," apologizing that they couldn't find me. A "note" found in her drawer, explicitly stating she wanted no funeral, no memorial, which would be in keeping with her personality. Why not a simpler ruse? Because he *is* a master—of human psychology as well. Because he sensed that I would have to see it for myself. To inhabit the fantasy with eyes and ears and sights and sounds if I were to be satisfied. So he had to do it the riskier way, the full staging—because despite the risks, *I* would be less risky that way. More accepting. More somber and docile. More fully convinced.

Or was it, at some level, just to see whether such a stunt could be executed, could be pulled off?

And what kind, what level of magician would attempt such a trick? . . .

Who would such a magician be? . . .

In my subsequent moods of nostalgia and longing and loneliness, when I would check the Internet for her, I'd read her single obituary again, and see nothing else about her, of course. But there wouldn't *be* anything about a quiet, self-effacing midwestern woman on the Internet anyway, only some old photos from before.

And of course, it would never have occurred to me to look for my *own* obituary. The one she had just shown me. Would I find it now on the Internet too, there to assure and convince any of my old acquaintances of my status or whereabouts—or lack thereof—should they get curious? But mostly, of course, to convince *her*. It was a parallel stunt pulled on both of us, an elegantly parallel deception. Like mother, like son. I was sure now, though, that when I searched the Internet for myself, there I would be—or wouldn't be. Only the obit. With no other presence, of course, because of my professional, thorough job of erasing any other presence, anything about me. Christ, I was doing the patrol job of assuring my own electronic death. Safeguarding the deception myself!

What kind of magician would periodically check, to make sure that nothing newer about my mother or me appeared? Would know how I trusted the Internet, how it was my alternative reality, my only reality as far as my past, because the demands of my job precluded any physical return. What magician might that be?

All those thoughts surfaced, disordered, hellish, in the minutes and hours that followed. But for now, it was something bigger, more stunning and remarkable: a past brought back from oblivion. Inhabiting it like it was yesterday.

The irony did not escape me. Twenty years spent peeking and poking into other people's pasts. And yet never peeking or poking into my own.

. . .

The flood of my unalloyed joy. The rushing current of my fury. For her, the miracle of seeing her son after so many years—years she'd thought I was in the ground. And for me: years I had lived duped. Replaying the ease with which it was done. How he had preyed, so ingeniously, so specifically, on an only child with a single parent, a parent who kept to herself, a private person, nearly a shut-in. A kid who had already retreated into the alternate world of computers, of hackers, a kid who lived at the keyboard and nowhere else. A kid withdrawn from the world. Perfect prey. When he approached me in that off-campus coffee shop, he already knew all of it.

My joy and fury rising together, contrary forces, pressing against each other so hard they leave me paralyzed, forces pushing isometrically against each other to leave me stunned and frozen.

Twenty years, and no change. The house, the yard, the furniture, the views, all as it had been. And did this say that twenty years had been stolen? Or that twenty years hadn't passed at all? (Like a prisoner who walks back out into the world, and nothing is changed, and everything is changed. It all looks the same; it all looks different.)

"I can't . . . I can't believe . . ." she manages in a whisper, emerging from her own shock and paralysis, sitting up straight in that ladder-back chair in the dark front hall—the same chair where I piled minerals I'd collected and tossed my sweatshirt and set down the Matchbox cars I'd been playing with in the dirt outside. "All these years, as if in a flash . . ." She blinks her eyes as if seeing it, literally experiencing it that way, and confused by the idea. "Just a flash." She keeps her hand pressed over her heart. As if to test, to continually reassure, that it is beating, that this is real.

I say nothing. I'm still too stunned by events. I never doubted her death. But here she was. Still here. As if waiting for this moment.

We can do little more than look at each other. Stare mutely in disbelief, and slow, creeping, fundamental comprehension.

Over the next few minutes, the next few hours, as we head arm-in-arm into the kitchen and she makes us mint tea and tuna sandwiches and we sit together at the little kitchen table with the morning light flooding in rich and full around us as if it too is a stunned witness to this turn of events, it is hard for me to get past the fury. It is hard to get past the sense of loss. The sense of insult. How he took over—cold guardian, father figure—and handed me a tainted ticket to the world.

"I know who did this to us," I tell her quietly. "I'm starting to see how it was done to us . . ."

She looks at me horrified. "*Did* this to us? What do you mean?"

And I realize that it has not even occurred to her that what happened to us was purposeful. She assumes, I can see, it was a series of accidents, miscommunications, official mistakes, bad luck, in a life that has known its share of them. Of course she thinks that—this sweet, simple, private midwestern mom, after all. A plan, a purpose, is incomprehensible.

I am about to explain it, to tell her who it was, who was behind it all, to tell her more about Wallace the Amazing than she would ever guess from television. About his success and the cold calculations and manipulations that make his success possible—and that she and I have apparently been part of it, pawns in it. But is there anything to be gained by doing that right now? By sharing it with her? By bringing so much darkness into her reunion with her son? At some point, maybe. But not right now.

(And proof of the rightness of holding my tongue? That in those next few hours, I can hear my mother—ever private, ever reserved—weeping behind the bathroom door for several minutes, before composing herself, coming back out.)

In my confusion, my stunned fury, one thing is clear. I will help Archer Wallace. The real Wallace. Duped like me. I will help him. We will finish off Wallace the Amazing. I am his creation, his mechanical monster. So I'm the perfect creature to turn on him.

His little trick, his deft little turn, twisting my life like a picture card (a jack, a knave) around his practiced magician's fingers. It makes everything around me feel like a stage set. Makes the past that surrounds me here in the hallway, the kitchen, the dark little house, feel unreal, since it had been scrubbed away, ceased to exist for me until a few moments ago.

Everything has happened. Everything has changed. Nothing has happened. Nothing has changed. Despite the unvarying geography, the utterly predictable house and porch and shutters and fence and side chairs and breakfast table and a thousand other visual and physical markers and assurances, there is this enormous sense of dislocation of time and place.

Wrinkled, curled in on herself, as if patiently preparing for life's last lap, quietly resigned to her final years on earth, my mother is suddenly brought alive. The years peel off; a new light in her eyes lifts her, enlivens her, animates a much younger being.

I return to what is relevant. To what is simple and primary, here and now.

"I . . . I didn't know, Mom." Half-formed, abject, apologetic. "I had no idea . . ."

"Of course not," she says, her own words forgiving, her voice so familiar, speaking to me quietly across the decades. "How could you? How could anyone even imagine?" Looking at me closely, like a specimen. And then beginning, intuitively, to rebuild our bond. "But now we have to deal with it, Charles." Blinking, as if to clarify the blurry thought for herself, clarify the necessary action. "We have to go forward. Repair what we can. We'll always share the loss. Now we have to share whatever can be salvaged, whatever can be gained . . ."

We are not mother and son, we are instead survivors of a primordial disaster, of a shifting of planets, a teleological tsunami.

I am looking back over the years, past the wrinkles to the eyes I know but have never looked at so closely. It feels invasive. I turn away.

And then, she's trying to rein it in for us, to normalize it, as if we *are* just a mother and son reunited in an old farmhouse on a dusty nameless American plain—exactly what we are. "Your jobs, your friends, your life . . . I want to hear it all," she says with a warm smile. Settling back in her familiar kitchen chair. Feeling, it seems, with a crazy, impulsive optimism, that we can simply catch up on twenty years. That we can happily, merrily fill in the blanks over tea and tuna sandwiches. She looks at me, a look filled with a mother's essential pride, admiration, joy, at an adult child's mere presence. "Having you suddenly here in the kitchen again, Charles. My kitchen. *Our* kitchen. It's . . . it's . . ." She searches for a word. "It's like *magic*."

I stare at her, shocked and stricken-looking enough, I guess, that I take the warm American plain smile away from her.

Magic. If only you could spit at a word. Chew it up, grind it into dust in your teeth, spit it out, bury it in the dirt with your boot heel. The long-dead mother alive; the unchanged landscape and details that I haven't laid eyes on in twenty years; the return, the awakening of a former self; the fact that it is all at bottom a deft, fairly simple trick—it all conspired to create a sense of unreality, of a waking functional dream state, wherein I was observing events as if from elsewhere, as if from afar.

He has induced this dream state, this kind of coma, a drug trip, wherein bounds are fluid, conventions are altered, physical and psychological rules get stretched and suspended. Does he too, wearing his adoptive self, experience this dream state? Does he know what he has unleashed?

So the Amazing has pulled off his scam, his act, not just on the Internet, where lies can be composed, alternate realities can be constructed fairly easily. No, he has done it in reality, in *my* hometown, for God's sake, altered reality. My mother's and mine, at least, and all of those acquainted with us.

To expunge someone from the Internet, that is technology. That is expertise. But for me to stride into a past that had been obliterated, that existed only in my imagination and is now fully restored in front of me, surrounding me, reproduced as if out of thin air—for someone to achieve that, is high art.

Magic?

Sure, Mom. Magic.

TWELVE

And so it is only appropriate, wouldn't you agree, that the magic continues. The dream rendered into reality, reality into dream.

Archer Wallace and I wait in glimmering dusk, beneath an otherworldly sunset of maple red, tangerine, and buttery gold, outside the gates of Shangri-la. Its spiral turrets and gleaming whitewashed flanks, sparkling jewel-like in the sunset, are familiar to me. I have seen this stunning stucco castle—studied it—on several pages in *People* magazine. Glimpsed its sumptuous colorful interiors in a spread in *Architectural Digest*. A sultanate in the desert. An oasis rising from the sand and scrub. I have never been here. I have never risked coming so close to it. But now, all bets are off (or on). Now risk—the big payout—is part of my vocabulary. After years of observing Las Vegas from a cool distance, I am in it—for the big payoff, with all attendant risks.

I know the gate code and door codes and alarm codes. I supervised and reviewed much of the security for him, set up and informed my boss how to create and maintain the security he craved, so I now have a level of access I never even thought about. (Unless he's changed the codes, but I would have known about that.) I know where to park the car so it can't be seen by the cameras. I helped set up the cameras—aiming them, adjusting them remotely—years ago.

We are waiting here outside the gates until Wallace the Amazing's show begins. We know he'll be out of the house for those hours, onstage and preoccupied and therefore out of the way. It's the one thing we can count on.

We sit silently in the rental car. There is nothing to say at this point. The plan is clear. We have been over it repeatedly. Unnecessary to verbalize it further. Its contingencies drilled into each other.

As Wallace's show begins at eight, just after nightfall, our show begins too. Archer Wallace and I scurry silently toward the front gate. I punch the keypad—first the code to cancel the previous code, then my new code, then confirming the new code, and the gate swings open.

We are hoping no one happens to be watching. But why would they? We are assuming, but we aren't sure, that his family is gathered around the television for the broadcast. Assuming it's their nightly ritual.

As we approach, silently, the glow of a big-screen television tumbles out of a bay window into the courtyard. Just as we imagined. So far so good.

The huge TV blares. It brings Wallace the Amazing practically life-size into his own living room. It masks the sound of my pressing the front door keypad and gripping the gold (yes, eighteen-karat gold) latch and handle with both hands, and pushing it gently open, and presumably it masks the sound of our footsteps. Wallace's own voice, confident, polished, booming through the home-theater speakers *profundo*, provides the real Wallace and myself the auditory cover we need.

Edging the front door open only as much as necessary. Up the half-dozen broad, grand entrance foyer stairs. In front of us, the family is sprawled like pashas on huge couches and colorful mats, watching rapt, as rapt as anyone in the show's live audience. They have seen the tricks a thousand times but don't know how they're done, and seem still as fascinated as ever to witness them. Or maybe now it's just to hear the funny, sordid, or unpredictable details of audience members' lives.

Archer Wallace draws his gun. I draw mine. (I had initially refused to carry one. This was going to be the end of our cooperation, the end of our plan, but Archer Wallace proposed a compromise. What if I brandished a gun with no bullets? I relented.) By the time the Wallace family becomes vaguely aware—senses something, turns—we are behind them, guns to their heads. Archer's gun is held to the head of the maid. Mine is held to the head of Sasha, the Amazing's amazing wife.

Archer Wallace is coolly proactive. "Everyone stays quiet, and no one gets hurt. Not a sound. No sudden movement. Got that, girls?" His health and appearance have improved markedly over the past few days. He acts strong, authoritative. As if all his strength, his energy, his whole being, has been waiting for this chance for action, this overdue revenge. *"Everyone stays quiet, and no one gets hurt."* Hearing that cliché aloud only makes the scene more unreal for me. Like it will all cease to exist in the next moment, turn out to be merely—and poorly—imagined.

The two daughters, Amanda and Alison, nod mutely, obediently.

Wallace the Amazing squints out into the audience sternly. As if he can suddenly see us. As if he is watching the action in his home but can do nothing about it. Life-size, as if he will step off the screen into his own living room, to defend it. But of course, he calls on someone. "You play the viola, don't you?" he says. "A Carpini viola." Viola repair bill, I remember.

Sasha looks in anxious, contained horror at me. She has no idea who I am, of course. No idea about my relationship to her and her family. No idea that I am a significant reason she is living in this sultanate, in such surroundings, in her lush life. To her, in fact, I am the precise opposite. A common thief, probably drug-addled, who with the capricious pull of a trigger will take this lush life away. I have spent years watching from afar the fruits of their marriage, the births and growth of their daughters, the living of their lives. She has never seen me and—given that she presumes her husband's tricks are indeed magic—never even imagined me.

"Just tell me what you want," she says to me, doing her best to contain her bile, to hold check on her fury and her fear, for they are working together in her, churning. I can see them both written across her face. She addresses it to me, as if intuitively singling me out for its existential meaning—*Just tell me what you want.* Taking charge for her daughters, dangling the possibility of a practical, civil solution, intending to get us out of there as quickly as possible.

It is Archer Wallace who answers from across the room. "What we want your husband is going to have to provide, Sasha." Using her name, to show we have done our homework.

He grabs the maid's arm, pulls her up, and, keeping the gun to the back of her head with his other hand, guides her across the room to where the girls are. He pushes the maid onto the couch between the teenage girls. Everyone understands this is to put them all together to keep an eye on them more easily. Everyone senses this is planning, professionalism. It seems to make them relax a tick, reassure them. Seems to say that this will be over soon, without incident, that the thieves will take whatever it is they want, and disappear into the desert as anonymously as they came.

Then, in an unforeseen instant (unforeseen by Sasha and the girls, anyway—I had been anxiously, literally "foreseeing" it all too clearly), Archer switches the gun to the back of Amanda's head, pulls her up off the couch as brusquely as he pushed the maid down onto it. I can see the fresh horror etch onto Sasha's face.

"Oh, no . . ." Faltering syllables as Sasha puts it together.

Wallace cuts her off. "Nothing's gonna happen if your husband does what we tell him. It's reasonable. He'll understand. It's evening the score. You ask him to explain it to you." The real Wallace sounds reasonable but firm. Understanding but authoritative. He plays it perfectly, I have to say. "Don't do anything—no police, no screaming, no panic—until you talk to your husband. Do you understand?"

No response. Staring.

"Do you understand?" With more force, with threat. This disheveled tuft-haired ghost—now he looks crazy. Reckless. And unafraid.

An alert nod of obedience from Sasha.

It is not the time, but I can't help myself. I look at Amanda—the shape and color of those swimming brown eyes, the tilt of her head, the relaxed posture that signals serenity and stillness amid surrounding turmoil. I can't help but admire her. She is terrified, yet she is also alert, fascinated, observing, somehow calm. Calmer than her sister, Alison, who is literally shivering in fear, and her mother, Sasha, standing immobile, paralyzed with panic.

While Wallace the Amazing closes his eyes onstage, wrinkles his brow in concentration—as if somehow seeing us, envisioning us, an interruption, a dark spot on the periphery of his thoughts—the real Wallace and I begin to back out of the family room.

The maid makes a sudden, protective move—to bolt from the room? grab a phone? pull an alarm?—and I swing my gun to her, and she screams, and Sasha screams in chorus, and Alison, the other daughter, begins to weep . . .

"Hey!" Wallace yells. "Hey!"

And another scream goes up, and Wallace fires.

Into the ceiling.

It silences them all bluntly and immediately.

As we cross the threshold of the front door, Amanda held between us, we are crossing another threshold, I know. From nuisance to menace. From annoying pest to deadly predator. A threshold where the police—the real police—could now be summoned, if that's the way the Amazing Wallace decides to play it.

From theft of identity, to theft of child. The story's dark new arc.

She is a beautiful young girl, Amanda. I glance at her in the rearview mirror. Archer Wallace sits beside her in the back while I drive. The gun is dangled casually in his right hand, exposed as a reminder to Amanda—and perhaps to himself. By previous agreement, Archer Wallace and I are silent. We don't want to supply any inadvertent clues.

I have mixed feelings about all this. Terror at our actions, of course, terror at the possible outcomes, each worse than the next, but tender feelings also. Amanda has never seen me. I am sure she has never seen even a picture of me. But I have watched her grow. I have seen her from infancy, watched from afar as she has taken her first steps, swallowed her first spoonfuls of solid food, spoken her first words. I have checked her grades, zoomed in on class photos and soccer and swim team photos posted online, kept an encouraging though watchful eye on her. This was my surrogate family, all the family I had, the family that I had filled in for mine, though this was my first time of course (and no doubt my last) in the family home. The routine details of her childhood—riding a two-wheeler, splashing desperately but triumphantly through her first lap, scoring her first soccer goal, smiling with accomplishment after the final note of her first oboe recital—she was the human marker by which I had measured the passage of time; in truth, the marks were penciled onto my soul like the carefully penciled slashes marking her height on the jamb of her bedroom door. These details of her upbringing are how I was able to bear it. And before you think that there is some perverted attraction or avuncular affection that goes inappropriately over the line, let me add: I now have the chance to get to know my daughter.

My daughter, because she is. My sperm, my DNA, my biological offspring—and this known presumably not by Sasha, or Dominique, or any other "detective." This known only by the Amazing and me. When his low sperm count and inadequate motility interrupted his plans for a perfect existence in a perfect oasis in the desert, he knew he did not need to turn to the inherent risks of a sperm bank. He had already, as it happened, intensively researched a candidate. Smart, proficient, loyal, alone in the world, already in his employ. Wallace engineered the sperm drop— my milky-white contribution in the cold cylinder, where Wallace picked it up a minute after I had left it for him—and it was his own specimen, as far as the world of medicine knew, with finally, miraculously, a viable sperm count. (The mysterious rhythms of reproduction still not thoroughly understood, but it happened all the time; couples couldn't conceive and then, suddenly, inexplicably, they did.)

Certainly it helps explain, doesn't it, why I felt my relationship with Wallace was so special, why I could not even imagine there could be another in my role. Certainly it explains my trust in him—because of his utter trust in me. His apparently profound and thoroughgoing admiration, sealed with the ultimate compliment. *I want you to be the father of my child.*

Perfect for him. Because I had already proved I knew how, that I had the discipline, to keep my distance from his life. That I could respect and honor a bargain, a deal, utterly. I had proved it day in day out, year in year out. So I was the perfect candidate for surrogate fatherhood.

And in the context of my ongoing years of service and my relationship, it was the simplest, smallest thing ever asked of me. Nothing to it. I hardly gave it a second thought, said yes immediately, no big deal, happy to do it. Ejaculate into a container, drop it off. Hardly a precious possession of mine, that single successful spermatozoon. I have billions more, and only occasionally any place for them to go. It was a favor that took no real effort, that, in fact, was its own small pleasure—for once, masturbation with some greater purpose. As far as how I might feel about a child who I knew was mine, I had no idea; I had no point of reference for such feelings. I imagined they might be intense in some new way. Or that I might just as likely have none at all. It turned out to be the former: unexpected, powerful, relentless feelings of interest, joy, pride, and, most of all, connection.

So when Archer Wallace had proposed the kidnapping, I had little choice—I had to be there to protect my daughter from harm, to be there whatever happened, come what may—but it was also the chance to be with her finally, to get to know her a little, if under the worst possible circumstances.

From utterly selfless to utterly selfish, in one short step.

So Wallace's two "detective" employees each have an extra connection to him—one his mistress, one the father of his child. Part of his method? Keep us close, keep us loyal, keep us protective, keep us interested? Now you can understand, that was part of the shock when she said she slept with him. It was another line of parallelism between us. We were not just both his employees, but both something much more—much more "connected."

Connection, connection, it is all connection . . .

My sperm—creating his fatherhood, and guaranteeing my loyalty, in a single ejaculatory stroke. A way to be sure I'd stay in his employ. To dutifully do what would ensure the welfare of my child, because my child was in his charge. My sperm donation—a useful, convenient solution—and one more tactic from him. In light of my startling visit home, I saw the degree to which his whole identity was in service of his stage act—helping to protect it, to insure it. So why not the paternity of his children too? It made the threat of the blackmail—of bringing down the act—all the more powerful.

As for his other daughter, Alison? Not mine, I knew. Not the efficient second use of my frozen sperm, because there was not a trace of resemblance, in look, movement, or (in my admittedly prejudiced view, anyway), in personality or intelligence, to me. (I had followed the girls' upbringing, don't forget. Followed it like a detective on a stakeout or a tail. A lifelong stakeout. A forever tail. I had held my breath, waited anxiously, when Sasha was rushed to the hospital near the end of her pregnancy with Amanda, some sudden problem with the fetus. The hours I spent pacing in my condo like an expectant father, until the crisis had passed. My ineluctable caring, my investment of feeling, right from the start.) I knew—knew as a father can know—that Alison wasn't mine. There was someone else. But if not Wallace (because maybe his sperm count, his low motility, had been overcome by the time of Alison's conception—a different period in his and Sasha's life, the pressure off), then who? Who would be that close to him? Or was that part of his consummate tactical genius too? To keep me anxious, nervous, about who it might be?

And I see that for me—especially, particularly—my filial connection to Amanda means so much, because it is evidence of my existence. Evidence of my presence. Proof of my existence beyond an anonymous sterile condominium, beyond a half-life of screens and keyboards. Without Amanda, I remain pure shadow. A mere extension of the digital. In a sense, hardly existing at all.

Did Wallace sense how important it would be to me? The extra protectiveness, the extra loyalty, it would engender?

Wallace the Amazing and I both understood that Amanda and I would never meet. Or that it would only be after his career, in her adulthood and my dotage, if even then. He would have named me her godfather, he let me know, if we lived in a world where our connection could ever be known. That was the debt he felt he owed me. Or was it just one more tactic?

· · ·

In a city of fifty thousand motel rooms, it is easy to find a safe place to keep Amanda, at least in the short term, as long as we usher her into the room unseen. Pop on the television, give her a pile of books, an endless supply of junk food, bar the bathroom window so she doesn't contemplate anything foolish on her occasional peeing breaks, and then we will wait. Wait to hear what comes first—wailing sirens at full alert, or a discreet phone call to the untraceable number we left.

Is it a safe motel room?

Depends on what you mean by safe.

We open the motel room door to hustle Amanda in, and there are the Stewartsons, waiting for us.

As previously planned, carefully arranged with me.

Archer Wallace is disarmed in seconds—professionally, in a blink. Not even adjusted yet to the dark of the motel room, its blackout shades and blinds drawn, hardly aware of it even happening, he's relieved of the gun that he so effectively and aggressively brandished, that he had stowed in his pocket during our check-in and for the necessary double-handed moment of inserting the key card and opening the door.

Not too smart.

His awkward, flailing, unthinking protest is met with a fist across the side of the neck. A blow I fully recognize as a veteran of it. Swift, sobering, decisive, only needed once—one warning punch all that is necessary.

And I happily hand them my gun too—no bullets, only a prop anyway—glad to be relieved of it.

What choice do I have?

I knew that Wallace and I could not pull it off without the Stewartsons following us. That they would be watching me, watching us, no matter what. Even when I found Wallace at the eldercare facility, they were close behind me, barely shakable. Even though I know Vegas like no one, I didn't think I could lose them—or if I could, it wouldn't be for long, and they'd only come back madder and meaner.

And I could not forget the beating I took last time. It was exactly as memorable as they hoped. It achieved what they wanted, I know, redirecting, refocusing, my behavior and actions. Their carefully calibrated escalation of violence with each encounter. I was painfully (ha-ha) aware of that measured escalation. I could too fully anticipate the next lesson. And the only way to avoid that next encounter was to bring them Archer Wallace, and fast. Risky enough, the lost hours of my quick and startling side trip to my mother. Hard enough to hold them at bay during that. So really, what choice did I have?

So I have delivered the goods directly to them. Amanda, their bargaining chip, and Archer Wallace, who crossed them. He and I are taking the risks. The Stewartsons and I will reap the rewards. An arrangement the Stewartsons liked immensely when I filled them in on Archer's plan the day before. Letting them avoid the risk of actually kidnapping Amanda, letting it happen from a safe remove, no risk of video cameras capturing them (they didn't know about my extensive knowledge on that) or of being seen, leaving them less exposed.

"Nice work, boys," says Dave Stewartson—highly arch, broadly sarcastic, a movie-gangster imitation. With a little nod, he adds, "We'll handle it from here."

In a few moments, Archer Wallace has come full circle.

Gagged and handcuffed to the tub and sink in the motel bathroom.

Back where I met him. Back where he began.

• • •

And now that the Stewartsons have Amanda, Archer Wallace has lost his value. That was part of the appeal of Archer's kidnapping plan when I told the Stewartsons about it: no more worrying about, dealing with, Archer Wallace. He was no longer a picture card, just a mere deuce or three in this high-stakes poker game. The nothing, the nobody, that he was when the Stewartsons discovered him. Worse than that, because he is now expendable, and the Stewartsons seem entirely comfortable and vaguely experienced with various forms of "expending." They won't leave him chained to a motel tub and sink forever. What will happen to him?

What choice did I have?

Better, I had decided, not to contend with the Stewartsons' practiced violence. Better to prove myself to them, get the credit I may need to exercise later. Better not to have them enter the Wallace fiefdom, the Wallace Shangri-la themselves, and do something foolishly violent, their instinct, their default setting, I knew by now. Better to acknowledge to them that I had found Archer, that he had this kidnapping idea and I thought we should go through with it. That it might be the only sure way to get Wallace the Amazing to respond, to act, to deliver.

The discussion of the idea with them had been concise, focused, professional. Wallace the Amazing didn't seem to be taking the threat of his false past and stolen identity being revealed very seriously. The Stewartsons were beginning to understand the same thing I was—that he was above all a showman, and this would become part of the show. This sideshow was not merely a distraction and annoyance, but would feed directly and usefully into the main event. What were the consequences of revealing his identity? The threat of the loss of his fortune. Of his show. But only the threat. And only eventually. And on the way to it, years of litigation. Teams of high-priced Las Vegas lawyers. A circus of a court case. Publicity you couldn't buy. A colorful, hidden past, which would create intrigue, excitement, and who knows, enormous sympathy? (The lawyers' investigations would probably bring out all kinds of nuggets from the past, which would only excite more interest.) You couldn't say what the outcome would be. And he and his brand and his influence seemed to be so well established in Vegas, who knew how well or how fairly the litigation would go?

The Stewartsons had assumed that it was worth at least a few million bucks to Wallace the Amazing to make this little problem from his past go away, given his stature now. For a few million bucks, why jeopardize it?

What they hadn't figured was that Wallace the Amazing might not take it seriously at all. Might welcome the threat of exposure. The challenge of litigation. That he didn't really see it as very jeopardizing. Because he could hold them at bay, duck and feint, go on with his act, even incorporate it. Frustrate and infuriate them.

So the threat of exposure seemed to take a backseat. Kidnapping seemed stronger. Traditional. Tried-and-true. No matter how he genuinely felt about his own children, he'd have to deal with it, one way or another. He couldn't simply let his daughter be taken. He'd have to try something, do something, to get her back.

(And once kidnapping was the plan, I had to be the one to do it. To engineer it, to oversee it.)

• • •

I know. First, my partnership with Wallace the Amazing. Then, a partnership with Archer Wallace. Then, a partnership with the Stewartsons. Always, a path of least resistance. A path of agreement, of docility. Secret partnerships, that no one else knows anything about. Don't think I don't notice the pattern. New partnerships before the old ones have dissolved. Saying yes to everyone. Accommodating everyone else. Never doing it on my own. And is it now primarily to best protect Amanda and myself, as I tell myself? Or is it the need to stay the beta male, keep to the background even when I am forced into the foreground? A man of changing loyalty—because a man of no loyalty? Or of enormous loyalty to his own daughter, and I see this as the only way to protect her. To be there for her—literally, finally.

A man of no relationships. Inexperienced, incompetent with relationships, with friendships, with loyalty, with belonging. Cut off from all social interaction. So what do you expect when relationships are demanded of me? I don't know what to do, how to treat them, how to behave. Promiscuous in alliances. What do you expect?

I can't bring myself to even exchange looks with him. My doppelganger. Fortunately he is back in the bathtub. Out of the way. How far out of the way remains to be seen.

And now I have kidnapped my boss's daughter. What a sorry banality. What a low-class, sordid revenge.

Or if you prefer, I have kidnapped *my own daughter*. Still a banality. Like white-trash couples who use their kids as pawns in divorce proceedings, in love triangles, swiping them from each other in Walmart parking lots or from school playgrounds in situations of increasing and surpassing sordidness.

And the only solace, and the cruel irony—and it is considerable in both solace and irony—is that I get to know her a little. This truly wonderful young girl.

I look at Amanda. I can't help myself. Bright, alert, yet managing to remain calm. (I had gotten the inkling, in those few swift, chaotic, purposeful moments inside their home, that she was the smart one, the calm one, and it turns out I am right.) Terrified of course, but hopeful. She is executing the best strategy, pulling off the best trick of any hostage—making her captors, or this captor at least, feel horrible about the turn of events.

The calm one. The smart one. And unquestionably the beautiful one. Big eyes, ethereal, flawless complexion, despite a childhood beneath the harsh Vegas sun. And as we check into the motel room, move around it cautiously, I see that she knows it about herself. Her smarts, her calm, her own beauty, are not lost on her.

I don't tell her, of course, that I know her friends' names, have checked on the safety of their homes and the relationships of their parents. I have checked on her safety and comfort at school. I have been her silent, unseen, and unknown protector for all her fifteen years. I have been her silent, unseen surrogate parent, and now, as of an hour ago, I have taken an utterly opposite role: very much seen, in behavior that is far from parental. And I don't know if I'm managing to hide my paternal concern for her—I don't know if anyone could do it completely—because she seems to somehow sense (and why wouldn't she?) this special connection, this special concern. And she looks at me with questioning eyes, with a slight tilt of the head, as if waiting for me to explain myself, waiting for me to right things, to release her, to bring her back home.

"You need a sweater?" I ask her. "Let me know if you're cold. I'll get something for you."

"No, I'm fine. But thanks." Then looking up at me, quizzically. Gauging me for a moment—judging my capacity for sympathy, for humanness, for her own safety—before asking what she's clearly been wondering. "Do I know you from somewhere?"

It startles me a little, of course. But she doesn't know me. She couldn't. I've spent my life carefully out of her sight. I shake my head no.

"You're not, like, some distant uncle or something, who I've never met?"

Jesus. Her power of intuition. I shake my head no.

"And this is just business, right? Get money from my dad, leave us alone after that?"

"Something like that, yes."

"And you're not gonna hurt my sister or my mom? They're out of the picture now, right?"

"Right." Adding, "There's no reason for anyone to get hurt."

"But sometimes things go wrong in kidnappings," she informs me. "You always read about that. People panic. Somebody tries something stupid. Stuff can go wrong."

"Your dad just has to follow the directions."

She looks tentatively up at me. "You've got a nice smile." Smiling a little herself. "Whoever you are."

And do I have the nerve to hurt her, if need be? Fortunately, the question is moot. My partners will be more than glad to do her any injury, if that's what's called for to get their money. The question is, how far will I go to avoid that, to defend her?

The answer is, far.

Only days before, I was held. And now, she is. Which gives me even more empathy, even more identification with my victim, probably a dangerous thing. Probably a very dangerous thing.

I don't tell her all I have done on her behalf. That I have been there, at the protective periphery, for all her birthday celebrations, her preschool and elementary school graduations, that I have looked in on the privilege, observed from just outside the candy shop's plate glass window.

And with her now so close, so real at last, cloaking her own fear admirably in quiet bravery, but her eyes betraying it—eyes on mine questioningly, and my eyes on hers—the motivating, propulsive rage that pushed me so forcefully into Shangri-la is diffusing, softening, confusing me. I don't know if I am going to rob them or protect them, Amanda and her family. To finally and fully bring them down, or to make sure nothing happens to them. Am I going to see our plan through, or foil it in the end? I honestly don't know. Because I don't know who I am anymore. I don't have any values, because who I was, all my values, were in the job I was doing, the circumscribed life I was living, and suddenly both are irreversibly disrupted. I'm displaced, and I have nothing to fill the vacuum.

"You're sure I don't know you from somewhere?" she asks again, quietly, when no one else is near us. Not playful. Direct. Puzzled. Deadly serious.

If you don't know who you are, then you don't know what you are doing or about to do. A precise, ingenious, quick biographer of other lives, I've been set utterly adrift in my own.

And then, I hear Amanda praying. The daughter of the Amazing, who knows there is nothing out there, praying. They have grown up going to church, Wallace and Sasha taking the girls fairly diligently. Vegas churches—how anomalous, how absurd—and yet they are huge, their congregations loyal and dutiful, as if to bask in the absurdity, establish a beachhead in it.

Or does Wallace, from his years onstage, simply recognize the childish human need for belief, belief in some kind of beyond, for all the human comforts it supplies, the human needs it answers, the human ego it assuages—a confirmation of our species' special place in the universe? He would hardly deny that to his daughters for the sake, and rigorousness, of grim reality. He coddles them in expensive luxuries and comforts; why should he deny them this essentially free one? They can grow, they can decide on their own at some point when they are older. As he looks out on his audience—delighted in the magic, awed by his connection to the beyond, shaken and shivering in the naked demonstration of its power—he looks out nightly on the sheer heft and force of this need to believe. Its sheer muscle and bulk, if not its monstrousness. He makes his handsome living on this need; he is hardly one to deny its force and size and power.

Amanda, my daughter, is praying.

Silently, I join her.

Prayer? Me? Sure, why not? If only for the sense of connection. In sympathy, in unity, with my sweet, frightened daughter.

THIRTEEN

But I am, of course, doing much more than praying. You know me by now. I am working diligently at the opposite end of the belief/faith spectrum—at the end where it is all facts and data. As soon as I left my mother's house, I had opened my laptop and started.

I knew he was scrubbed from the Internet. Part of my job was to scrub him. To maintain the aura of mystery, to endlessly rewrite and reconfigure his past, to leave it in vague mists of southernness and poverty and a mysterious extrasensory gift. Part of my job was to keep him that way, but he had done a pretty creditable job of it before I even arrived on the scene. A quick look revealed how well he'd done. Tens of thousands of pages referencing the Wallace of today. But little to nothing of a verifiable past. Compared with audience members, whom I could trace back carefully, methodically, step-by-step, his life began fully formed at thirty, as if he had sprung whole from the soil one night. But that absence, that emptiness, made all the more apparent that there were answers, there was truth, hidden back there. And, ironically, *I* had finished the job, completed it, as only a professional could, as he knew only I could. And now that I desperately wanted to know more, to discover the truth, the truth had been expertly disposed of, erased, stolen away from me. *By* me. Writing the biography of no biography. Letting any observer's imagination write it his or her own way.

Now I had to somehow resurrect it.

At this stage, a real detective shuts down his computer, steps away, and goes and looks, cruises the neighborhood, searches door-to-door, chats casually with the kids hanging out, asks questions, finds old relationships, slouches low in the driver's seat in a car across the street. All of which I was willing to do, but couldn't, of course, because I needed to continue to deliver the data to Wallace the Amazing, without interruption, now more than ever, so that he would not suspect me of being involved in taking Amanda. Could I learn anything in a day or two? Ask the favor of Dominique again? But it wouldn't be a quick, focused errand with a specific destination, like seeing my mother. It would require time—days, a week, poking around, getting familiar, exploring.

If I was going to learn anything, wouldn't I have to go back to the South, figure out who he really was, where he came from, find his roots and the roots of this overwhelming and total and perfect theft? A theft so complete and overwhelming and perfect that all trace of it had apparently disappeared. Had been reconfigured and remade, truth and actuality buried deeply and shunted aside. It meant I had my work cut out for me. Who had he touched; who knew who he really was?

• • •

But I can dust for digital fingerprints. As if discovering the latent fingerprint on the LED screen, finding a faint track in the digital dirt, stumbling onto the missing person's sock, or a slipper, in the thick digital underbrush. I was the right person to bury it all—and I'm the right person to unearth it. So it is that my fleet expert fingers pick up the first traces, the faint whiff, of Wallace the Amazing before he was Amazing or Wallace. Returning to those archived newspaper articles about Archer Wallace, mining the smallest details of the reporting, winding out from them in several directions—archived school records, birth records, drivers' licenses, tax records, all the techniques I have perfected over twenty years. Once I have the scent, my sensitive Internet nose can follow it into far corners, opening the dusty, digital attic trunk, unpacking the old albums, peeling it all back, laying out the startling biography, until I am staring at it, spread out in front of me, in amazement.

Ready?

Oh, I doubt it.

Born: Edward Lambent Corder. Grade school: Oklahoma. Junior high: Texas. High school: Arkansas. Father a roustabout, field hand, and drunk. Rented shacks, plywood floors, outhouses, dinner brawls. Which accounts for scant to nonexistent school records, rental receipts, bank statements. Living on America's margins, and yet there could be no truer or deeper American. His myth gets to have it both ways.

And then, South America. Tanker stowaway. He chose the only place more difficult to track him than the rural United States. Primitive, recordless South America.

And there, at a certain point, the record ceases. Disappears. Stops like tracks in the middle of the desert. There most would leave it. Most.

I dig further. I don't give up. I scrape away the sand and dust from the digital artifacts. I stand at the end of the track, the terminus, the end of the line, look out around me, search for movement, any movement on the horizon.

And eventually, I stumble across it—something so unpredictable, so out of the ordinary and odd, it's as if it's planted there for me. Something too, that is extraordinarily strange to have found its way onto the Internet, into technology's orbit at all. A trail of clues have led me to old journals, uploaded now as artifacts and mementos, of college kids backpacking through Peru and Bolivia—one of them not too stoned to remember a few names, to make a few coherent notes.

The name that the college kid jots down is extraordinarily weird. Dos Sequiantos Nas Tas Tasa. With the help of the Internet, I translate crudely from the Indian dialect: Dizzy Blue Fish.

A shaman.

Young Eddy Corder—apprenticing to a shaman? Living for months outside his jungle hut, sleeping on the jungle floor? But that's what I'm able to piece together from one of the journals: *There's this strange kid here from Arkansas I think, been hanging out here forever, talks dialect with the tribe, wears a shaman necklace, gets invited to sleep in the headman's hut—spooky stuff.* A shaman can be a medicine man, a pharmacologist, a hypnotist, a mystic and reader of signs, a semiologist, a sage and a counselor. But most of all, isn't a shaman a showman? Isn't he a native tribe's ancient, traditional version of the Amazing Wallace, astounding with his interior knowledge, his command of the unknown and unseen?

(And thinking about those college kids, and about the Amazing Wallace's previous, less layered, more innocent identity, I get a picture— the detective's vague, amorphous intuition, like my own shamanistic vision floating up from my unconscious—of a young couple traveling through South America at the same time and coming into the orbit of Dizzy Blue Fish and his American apprentice. The presence of both the young Eddy Corder, and this young, attractive couple—all of them with previous names, all in South America together. Possible? Significant? Mere coincidence? Useless speculation?)

What I find on the Internet knits myth and reality, a peculiar and unique fabric of the deep jungle. But I can't help thinking of the shaman, and the shamanism, in the context of what the Amazing Wallace does now. Because the shaman is both showman and authentic healer. The shaman's stunts might be fake—techniques for, a mastery of, group hallucinations? Is that all he has accomplished? But practicing authentic healing arts too. Using ancient ingredients that have made their way into our most effective and powerful modern medicines. The ingredients we have turned to, to study at the molecular level, to reassemble, imitate, duplicate in the lab.

That's why my cynicism, my lack of belief, my rational self, hits its greatest challenge in the idea of shamanism. One side of me thinks it is merely sorcerers' tricks and techniques—of misdirection, stagecraft, group hallucination, perfected over centuries—from which they derive their power. But another side of me looks at the record of healing, the adoption by western science of many of its ingredients and treatments. It leaves me split, and baffled. Does this, after all, add to the myth of my employer? Or does it detract from it, begin to unravel it, begin to reveal the truth behind it? The tribal shaman is in some ways the inverse of Wallace the Amazing—poor, primitive, naked, with none of Wallace's wealth and sophistication and comfort and modernity (or my technology). And yet they are brother practitioners, engaged in the same sciences and disciplines, as much as I can understand them at least. You would think that the timeless, changeless Amazon jungle and ever-morphing Las Vegas (famous for dynamiting buildings, throwing new billion-dollar projects up like joyously tossed newborns, altering its face, updating its appeal) would have nothing to do with each other. You would think an ancient tribe, fixed in time and place, untouched by modernity, and a modern tribe of extreme transience, devoid of tradition, each generation freshly made, would have no connection. And yet they are expressions, mirrors, of each other. And in that there was, I hoped, a detective's clue—not a conventional clue, to breaking an individual case, but a broader clue, to understanding human impulses, and needs, and maybe even a little of mankind, and maybe a little of myself.

What has Wallace the Amazing taken from the jungle and brought to the desert? And what are the Stewartsons actually after?

Once you have the thinnest thread, you can follow it. You are like a child in the woods, following a piece of string—diligent, preoccupied, focused.

So I'm eventually able to piece together his travels. The point being, there were numerous stops first. By all indications, with other shamans. *Questos Ayee Terracoatl. Bonduto Pen Losoviostandododoah.* "The Mud Man Who Sings." "The Stooping Triple Ghost." Brief stops, compared with the months he eventually spent with Dizzy Blue Fish. Which tells me these others, these initial shamans, weren't satisfactory. That they were false in some way, cons and scams that ultimately had the curtain lifted, that ultimately revealed their powerlessness.

Which tells me he was looking for some level of authenticity. For something deeper. He was—as only a young, brilliant, dispossessed youth can be—a searcher after truth. Ironic, that the search for truth had led him to tricks, to a complex, compelling scam. A dark notion floats above me, half-formed: Is that irony, that paradox, part and parcel of the truth he found?

FOURTEEN

And now, out of the South American jungle, and back to blackmail. A golden age of blackmail, really. E-mail, cell phone text, Twitter, Facebook—the communication is instantaneous, the levels of identity protection multiple and safe. A blackmailer can hide behind a wall of passwords and screen names, deploy an arsenal of hacking expertise. Proving at the same time that he knows your most personal information and movements and that he can reach you anytime—with a frightening aggressiveness that is this era's version of a pointed gun.

And now, thanks to sweet Amanda, the next e-mail message to the Amazing Wallace has force. Its every word will be searched, analyzed, internally and externally debated, examined for clues to more information, parsed for more comprehension, like the faithful searching their Lord's utterances.

> We have your daughter. Our strong advice: please accept and presume that we do, so we don't have to start sending tips of ears or sections of fingers or slices of toe.
>
> Here is what we want. Ten million, deposited to

an offshore account we have just opened expressly for the purpose. Yes, they're cracking
down on offshore accounts, but we'll have the
money in and out of it before it's an issue, before the authorities even know what happened.
At least, you better hope so—that's the only way
you're getting your daughter back.

Ten million. A nice, clean, round, nearly symbolic sum. Of
course, a ransom, or any sum for that matter, must be placed in the
context of its time and place. Ten million was enough to radically
change lives. It was a sum that covered, made possible, an invisible
Caribbean or Malaysian or South Seas off-the-radar pirate life. It
was also a sum on the fine line between a man of Wallace's assets
trying to retrieve it—insulted, vengeful, furious—and just as easily,
just as foreseeably, leaving it alone, paying the ransom to get his
daughter back, eating the cost, accepting and declaring the loss,
and then trying to forget about it, and eventually all but succeed-
ing. Ten million. It was not too little to ask of Wallace; it was not
too much. A sum that provides initial shock, literally breathtaking
at first, and then, as the payer immerses in the practicality of cob-
bling it together, it loses its shock value. Like a charitable request to
a big donor. The donor is initially stunned and appalled, but then
begins to think it through, to sort through the mechanics of actually
doing it, of putting those assets to work, of seeing tangible results
for those assets.

Ten million. A sensible sum. But for me, problematic. Because
if the Stewartsons were going to respect our deal, their $5 million
promise, that meant they were splitting the proceeds with me fifty-
fifty. That was absurdly fair-minded on their part. That is *not* who
they are. It signaled to me—strongly—that they had no intention
of splitting the money with me. Their gentlemanly fifty-fifty was
practically a mockery, a duplicitous smile, before they dropped me
in a gutter somewhere.

Or, they weren't actually interested in the money at all. That fifty-fifty was fine, since it wasn't really about the money. Which raised all kinds of new questions. Even more problematic.

• • •

Within minutes of the e-mail, I get a message from Wallace the Amazing—coded, virtually untraceable, through our usual back channels of staged financial statements and skein of protective websites. An inverse communication, a mirror, a corollary.

> Help me find her. Please help me find her.

The father, the human behind the mask.

> You're the best detective. You prove it every night. You saved me from Big Eddie and his thugs. I'll do anything, give you anything in return. Name your price. She is everything to me. And of course, she is everything, even more, to you. Help me find her. For me. For you. For us.

"You're the best detective." Careful. Intuitive. *"If I know you, Chas, you probably even have an idea of where she is already."*

Of course, I feel awful, worthless, contemptible, that he has turned to me in his hour of need, turned to my faithfulness and loyalty, which is apparently still unquestioned. And yet look how I have treated it the past few days, how I've turned on him after a lifetime of support. After he has provided a life to me.

(A life he deceived me into, securing the deception by taking my mother from me, erasing her—and for good measure, taking me from her.)

And of course, I see that I could have his eternal thanks in the form of a reward. *"Name your price."* And it occurs to me that I may now be in a position to collect on both ends—as perpetrator and rescuer; as criminal and hero; snake and saint. Take my cut of the ransom, *and* my cut of the reward. (But how exactly? If there's a ransom paid, there won't be a reward. And if there's a reward, then there won't be a ransom. But that's a conventional view. I am starting to imagine scenarios that have both—the ransom, then the rescue.)

This is Wallace the Amazing, however. Not to be underestimated. Is he turning to me in ignorance, or does he suspect that I am involved, that I have a hand in this? Someone waltzed into and out of his home, after all, someone that Sasha and Alison have presumably now described to him, though as you know, I am unremarkable, nondescript, usefully generic. There wasn't much they could say beyond height and build and race, and there was no photograph he could show them—"This guy here?" He is giving me a chance to redeem myself, to set it right, and sending me the implicit message: no harm, no foul. Showing his love. Giving me another chance. Or demonstrating his absolute faith in me. Like a god of forgiveness.

But he took away my family . . . why shouldn't I take away his? (Or take mine back?) Why shouldn't there be biblical justice? An unforgiving Old Testament God would be quite at home here in the desert. Amid the rigidity of the slot machines and cards and games. You win or you lose. *X*s and *O*s. Digital, antipodal, polar, Manichaean. *Vegas think*, I call it. All or nothing, winner take all, winners and losers. Blistering hot or freezing cold, like the desert itself. Bright day or black night. No subtlety. No shades of gray. No nuance. People come here to avoid nuance. To escape nuance. To get away from the unclarity, the anxiety, the fog of gray. That's the Vegas way.

Wallace sends me his private plea but delivers no response to the Stewartsons' e-blackmail. They had expected it within moments; we have his daughter. But the hours drift by, and nothing. That's how I would have played it too, if I were Wallace. It is annoying, frustrating for the Stewartsons. Did he *get* the e-mail? How could he not respond? What's he working on *instead* of responding? Is it possible he doesn't care about his daughter? That he's willing to let her go? Be exposed for the fraud he is, give up his career? They pace, they quarrel, they second-guess. They check their watches nervously. They regard each other accusatorily. *Wasn't this your idea?*

We watch the show that night. To see if there is any hint from him. To see if he's distracted, or off. To see if there's any indication of what's happened to his daughter, to his family.

Oh yes, there is.

The act proceeds normally. Elicits its usual quota of oohs and aahs, its audience swooning. It picks up pitch as it proceeds, as the hour rolls powerfully, ineluctably, to its climax, an entertainment freight train gathering momentum. And then . . .

"Ladies and gentlemen, this is a special night. Not a special night I relish, but a special night nonetheless. Because you, this audience, will bear witness to my most spectacular demonstration ever. My most *important* demonstration ever. The one closest to my heart and my soul. A demonstration that *has* to come out right."

A buzzing murmur rises, then falls to a hush.

Wallace hangs his head, looks at the audience as if at a friend across a cocktail table in a dark bar.

"Last night, my daughter was kidnapped." Gasps. Mutters of incomprehension, until he nods. "Taken from our home." He lowers his voice a little, removes the showmanship from it for a moment. "In my world of goods and possessions, a world you've seen I'm sure in magazines, a world of wealth and amusements, my daughters are my only true treasure.

"I did not call the police, because these kidnappers are professionals. They are professional extortionists, who, of course, want money for her return. They warned me not to get the police involved, and now of course the police will know, but the police will not be able to make any progress in finding her. These people are polished pros. It is obvious to me that the police, though well intentioned, will be powerless.

"So here's my chance. Instead of predicting driver's license numbers and the amount of change in pockets, and telling a dog's or an aunt's name or the color of your car or your curtains, here is the ultimate test of the mentalist. To find his own daughter. I can't say whether the anxiety and stress of the situation will inhibit my process, will block me. I confess I fear that enormously, as I have been concentrating as you can imagine for the hours since the kidnapping and have gotten nowhere. But I must learn in these next hours to put that aside, to somehow focus. I may have only my own powers of mind to call on. I will need, in these next twenty-four hours, to call on every scrap and crease and corner of them.

"And that is why I am enlisting *you*. Every one of you in this theater tonight. Because while I have struggled over the years to convey anything comprehensible about my gift, my process, how I work, what precisely is going on in my mind, I *have* conveyed one fundamental element of it: the notion of connection. You know at least that I work by some version of connection. And I need that connection now. I need you all to visualize, to imagine, to empathize, to not only picture my beautiful daughter but to feel, to absorb, my love for her. To feel my connection. Because it is the power of all of us together, the allied, multiplied, manifold power of your concern, your anger, your sympathy, your focus, that I will tap into to see her, to find her, to connect with her.

"So I want this audience, *need* this audience—this exact audience, every one of you—to reappear here tomorrow night, when, I swear, my daughter will join me onstage. I will produce her here."

Momentarily fragile, bitter, human . . . "I have always vowed to keep my family separate from my working life, but this kidnapping has forced my hand."

Quickly casting it off, finding his familiar register of intensity, clarity, power . . . "To the kidnappers, yes, I know you have her, yes, I know what you want, but I'm not giving you the satisfaction of following your instructions, dropping a black case of cash at the intersection you designate. I'm *not* doing it . . ."

A wild response from the audience. Unbridled, unleashed endorsement. A wild stampede of pure will, defiant support and brotherhood. The troops roar their loyalty to their general.

The lights on the stage black out. A photograph appears—the backlit image huge, a hundred feet high—of Amanda, smiling. A thousand acolytes in the live audience take in her deep-brown eyes, her pretty face. Plus the millions watching at home. Maybe someone has just seen her. Not a bad move, Wallace.

"Her name is Amanda. She's everything to me. And the question—not a rhetorical question, not a stage question in a Vegas stage act, but a real question—is whether my powers will work when I need them most."

The familiar voice, no longer bathed in light, but materializing out of the darkness: "Amanda, I'm coming for you."

Here in the motel room, as we watch, it is hushed and stunned.

Except for Amanda, who looks at me and smiles.

Incorporating his daughter's kidnapping into the act. Cold-blooded and risky, but maybe ingenious in ways I hadn't ascertained yet.

Turning the kidnapping into a tent show. Into an occasion of faith. A religious experience. A noble moment of community.

• • •

The message to me couldn't have been more explicit. Somewhere between a plea and a boss's order. Clearly, I was on it. Maybe he had put Dom on it too, but maybe he deliberately hadn't, making this a pure and undiluted test of my loyalty, of where I stood. It was his challenge, his all-or-nothing Vegas bet laid on the table. *Really need you on this, partner. Don't know anymore if you're with me or against me—obviously someone waltzed into my home with the codes, and you're the only one who could do that, so I obviously suspect you. But it doesn't matter. I'll put it aside. Let's seize the opportunity together. Name your price—you can return to my payroll after this if you want, or not, up to you. A mentalist victory like this will put Wallace the Amazing over the top.*

Though it went unsaid, I felt it. Like a heat that singes my back, my forearms, my skin.

I was hiding in an anonymous motel room. But the spotlight was nevertheless, finally on me.

FIFTEEN

So now, all of Las Vegas—to say nothing of the rest of America—will be looking for Amanda for the next twenty-four hours. Those who saw the show, passing on the news to those who didn't. Replaying the show on the Internet, getting a good hard look at Amanda's photo.

And I'm thinking—as the Stewartsons are—that the mobilized army of the curious and the newly and sympathetically alert could easily include a motel clerk or maid who happened to see us hustling in or hustling out. Or had a vague awareness of something unconventional and inappropriate going on in Room 201, and now had a new focus on it.

The mobilized army will in a few minutes be wildly exchanging clues and sightings, and the police task force, already assigned, at their row of desks, will begin sorting through the flood of excited calls.

And the ingeniousness, of course, is that if Amanda is found like this, by conventional, terrestrial, cooperative, human means, the Amazing's "powers" will not have been tested. A higher power will have triumphed, he'll justifiably say—the power of human goodness over human venality.

And if she is not found—and his "powers" fail him in this instance—any rational public questioning of his powers, of the whole tent show, will be subsumed in, overwhelmed by, sympathy for a victimized father searching desperately for his treasured daughter. No cynics, no late-night comedians, will dare fly in the face of that. Filial love and duty and responsibility: the greatest power of all.

If she is not found—if his "powers" fail him in this instance—then yes, there is speculation anew about those mysterious powers, but about why they failed him here, not doubt of them as a whole. Those who believe in such powers will have explanations about his wanting something so much that it overwhelms the calm and stasis and deep serenity of mind required to perform his usual mental feats (and he can even reinforce this view with a few stumbles onstage). Those who know his powers are all a stunt will have sympathy, will see him suffer this object lesson, this moral accounting, and therefore will ask nothing further of him in the way of a fall. You've fallen far enough. You need fall no farther.

Outside the motel room, the pack of dogs is already spreading out over the city. Unleashed, a hundred thousand noses to the ground. Sniffing the desert air. Will some contingent of the citizenry start searching local motel rooms? Seems a logical place to start.

The Stewartsons can't send another e-mail. Now it will be traced. After last night's broadcast, the Las Vegas police—the *real* Las Vegas police—are now fully aware and informed about the kidnapping (if they weren't already, in some previous arrangement with Mr. Vegas, Mr. Insider, their favorite civic booster, the Amazing Wallace). They certainly have the technology for tracing e-mails. Police will now be watching all places of public access—library, Internet cafés, etc. They have the manpower and surveillance for that. (And the more I think about it, the Amazing Wallace probably alerted them just before his broadcast. The Amazing Wallace would have played the politics of dialing them into what he was about to do. To keep in their good graces. So they are part of the plan.)

In fact, when Dave Stewartson and I go to buy a disposable cell phone and a minutes card off the rack at Anton's, a local electronics retailer, and bring it nonchalantly to the checkout counter, we are in for a sobering surprise. The clerk looks up apologetically. "Sorry, Vegas police said we can't sell these right now. In fact, anyone asks for one, we're supposed to call that info into them." The clerk smiles. "I ain't gonna do *that*, but I can't sell you the phone. It's all inventoried, items and sales dates, and I'd be fucked, lose my job."

I watch Dave Stewartson take a breath. He looks silently, haughtily, down at the clerk. I know what the quick judgment is, running through his mind. *Do I trust this kid not to call it in, or is he gonna be a Boy Scout?* How will Stewartson handle this?

Stewartson smiles jovially. "So essentially, if I'm gonna get this phone, I'm also gonna have to find you a new job."

The clerk smiles. He likes this good-looking, smiling, charming guy, likes the wit, the engagement. This nontransaction has taken an interesting turn.

Stewartson continues: "So the next question is, how much do you like your job?"

"Not at all." No hesitation.

"Want to come work for me? I'll double what you're paid here."

The kid's eyes light up. "Doing what?"

"Everything. I've got a pretty good-size import-export business based in the area."

"Really?" The clerk clearly has no idea what that is but won't admit it.

"I always need clerical help, sales help, little of everything. I hire bright people, and I train them. That's been my business model for twenty years now. You'd have to show up Monday, eight a.m." He scribbles an address—God knows what address—and hands it to the clerk. Who holds it like the Sacrament.

The clerk nods. This is Vegas. This is how it happens. He's heard about this kind of thing all the time. Surprising—and not surprising at all. "Okay, I'll be there."

"And the cell phone and card?"

The clerk shrugs. He'd half forgotten them. "Sure." He looks furtively to both sides of him. "Know what, sir? I'm not even gonna ring them up. That's one way to not have the police getting in your business, right? Here. And thanks."

"No, thank *you*," says Stewartson, big, genial. And when the clerk looks at me—I am obviously a trusted lieutenant, a right-hand man of some sort—I nod approvingly to him, assuring him of the wisdom of his split-second decisiveness. Indicating my clear admiration of it. Good, quick thinking, kid.

And seeing the new cell phone slip into Stewartson's pocket, I think of Debbie's cell phone again. There's been no indication from the Stewartsons that they have it, that they did indeed take it off her kitchen counter. So has she in fact retrieved it? Or has she decided instead not to risk any more with that phone, that it's better to start over, with a new phone, a new phone number, cutting off any connection to her previous life with me, safely, practically, but also symbolically.

I think of how my own cell phone would ring, Debbie calling me from the road, one acting job or another, from Duluth or Anchorage or Philadelphia or Miami, her movement around the country reminding me so vividly of my own pre-Vegas existence. Checking in between filming setups or from her hotel room at night, with the news of her day, descriptions of the city she was in, the nice people she was working with. Nothing urgent or even memorable was said, and yet during each day spent locked in my condominium in front of my screens, it was my moment of intersection with real life. With actuality. With living, breathing humanity, channeled through a single human voice. It was the nothingness of those conversations that I missed; it was their lack of import, their casualness and simple contact, that was so meaningful. Their pointlessness was their point.

I would never, could never, bring Debbie anywhere near this tight, tense chaos of the moment. But after it is done, after it plays out one way or another, whether with millions and a fugitive's freedom or with a lengthy jail sentence, will I reach out to her? I feel more alone than ever. And find myself asking, with more frequency, with more longing, and despite the shadowy allure of Dominique, where is Debbie now?

Before Stewartson calls the Amazing, he takes from his luggage a little gray box—about four inches square—and attaches it to the phone with a thin red wire in a highly practiced way, offering a quick, sidelong smile as he does it. I've never seen one, but I know it's a voice scrambler. Further indicating what kind of employment background the Stewartsons have. America's cast-off warriors. In full post-patriotic mode.

Dave sits on the bed. Takes a breath. I watch him dial. I don't say anything, but I know from the first three digits that it's Wallace's private number.

A number I've always known. And a phone call I could never make. How does Stewartson have it? Why hasn't he used it before? But I know why—because even with a disposable phone, there are risks of being traced. Stewartson is taking on more risk. Feeling frustrated. Edging closer to the endgame, one way or the other.

The Amazing Wallace doesn't pick up.

Stewartson leaves a message. Short and punchy. "Pretty ballsy of you, Wallace. Pretty fuckin' ballsy. Offer still stands. Ten mil, we disappear, and you remain the Amazing Wallace, locked into your lie, taking your little lie to the grave. But you've set your own clock, haven't you? Offer runs out at broadcast time tonight. Which we're looking forward to, by the way. We thought we'd be exposing you. But turns out you'll be exposing yourself."

We hang up. We wait.

That night, Wallace the Amazing amazes the city and the world again, takes the stage, defiant of the kidnappers, defiant of their effort to derail his show, his routine, his entertainment. (I haven't supplied any information for tonight's show. I didn't need to. Because last night's same audience is returning, per Wallace the Amazing's directive. It was a pretty clear message to me. *To let you totally focus on solving the kidnapping, Chas.* Making it a priority, relieving me of my other duties, given my special relationship with his daughter—my daughter. Though perhaps sending another, sub-tler, inverse message to me as well: *I don't really need you, Chas; I can work around you. You're disposable, dispensable, so keep that in mind.*)

When it becomes apparent that he will continue to do a live show, despite his daughter's kidnapping, the ratings are greater than ever. During last night's show he brazenly promised to produce his daughter here tonight. I would have thought her absence would be seen as his failure, his inability, his empty bravado. But no, Amanda's absence only extends and expands his audience, builds sympathy and curiosity, heightens tension and drama. Wallace the Amazing proves his showman's instincts once again.

The kidnapping of Amanda Wallace hangs over the show, liter-ally. The massive projected portrait stays up throughout—testament of a father's love of his missing daughter, saying clearly she is on all our minds.

A couple of times, he furrows his brow, and says, partly annoyed but partly sympathetic to the theater audience, "Too many of you are thinking about the kidnapping. It's making you hard to read. We're all thinking about it. But try to put it aside for the next ninety minutes. That's what I'm trying to do. Don't let them win." Appreciative gasps, because *yes*, they *are* thinking about the kidnap-ping. Accompanied by sympathetic nods.

And toward the end of the show, he turns to the massive por-trait still floating above him—the tacked-up missing poster, the milk carton missive writ large, Vegas style—and turns back to the audience and turns to the subject at hand, the subject on every-body's mind, and ups the ante, stuns them (and us) again.

"Twenty-four hours. And nothing has turned up. Obviously these are professionals, and my instincts were right. In the past twenty-four hours I know you've been looking, for the sake of jus-tice, to return a daughter to her father. But the police have sifted through the clues you've turned up, and we're nowhere yet." (*"We're nowhere"*—all in it together. He's a master.) "So let me add some-thing tonight. Last night, I wasn't explicit about paying you for your help. About whether that would be a part of my thanks, my appre-ciation. But it will be. What's a daughter worth to a father? What do you think? You find her, and you tell me what's fair. You tell me. The reward is what you think it should be."

Gasps. Murmurs.

And a little kick in the ribs of the kidnappers.

Deliver her to me and pick your own dollar figure. *You* say what she's worth.

Turning the city and the nation, in effect, into a city and nation of blackmailers.

Saying, in effect, you're nothing, you kidnappers. You're one among a million blackmailers. And I'll pay any of them, gladly, anything, maybe more than what *you* were looking for, before I'll give you a dime.

So I sit with Amanda. Amanda of the beautiful swimming eyes, clear and nearly poreless skin, preternaturally calm demeanor. I want to talk to my daughter, but Dave and Sandi are always nearby. All I can do is try to smile reassuringly, and such a steady, affection-ate smile from a stranger has to be highly unnerving to a fifteen-year-old girl. So all I have is a neutral look, and I try not to look at her, that being the best I can do to reassure her.

Archer Wallace is still chained to the bathtub, bathroom door closed, bathroom light off. I have been instructed not to interact with him in any way. (Sandi and Amanda have the same routine for using the motel bathroom: light kept off, blanket tossed over Archer's head, when they're on the toilet. I face the other way, say nothing to him, when I pee. He rises to the level of a presence only when we attend to bodily functions. He must realize that. Sandi tosses him food or snacks periodically. His own bodily functions he must take care of right from the tub.)

While the Stewartsons check the motel perimeter, Amanda and I are alone for a precious few minutes.

She can sense, probably, that I am free to talk to her only when the Stewartsons are out of earshot. She probably senses that I *want* to talk to her.

"Just checking one more time . . . you're warm enough? I can get you a sweater, remember, or turn down the AC."

She shakes her head, smiles a little again. "You sound like a parent." She looks at me. "Afraid you won't get your money if you return me with a cold?" Then she frowns, her lightness suddenly gone. "It's kidnapping. I don't think you should be worried about colds." Cynical, realistic—but also indicating, oddly, perhaps, that she is thinking about what will ultimately happen to *me*. Now *that* is amazing.

I don't know how long the Stewartsons will be out of the room. "I saw an online video of you starring in your school musical. You were a pretty convincing Peter Pan."

"You've really done your research. Careful preparation. Congratulations."

"You were good, Amanda."

"Maybe I've got a little of my dad's onstage talent. Or big ego," she says with a diffident smile.

If you do, it's your own talent. It has nothing to do with his genes. Maybe instead you've got your real dad's diffidence, modesty, curiosity, powers of observation.

"Well, I think you should continue your singing. You have real talent. I've got a girlfriend who could be helpful." I pause, debating saying more, but press forward, can't help myself. "How are your teachers this semester?"

She looks at me. *Are you serious?* "Do you really expect me to answer that? To have some pleasant little conversation with you?"

I shake my head no—she doesn't have to answer. We sit in silence.

Until she looks up at me quizzically in a moment. Then: "Math's a bear."

Yes, you always have trouble with math.

Is she genuinely confiding? Or is this just a shrewd little girl deciding to keep the lines of communication open? I'll take it, either way. "The secret with math is, just spend a few minutes a day with it. Honestly, that's all it takes. It builds on itself."

She looks at me. Shakes her head a little at the absurdity of this exchange. Suppresses a smile. But we're both in on its absurdity. It's a shared joke. So I smile a little too. The smile she noticed before. A smile I call on now to somehow reassure her.

"How much?" she asks, suddenly.

"How much what?" But I know what she's asking.

"How much money are you trying to squeeze from my dad?"

"I'm not sure that's your business."

"I know more about money than you think a fifteen-year-old would. I'm a girl from Las Vegas, remember? Go ahead. How much?" Challenging me. Curious.

"How much are we asking, or how much are we getting?" I say. Resisting the urge to smile a little. Trying to steer away from specifics.

"Either."

"I don't know. We'll see."

"You seem to have trouble with math too," she says. And I see her resisting her own smile. Like me, it occurs to me. Like her dad.

We regard each other silently, blankly for a moment. Neither of us sure what a kidnapper or victim can or should say to each other.

"Nothing's going to happen to you," I say suddenly. It comes out unbidden, unrehearsed.

She looks at me, cocks her head.

"I won't let it," I tell her.

She stares.

Searches my face, my hairline, my eyes, my nose and mouth, as if picking up the scent of our biological connection. She stares into me, into my being, into my soul, and again seems to latch onto something. "Thanks," she says, genuinely. But her puzzled expression is asking again, *Are you sure we don't have some connection?*

"There's something weird going on here," she says. "Weirder than kidnapping. Isn't there?"

I of course cannot respond. Sharp little girl, she seems to pick up on that too.

"I can tell that you can't tell me," she says. "But it doesn't matter. There's something weird going on here."

Think zombie movie. We're holed up and hiding from the populace as if this is a zombie movie. Everyone is dangerous. The fan base is activated. We see news reports and videos of fans forming search parties. Accent on the party part. Drinks, hors d'oeuvres. A novel social excuse. Faces from the search parties leaning into the frame of the local news cameras, waving and smiling. They'll split the reward, they say on camera. Like lottery winners from a factory shift.

We track the parts of the city where the searches are going on, flipping between local channels to try to get coverage as complete as we can, but of course, we know the news coverage isn't comprehensive.

Although it is a city long on security—with security cameras in lobbies, on boulevards, in casinos, a city of metal detectors and pat-downs and gym-buffed guards, it is also, paradoxically, a city that's easy to hide in. There are more hotel and motel rooms per square foot than in any other city in the world, and no hotel or motel operator is very interested in much more than payment and a passing assurance you won't bomb or burn down the place. The issue in hiding is that you must hide intelligently. Not necessarily in an otherwise empty and stray motel, where you're more likely to be noticed, which would likely be included in any systematic search, but in a busy place where you're part of the crowd, where it's impractical to search. But maybe even in plain sight. Should the Stewartsons and I all become conventioneers? Blend into the ophthalmologists' convention? The gastroenterologists' annual event? And Amanda here, she can be my daughter, along on a junket, along for the ride.

If Wallace the Amazing doesn't respond in some way, I'm worried about what the Stewartsons will do to Amanda. They won't kill her. But they will blithely, eagerly, do something short of that. A finger. An ear. Something traditional. They are trained in maiming, highly versed in such tactics, and eager about it, and it provides a further way for them to test my loyalty, bind it with blood. I feel it coming.

Because by now I know who they are. Or were. Sitting with my laptop in the down hours with Amanda, waiting for Wallace's response, I've been able to follow the thin digital thread further—track their post-government, pre-Wallace career. An electronic maze, a warren, of military and federal government sites opened their digital doors to me just a crack, just enough, leading me twisting, turning, down narrow Internet alleys to a little discovery that on reflection isn't startling at all. They were part of a response team for US corporations whose executives were kidnapped in South America. They were the experts called in to recover the executive, and they have seen all the tactics from the other side, seen how well they work, how effective they are, know just how and when to deploy them. Their names are scrubbed. No Stewart Davidson, no Sheila Barton. But there they are, in photos on black websites that I managed to hack, depicted on a team of operatives. A whole little subworld of security firms, paramilitaries, mercenaries—and there they are.

No one comes in or goes out of the motel room. We have called off the maid service, but clearly in a change of shift there has been a miscommunication, because I hear a maid and her cleaning cart rattling up to our door, the maid humming vaguely to herself. She knocks, announces herself in English badly fractured with some kind of Eastern European accent, waits in an unrushed silence for our response.

Stewartson, annoyed, gestures us to be quiet, draws his gun, goes to the door, keeps his attention keenly on the door handle.

The maid waits a few moments, then knocks again. I would have brought Amanda to the bathroom, to join Archer Wallace in there, but there is no time, and it will look more obviously suspicious if we are seen in the process of locking a teenage girl in a motel bathroom. A foreign-born maid, with limited English? With any luck, completely unaware of, out of touch with, a Vegas stage show, or the televised images of a kidnapped daughter.

We hear the maid's key card slide into the slot and the beep of the door unlocking, and Stewartson says loudly, "It's occupied. *Ocupado!*" and before Stewartson can stop her, the maid enters, babbling to herself in some Eastern European language, still humming to herself, and only looks up after a beat, fear seeming to fill her eyes, as she sees the room is occupied. Extremely occupied. She is wearing a hearing aid, so she obviously couldn't hear Stewartson.

Now Stewartson flies at her, stands over her, gesticulating, but it's unnecessary. She is already backing out, apologizing profusely in broken English and her own tongue, pointing to the hearing aid in explanation.

But not before Dominique and I exchange glances.

I am, as you can imagine, very impressed with her performance. The hearing aid. The mumbled, concocted Eastern European dialect. I don't know, of course, what she thinks of *my* performance. Sitting on the bed next to Amanda, my hands snugly behind my back, as if tied. Trying to look like a victim, alongside Amanda. Dave and Sandi, occupied with the maid, don't even notice me.

Falsehood, inconclusiveness reigns. The moment is, shall we say, interrogative.

And tapping somewhere deep in Dominique's alert, attuned researcher/detective brain—does she notice similarities beyond our identical, vaguely imploring side-by-side position on the edge of the bed? Does our identical seating provide a clue to her unconscious? Does she take note of the similar scoop of eyes, the identical lower lip, the similar cherubic faces? And pick up on something that no one else in the world knows?

"Stupid bitch," says Stewartson, after he has slammed the door on the crazy, mumbling maid.

I don't know where Dominique stands, of course. Loyal employee and bedmate of Wallace, or has the discovery of my existence changed her, as discovering her is part of what changed me? And beyond that, isn't there the confirmation, the resurfacing, of what I thought I sensed before? A chemistry between us? A heightening connection?

And she—in parallel, a mirror—doesn't know where I stand.

How could she, since I don't know?

We gather for the Amazing Wallace's show once more. Once more, he seems to go on as if nothing is wrong, the consummate showman, and then, consummate showman, he sees it. *It comes to him.*

"My God." He falls to his knees, struck down by the knowledge. He can't contain it, as he must know he should, but he can't. It's too much, too burdensome. He blurts it out. It is knowledge pounding inside his head that must come out. "I see the door. The room number. Room 201. A motel." He pauses, bends his head to the floor. Looks up, stunned. "1508 Trailer Road. That's it. She's there." He turns desperately to the crew offstage. "She's there. Call the police right now. Right now. Go, go, go."

And he collapses onto the stage.

The audience gasps.

Some of the crew comes onstage to help him. A stage manager takes the microphone. "Please . . . let's all just wait a few minutes, all right?" The motel is only minutes from the theater. "Let's just take a deep breath here, and wait . . ."

The police arrive in force, en masse, tires screeching, sirens wailing, baying like excited hounds wearing buffed metal coats of black and white, plus Incident Command and SWAT—all barely ahead of the TV camera crews. We see it all on the television in our room, watch them surround the motel, watch the quick action, examine the methodology, compare this reality to the fictional version we have seen in dozens of TV shows.

It should have occurred to me that Wallace the Amazing, finding us through Dominique, would co-opt the moment first for theater.

Of course, we have moved. We are watching from a much safer place. A place no one will ever look for us, I feel sure.

Big Eddie's hideout house. In a Vegas development of hundreds of identical homes. Nondescript. Off the radar. Its identicalness to the houses around it, still its best architectural feature. And never occupied. Perennially empty real estate. Which I know from my reconnaissance of Eddie and his henchmen when they took Wallace here. When I saved him.

The site of my boss's kidnapping, which I singlehandedly foiled.

The site of his daughter's kidnapping, which I have cooperatively planned.

Big Eddie's unoccupied hideout house—where I have gone from hero to criminal.

In the wake of Dominique's visit to the motel, I suggested that we move. They thought I was being overly cautious, but I pointed out that the coincidence of the maid's screwup and her hearing aid was all a little too much for me. We discussed it; they argued about the risks of moving itself, I stood my ground, and prevailed. I assured them I had the perfect place. I knew of course this would endear me more to the Stewartsons, they'd trust me more—but mostly, I was afraid for Amanda's safety in a police raid. If the atmosphere was sudden, and intense, and unanticipated, I was afraid of what Dave or Sandi or a suddenly unchained Archer Wallace might do.

And if Wallace the Amazing knows that I'm involved in some measure (whether as perpetrator or victim), will he think to look here? He was brought here blindfolded on that night of course, but he presumably does know the location because he left here by crossing through the desert himself. Will it occur to him that we are here? I don't think so (it never occurred to you, after all, did it?), but I have to admit, there's a little piece of me that wants him to think of it. A little piece of me that wants him to find us. To end this.

The Stewartsons' car is in the garage. The house's curtains are all drawn. We transmit no signs of life. The only light inside is the television, which we are gathered around.

Back to the show. An audio patch to a police captain, his voice crackling across the stage. "Your daughter was here. We showed the picture to the night manager. He doesn't speak English—but he pointed to the photo and nodded and said yes and gave us the room number. You were right. But we missed them."

You couldn't ask for more drama onstage. But we had avoided it. And I had a little more time to decide where I stood, whose side I was on, and what to do about my daughter. Or so I thought.

• • •

As it turned out, time had run out—in a different way.

Dave Stewartson, seeing that my instinct about the maid had been right, starting to feel cornered by the Amazing Wallace's reckless aggressiveness, shows his own fury rising, unleashed, barely contained in the hideout's eerie dark.

In a minute, he is standing there with a bowie knife that I've never seen before—drawn out of the same black suitcase from which he had pulled the voice dissembler box—and he summarily offers me a choice I did not see coming, at a speed I did not see coming.

"Finger or ear," he says. Looking at me. As if the decision is mine. As if it's my call.

Finger or ear. The long, ignoble tradition of kidnapping—proof of both possession and commitment. Clarity of intent.

Stewartson is furious at his treatment as a criminal. In his mind, I see now, this has been a mission of rendering justice. (Justice for what exactly, I don't quite know yet.) He is cornered—by a city on the prowl for him. By a victim, a mark, who has reduced it all to stage antics, to a promotional opportunity. He's going to exact his revenge, put it back on track by going back to basics, to the tried-and-true. A return to tradition. As if the spirit of Big Eddie and his henchmen, the predilection to violence, inhabits this place.

"Finger or ear," he says again. He looks at me when he says it. To gauge my reaction to the idea. Still suspicious of my commitment? Or indicating he wants me to do it? "It's the only kind of motivation human nature seems to understand," he says, more pissed-off than philosophical.

I am genuinely confused by this. "But Wallace knows we have her. We hardly have to prove it. He's mobilized the whole city looking for her. You send a body part to prove—"

"That's not the point," he cuts me off. "The point is to send a finger or ear *even though we don't have to*. To demonstrate our intentions. To imply it's only a starting point . . . that we'll send her back in pieces, assembly required, if he doesn't stop fucking around and start listening. He's upping the ante . . . well, we are too."

Finger or ear. Traditional forms of kidnapping ID. Today, the Stewartsons could send an article of clothing, a lock of hair, a saliva sample from which to pull DNA. But it wouldn't have shock value, or implied threat. Proving possession is only partly the purpose. Proving seriousness of purpose is the larger part.

Finger or ear. Red or black. In this city of all or nothing, of win or lose, a moment where I can't step away from the table.

I am thinking at light speed. "Maybe someone else's finger or ear . . . so we don't damage the goods . . . don't decrease the value . . ."

He smiles, shakes his head. "A trick, you mean? A magic trick in the city of magic?"

I look at him, feigning ignorance, but I know of course what he's going to say.

"Not these days. Not anymore . . . they're going to DNA test it anyway, confirm it's hers. Standard procedure." Revealing, unintentionally or not, his conversancy and familiarity with official law enforcement.

"But DNA testing, even expedited, takes, what, twenty-four, thirty-six hours?" I point out. "By then the whole thing will have played out, our stand-in finger or ear will have served its purpose, we'll have our money by then."

DNA testing. It could show—show young Amanda, show the world—that Wallace the Amazing is not her father. That her father is "unknown"? That would be a good result, and not the result I expect. Because I imagine, despite Wallace's efforts at privacy and discretion, that my sperm donation, the science of my fatherhood, will inevitably surface in the glare of the case. In the process of verifying Amanda's DNA, won't a thorough investigation entail maternal and paternal samples? If so, it will come out that there is only a partial match, and therefore a sperm donor. In which case, is the "unknown" donor actually the father, trying to take back his own daughter? Who will apparently do whatever it takes to get her back? Aren't fathers like that? Isn't it obvious?

I feel the world—the crime—closing in on me. Circling around behind me, biting me in the tail.

"Yeah, expedited DNA testing will probably be at least twenty-four hours," Stewartson agrees. "And Wallace won't wait for the result; he can't afford to wait for *verification*." He spits the word out in disgust. "We'll get the money. He sees his kid's finger or ear in front of him, he won't risk waiting," Stewartson says. "I mean, come on, is this his kid or not?"

"The way he's stalling and grandstanding on us, maybe he's trying to make us think it's *not* his kid," observes Sandi.

"But he's onstage saying she's all he cares about." I point out.

"That's what makes me think he doesn't care. That he's just using this . . ."

It makes me wonder: How could Wallace *not* be more panicky? How could he not send the money? Does he know from Dominique that I am with Amanda? And as long as she is with me, is he gambling that I will keep her safe?

"Finger or ear?" Dave repeats, a little impatiently. "One of us decides, the other cuts." Unsaid—that this way, we're both complicit. In for a penny, in for a pound. Blood brothers.

I am looking at him calmly, searching my brain frantically, desperately, for a way to forestall it, for an argument he'll buy. *Don't damage the merchandise—rule number one. You're upping the ante, sending it into another sphere, why do that? Why not a substitute finger or ear? Let me find us one. As you say, Wallace will pay, it'll terrify him, he won't wait for verification anyway, so why not a stand-in? It's Vegas—why not a trick? The way he's already tried to trick us with the fake detectives, why not a trick in return?* But these are arguments I'm afraid the Stewartsons won't sit still for. Arguments that will do double damage, by making them question me again, where one swift slice of the knife will seem to seal my loyalty forever.

DNA testing—twenty-four to thirty-six hours. Whether and wherever and however the ransom is paid, twenty-four to thirty-six hours is my real deadline, I sense. Twenty-four to thirty-six hours to somehow play this out, to put this right. A private deadline, a ticking clock, a lit fuse . . .

"Let's go, Chas. What's it going to be?"

I have no choice. I'm trapped. Finger or ear. I have to do it. I have to deliver.

"I'll cut," I tell him. "You choose."

He ponders silently for a moment. "She's a pretty girl."

"Yes, she is."

A small moment of human consideration, of softness, from him? A small flicker of humanity to reveal to himself, to admit to himself? Or to banish ruthlessly in his consciousness, to vigilantly guard against in his decision-making. In this brief moment, Amanda's beauty could work decisively for or against her.

He weighs it a moment more. Makes what is probably a practical, and not an aesthetic, calculation. He shrugs. "Finger."

I know what you will say now, about my fatherhood, about my values, about me. But you need to understand the position I was in. The limited choices. Limited, desperate choices, as I pull on the latex gloves in preparation. One among numerous pairs that Dave has with him—more evidence of his career of professional invisibility, of leaving no trace.

We do it in the house's tiny interior downstairs bathroom, where the light can't be seen from outside, where I can wipe the tile, if necessary. We stand over the sink and faucets, ready for the mess. Sandi and Dave stand just outside the bathroom door, because there's no room for anyone else in here. Archer Wallace is chained to the sturdy old-fashioned living room radiator, a few feet beyond us.

There is no loose-floorboard magic escape to pull off this time.

It is hard to describe. Amanda's screams are horrific. Her eyes are jolted wide. She passes out, apparently in shock, slides to the floor. The blood is everywhere, more than any of us would have thought. There is in that moment, frankly, a confusion, a blunt chaos, of horror. Sandi, tough Sandi, wretches and turns away. Stewartson shuts his eyes, flinches. Even Archer screams out, "My God, no!" I think they could not believe that I was going through with it. I can't believe it myself.

I hunch over her at the sink as I do it—our shoulders together, our hands touching—I rinse and sterilize the area carefully, bandage her immediately, working feverishly, a desperate mess of bandage and white tape. That's the first thing, obviously. Everyone else seems too much in shock to help. (I didn't know if the Stewartsons had much experience with this. Judging by their reactions, they hadn't.)

My little girl. My little girl. But it had to be done. I had to save her. I had to save her.

My mantra. My mantra to bring myself to do it.

And when they lean closer, I exact from the Stewartsons the only small revenge I can, I suppose. I hold out the fingertip to them— red, severed, horrifying, covered in blood. "Go ahead . . . get it out of here." Before I go dizzy myself. Very dizzy. Heading for a bedroom, where for a few moments, not surprisingly, I too pass out in a heap.

You hardly have to be there. You know. We all know, don't we? We all know exactly. Shriveled, blackening already, it arrives in a package at that spectacularly turreted, pink-and-white sandstone, fairy-tale residence, that glistening sultanate in the desert.

Who knows what kind of a wail went up when they opened the package?

How loud the screams?

How many knees buckled?

I had done it to my own flesh and blood.

I had blood on my hands.

But probably, more blood—different blood—than you think.

SIXTEEN

A typical visitor to Vegas will remark wide-eyed and giggling on the "unreality" of the place. And yet the colored fountains pump real water. The miniaturized bowdlerized versions of the Eiffel Tower and the Pyramids are built of real steel and stone. Meals are prepared. People pay. It is arguably no less real than any other place. I don't know if Vegas represents unreality, or hyperreality, or an alternate reality, and I don't know if it really matters. I do know that being hunted in a city, hunted *by* an entire city, but a city filled with places to hide, as if this were all a big video game, ups the Vegas unreality/hyperreality/alternate reality quotient considerably. Of course, if we're caught—in fact, whatever the outcome—the consequences will be all too real. A degree of reality that I, for one, have not yet experienced in my largely, comparatively unreal existence.

She was a smart girl. I had the advantage of knowing how smart, watching her grow up, knowing her achievements, her inner calm. I only gave her the instructions once. How she needed to scream. Scream in horror, agony, fall to the floor. How it would be bloody, yes, but the blood would be from my own last finger. How I would immediately bandage her own finger, still intact, and she must continue to writhe, to scream, in the acting role of a lifetime.

Using all her considerable acting skills that I saw in her school show. She must trust me, that it's the only way. And then I realized, as I said it, I needed her to know I would do it. I needed a way to assure her that I could be trusted, that there was a reason, that this made sense. So I had no choice. I told her. *"Amanda, I'm your father. That's why I'm doing this. Why I'm doing this for you."* And that did it. That explained it. It explained her weird sense of knowing me from somewhere. Her dad wanted to help her. She wanted to help her dad. She knew now, knew more surely and knew at last, where the knife would fall.

And certainly the next moments—bloody, fulsome, rife with activity and terror and stagecraft—distracted her from anything but the overwhelming present. Or maybe her screams, her performance, had extra authority, an extra measure of distress and expressiveness. But I had no time to notice how she absorbed the news of my paternity, and more importantly, she had no time to absorb it either. A shaping fact of her life, slipped into her life as if in passing. No immediate reaction from her, any feeling hidden, subsumed. Daddy's little girl.

And if Dave had said *ear*? I wasn't sure. Her bandaged head would have covered it. I would have put the bandage right on. And my own longish hair, would that cover my own ear? No way. No chance. But that's gambling. It's Vegas. Bet it all on red, or on black. Vegas—where fifty-fifty is considered odds to actually play. Where rolling the dice is ingrained in the culture. Part of the desert air.

Have I been in Vegas too long? Buying for a moment, for an unscientific moment, into blind faith? A moment of pure belief? How could I? Did I believe somewhere in me that perhaps someone, something, some universe, some agency, was watching over me? Hard to say. Because if he *had* said ear, would I have worked out something else?

The point is, he had *not* said ear. I had slid all my cash, all my "credit," all my winnings, all my faith, onto red, and it had come up red. Bloodred. An act of faith. An act of faith that Vegas had rewarded, that makes it the desert town, the epicenter, of faith and belief.

(Spending years in Vegas, doing a show like ours, you get curious about the other shows. About other tricks, how they pull them off. You make the rounds of the other venues. You become a connoisseur, a lifelong student, a casual scholar of magic. You eventually figure out many of the tricks; I couldn't risk getting to know some of the other performers and technicians, or I'm sure they'd have let me in on things. Many you figure out, some you can't, and it returns you to the larger question, the original question: Is there magic in certain cases? But the point is, I had observed as a hobbyist, with a professional interest in the competition, with a scholar's focus and curiosity, the local customs and flavors of entertainment, and I had learned a few things from the various shows. Learned about blood flow, and knives and blades, and diversion, and directing attention. Learned about the optimal angle at which to slice to minimize bleeding, and about the elevation of the finger I would need, when it would seem of course that we were elevating Amanda's. Learned about surgical superglue, latest tool of the ER, and that the office-supply-store version is a perfectly adequate substitute, fast-sealing, practically invisible. Learned enough.)

And what about my own missing fingertip? How is it possible for me to believe, to have faith, that the Stewartsons won't see it? Won't see a missing fingertip? Isn't that a unique expression of blind faith?

Keeping my hands in my pockets. Using my other hand for any observed activities. Moving my hands quickly. But no one is looking at them anyway. No one is expecting a missing fingertip. The only hand that attracts any attention is Amanda's bandaged one. It is a matter of expectation, of focus. These are the lessons of Vegas stages and audiences and observation. A lifetime observing the art of misdirection from the stage performances of Wallace's competitors.

Think about it—if a friend of yours was suddenly missing the tip of his pinky finger, would you even know? How long would it take you to see? Would you ever?

Plus, we are hiding in the dark in Big Eddie's house now, keeping lights down, curled into ourselves, thinking obsessively about detection, thinking about the world outside us, all looking for us. Drawn shades and curtains. Occupying the shadows. Staying out of the light. A helpful environment of concealment.

And I keep my fists curled in slightly—like millions of people do naturally. And if either of the Stewartsons happened to look, they would only assume I always kept them curled in slightly like that, and that they had just never noticed.

And I am no longer delivering data. In such close proximity, in such tight quarters, I can't. So the Stewartsons don't see, and won't see, my fingers on the computer keyboard. No typing. No data entry or data retrieval. No search. That constant in my life—like a heartbeat—suspended. So I am already forced to be a different person. To be someone new. Someone missing his previous self. So missing a fingertip is nothing. A trifle. Symbolic at worst. Symbolic at best.

And will the fifth-finger fingertip of a middle-aged man really look enough like the fifth-finger fingertip of a fifteen-year-old girl? Absolutely—at least in the short term. Stop now, and take a look at your own. Except for outliers like Big Eddie's thick gorilla joint, so many of them—just the fingertip—are indistinguishable, pretty much the same, especially with a squeamish, cursory look. And in this case, even more so, because our last fingers—small, curved-in slightly, nail slightly arched in the middle, similar slight cuticle smile—are the same genetic material. The same genetic inheritance. Posture, fingers, hands, shape of lower lip, slight twist at edge of eyes—all obvious genetic connection, all predetermined, all the stuff of relatives' remarks at a million family events every day across the globe. Like father, like daughter—right down to the fingertips. Or alike enough, at least.

A case in point about misdirection. One that already proves my point. A single fingertip, drenched in blood, shriveling already, briefly revealed in its shroud of paper towel or linen rag, was enough to fool the Stewartsons.

But when it goes to Wallace the Amazing, will he unwrap it, examine it closely, see—immediately, probably, presumably—that it is not the fingertip of his daughter, a fingertip from a hand that he loves, that he has held since childhood, whose fingers he has kissed and counted and sang to in her childhood crib, in a rocking chair while feeding her, in silly made-up finger-counting games with her curled in his lap, a finger that he knows so well? Or will he think that my small and fortunately hairless fifth fingertip is her middle or index? Will the father's emotion and expectation of the moment overwhelm him, make him process the information, the evidence, a certain way?

Or will he not have the heart and stomach to even look at all, for anything more than a grimacing sidelong glance, before he releases it directly to the Las Vegas police crime lab, which will examine it closely enough to see that it is *not* the finger of a fifteen-year-old girl, but will nevertheless dutifully and systematically and now quite curiously run the DNA (retrieving the necessary "A" sample from Amanda's hairbrush or toothbrush or underwear or used tissues or any of a dozen places in a fifteen-year-old's sloppy bathroom) and see—confused, befuddled, excitedly calling over a supervisor—that the DNA is *yes*, a significant match to that of the female hostage, but *no*, it is not her finger. And will they even share this finding with Wallace the Amazing? Because the finger, that of an adult male, *is* indeed a DNA match, but her father, Wallace the Amazing, seems to *have* all his fingers, look there onscreen—so what is this stage performer, this magician, this Vegas act, up to exactly?

And if they do share the information with Wallace the Amazing, then he will certainly know my whereabouts—and will certainly appreciate my effort to keep his (my) daughter in one piece. Literally. And will understand why I've been too busy, too preoccupied, to deliver my daily data. And yet he still won't know any better my motivation, which side of the fence I am on. I don't know whether motel-maid Dominique reported back to him that I am a captive of the Stewartsons—or that I was merely trying, in that surprised moment in the motel, to appear like a captive.

All open questions. And all to be answered I figure, one way or another, in the next several hours. A fifteen-year-old hostage's life in the balance, they will start to run the DNA tests immediately, helicopter it to the Reno lab, call the lead technician back from lunch and the medical examiner off the golf course.

• • •

In the dark, we watch the local news station (KIXP, on high alert since the kidnapping, local reporters perched eagerly for stardom) breathlessly inform the public about the receipt of his daughter's finger by Wallace the Amazing—sent by anonymous overnight package, signed for at the door as you would sign for any delivery—and Wallace handing it dutifully over to the police and crime lab for further examination. No photos allowed, only descriptions, graphics, and graphic descriptions; the tip of my last digit enjoys an instantaneous fame that the rest of me has spent a lifetime steadfastly avoiding, as the rest of my hands watch in folded congregation in the house's dark, which is stuttering and glimmering in the television's fractious glow. My fingertip at center stage, but true to my own history and character, disguised. Unknown. For now.

The breathless, overdramatic reporting on the kidnap victim's fingertip, only helps confirm that version of events in the Stewartson's—in everyone's—minds.

I am popping the extra-strength aspirin and painkillers we got for Amanda. They're working for the pain—and the Stewartsons see the supply dwindling, and it confirms for them Amanda's mute suffering.

Sandi approaches Amanda to change the dressing on the wound.

"NO!" Amanda screams. "Don't come near me!"

"We have to," says Sandi. "Or it's going to get infected."

"NO, NO!" Screaming . . .

"Hey, hey, keep it down," Stewartson hissing, again nervous about the noise being overheard.

"No, you're not touching me." Frantic. "No way, no way . . ."

Dave and Sandi shrugging.

"Maybe we don't have to change the dressing. Maybe it'll be okay. It'll be over soon," says Dave.

"Maybe," says Sandi. "But we don't want an infection. We can't have a sick kid on our hands. That's a complication we don't need," she says, annoyed, before letting it drop. She addresses Amanda warningly, like mother to daughter. "If this goes on another day, I'm changing the dressing—and I don't care how much you scream and cry."

It's an impressive bit of acting from a fifteen-year-old—impulsive, effective. But then Amanda looks at me, and I am suddenly terrified of the solution she might propose: *"It's okay for* him *to change the dressing."* The guy who *cut* you?—the Stewartsons would ask—you want *him* to change it? Arousing suspicion where so much credit has been built up, so much suspicion has been settled. But after staging her fit, Amanda says nothing more. Keeps her mouth shut. Silent. Observing. That's my girl.

"Tests have confirmed that the DNA of the fingertip matches the DNA of Amanda's father, the well-known Vegas stage personality Wallace the Amazing," the police spokesman says flatly, over his bifocals, at the brief, quickly convened news conference, and doesn't elaborate. "We'll keep you informed of any further developments."

No shocked announcement. No gasp of confusion. The drama of the cut-off finger, suddenly itself cut off. I had imagined, looked forward to, the shock and surprise of the DNA test results, but I wasn't really surprised at this announcement.

It amounted to a tactic, and I had to sort out what the tactic was. And while I was not surprised, I was at some level disappointed, because I wanted my fatherhood acknowledged—if only shrouded in mystery and question.

It feels like a report sent directly to me.

But a report coded, vague, awaiting interpretation.

Because the report has *not* said what they must know. *"The DNA matches that of the daughter, but it is not the finger of a fifteen-year-old girl. It is the finger of an adult male. And Wallace the Amazing still has all his fingers."*

My paternity—at least as far as the public goes—remains a secret.

Which unfortunately, opens up a raft of possibilities:

Are the police keeping their findings a secret, at Wallace's request? Part of a tactic to crack the case?

Or keeping their findings a secret *from* Wallace, for the purposes of their own investigation?

Or a last possibility—so remote, so hard to fathom, that I could not then wrap my mind around it, could not and did not send my thoughts down that path. That the DNA of the finger they tested had nothing to do with father or daughter. That it was, in fact, the DNA—the fingertip—of an interloper. A deluded interloper, fooled into loyalty, loyal to the point of foolishness. A fool who had masturbated into a container, stealthily delivered its sacred contents, as part of a ploy to ensure that fool's commitment. To keep that fool forever in close orbit. That, in fact, there was never anything remotely wrong with Wallace the Amazing's sperm.

But at the moment, for me, it was too illogical. It contradicted too much in my experience, in my memory, in my vision of myself and of the world. This last possibility—I had too much faith to even entertain it.

It begins to happen fast now.

Fast enough that we don't have to change Amanda's dressing.

Fast enough that I realize quickly: it's probably being done at this pace to avoid the accompaniment of the Las Vegas police. To respect, return to, the Stewartsons' original parameters. The message contained in the message: *Let's get this deal done.*

The curt phone call of arrangement, from a disposable cell phone found, eventually, in hotel trash. No fear, or surrender, or annoyance, in Wallace the Amazing's voice, no gloating, no victory, no excitement, in Dave Stewartson's. Just focus on clarity of arrangement. And as multicolored letters cut from various printed sources are a thing of the past, so is the classic victim-for-cash exchange on a lonely bridge or beneath an overpass or at an unguarded border. Too risky, too easily observed, too easily foiled or gamed by either side, fraught with peril. Now, it was a checking or savings account (or several, if required by the size of the deposit). Hidden and untraceable in a multiplicity of web addresses, the transfer of funds has come a long way from a briefcase full of cash. It is electronic, a matter of hitting "Send."

Or, in this case, something even better.

"You're going to purchase ten million dollars' worth of shares of blue-chip stocks—Ford, Coca-Cola, Cisco, Exxon—and public-spirited personality that you clearly are, transfer them immediately to the Stewartson Charitable Trust, which was incorporated two days ago . . ."

Dave Stewartson, I am suddenly quite sure, has both his accounting and law degrees from some academic degree mill, some night program, like so many FBI agents and intelligence operatives, so many in his line of wet work—skirting legality, crossing borders, transferring and tracking payoffs.

A charitable trust—allowing the immediate transfer of stock ownership, of large blocks, without arousing suspicion. And by the time the IRS investigates or challenges the legitimacy of the trust—typically a matter of months if not years—their finding would be irrelevant, the money and trust administrators long gone, overseas, floating blithely, untraceably, island to island beneath a warm Caribbean sky. I know without even looking, and I will confirm it for myself later, that the laws of the State of Nevada are particularly conducive to such a trust. To a streamlined establishment and accommodating execution of such a trust, as they are similarly accommodating to the laws of marriage, divorce, property, and almost everything else.

"The moment the money hits the charitable trust account, you will hear from your daughter, calling on a disposable cell phone, who will give you an address and a time where she can be retrieved. She will give it to you only once, you will repeat it back once, so we know you have it, and then we will destroy the cell phone. Do you understand?"

Silence.

Stewartson says it again. "Do you understand?"

"Yes."

Dial tone.

Concordant. Mellifluous. A steady, confident final chord.

Stewartson and Sandi look at each other. Eminently pleased with themselves. For the two of them, in that moment, there is no one else in the world. I know at last, with certainty, that Archer Wallace and I, for all our essential contribution—maybe because of our essential contribution—are going to be cut out of this. The clue here is control, control of the assets that cash would never provide. I can tell only from the look that passes between them. I am enough of a detective to detect the ice in their veins.

A charitable trust. Hah. And they are its fiduciary officers. Typical Washington-trained operatives. But clearly this was a legal and protective tactic. Money to be used for charitable good is not scrutinized so closely, nor so promptly, as it would be going into the account of an individual. There is the curving, complex line of bequests and grants, eschewing and delaying the immediate scrutiny of the IRS and its investigative arm, or at least throwing any investigation to a less aggressive or less competent investigative arm. Something the Stewartsons have thought through. Charitable trust. I can't decide how deeply they relish the irony. Or whether they've even considered it.

A charitable trust. Does that seem particularly clever? It's not. It could be anything. Lots of options. The formation of an online bank with only one account on deposit. The formation of a corporation, with shares of stock. An investment in an Internet start-up, and the money disappears immediately into the operating costs and the sloppy bookkeeping of a bunch of twentysomethings. A major donor gift or pledge to a hospital that doesn't actually exist. A series of college tuition payments to a school created on the Internet. The switching of funds, the press of a button, and importantly, the confirmation of that switching of funds. As personal identity becomes more fluid, leakier, polymorphous, financial identity becomes tentacled, sinuous, octopean as well. Corporate shells, layers of financial possession like layers of clothing, and they require a different kind of technocrat to unravel them—forensic attorneys working alongside forensic accountants.

Such an exchange used to take place with the blindfolded girl on one side, the paper bag or briefcase on the other, where all interested parties had an unobstructed view and a clear shot. Now the trigger is the "Send" key—though a finger still hovers and rests on it, just as itchy, just as decisive, just as lethal, just as final.

Stewartson stares at my laptop's screen in the dark, merrily hitting the return to scan down, smiling dumbly like a kid, nodding, smiling . . . and then tossing the laptop against the wall.

"What?!" says Sandi.

"Christ!"

"Didn't Wallace do what we said?" she asks.

"Yes"—sarcastically—"exactly."

"So what's the prob—"

"Exactly what we said, yes. And then some. Added a little rider to the agreement." He looks ready to throw my laptop again.

There was the transfer agreement. But there was something about Amanda . . .

Stewartson explains evenly, trying to hold his temper. "When the money hits the account, it goes in trust to the benefit of Amanda Wallace, a minor—with her signature and identity required to release the funds. If her signature and identity are required, and confirmed, then he knows she is alive, and he knows she is in a bank, in plain view, in a public place with other employees around, and will presumably remain there until he comes to pick her up." Stewartson looks at us. "And since she's a minor, of course there has to be a guardian."

And he's appointing me the guardian. It's my first thought. Which would be logical, of course, if Wallace knew exactly where I stood. But he is shrewd enough to know that even with my sacrificial finger, my loyalties aren't necessarily clear. A finger might be worth a few million to me.

"And here's the interesting part," says Stewartson. "He's letting us pick the guardian."

Stewartson looks at Sandi, at me. "Maybe this is only to create a little dissent in our ranks. Since access to the money will only be in one of our names. It's like, who takes the suitcase when everyone scatters after the robbery. Goddamn him."

Sandi squints her eyes. "Whoever we pick and inform him of to put on the account, that guardian will ultimately have to show valid ID. Driver's license. Passport. On a transfer like that, the bank will check. If it's you or me, they'll have our name. A way to start tracing our identities . . ." Admitting in front of me for the first time, the winding path to who they truly are.

Stewartson sits, frowns, looks at me. "It could be you. In which case, we won't let you stay there with her like a guardian assuring her safe pickup, after the wire transfer. You'll leave with us, so we can keep an eye on you, make sure you complete the transaction, transfer the money over to us. We can make you an officer of the trust this afternoon so you can do that." He looks from me to Sandi. "But I don't like it."

Sandi doesn't seem as bothered by it. "Amanda signs, and we simply leave her in the lobby of the bank branch, a branch Wallace won't know until he's called and told. By which time we're long gone." She looks at Stewartson. "He did it this way to protect her. He did it to make sure he gets her back in one piece. He's a father. You can't blame him. By that point, we know we have the money. We have the evidence of it. By then, nothing can happen. He's building in a little insurance for his daughter, that's all."

"He's trying to change the rules at the last second . . ."

"He's trying to get his daughter back," says Sandi. "And the point is, he's obviously willing to pay." She smiles. "This is okay. It tells us he's past the hurdle of paying. Now he just wants to get his daughter back. I say we go with it."

"That's what he knew we would say," says Stewartson, resentfully. "He knew we'd accept it . . ."

"So what? So what if he knows we'll go for his change in the rules. We're still getting the money."

And I know Wallace, pushing the deal as far as he can, to give him as much leverage, as much opportunity as he can get, and still get his daughter back. Calculating the degree to which the Stewartsons will bend—and if they will bend this much, preparing to bend them next just a little bit more. Master of motivation, of the behavioral arts.

"What do you say?" Asking me.

They are looking at me as if they truly value what I have to say. I take a breath. I look at them. "Putting the guy's arrogance aside," I say. "It's choosing between splitting ten million bucks, or killing a fifteen-year-old." I look at them, shrug. "I'd go with the ten mil."

They smile. Toothy, fake, criminal smiles, both of them.

SEVENTEEN

We drive to the bank, First Desert—gleaming nondescriptly in the Vegas way, beneath the Vegas sun, a branch office in a strip mall in a residential section of greater Vegas out past Henderson and Silverado. Dry cleaner. Deli. Dentist. Eyeglass store. Ice cream shop. H&R Block outlet. The bank branch's sun-blackened plate-glass windows are covered by huge orange-and-green signs proclaiming attractive CD rates and streamlined loan processing. In the parking lot, the white parking-space lines glint as if painted yesterday. The sun bouncing off the bright angles of surrounding white and silver Toyotas and Nissans and Ford pickups burns your corneas as you get out of the car. The shimmering heat of the macadam rises up to you like it's been waiting for you. Waiting to engulf you in its thin air, to let you fight a little for your oxygen. An oxygen-depriving welcome to the real Vegas.

The permutations of approaching events are dancing in my head, a titillating, overstimulating, harlequin Vegas stage show in my brain.

By now, presumably, Wallace knows that, whether fellow victim or perpetrator, I am with Amanda. (And is he more comfortable now knowing I'm with her, or is he more nervous?) By now, presumably, the police have processed the fingertip's DNA against a control sample of Amanda's DNA. It's not an exact match, of course, because it's not her fingertip—but the issue for the police is, it's not *not* a match either. Closely correlated. Closely related. An adult's last finger, and yet all ten digits are on Wallace's hands. Some other unknown relative? Why hasn't Wallace informed them of that possibility? Is he cooperating, or isn't he? Perhaps the police have withdrawn entirely for the moment, amid their own confusion about the DNA results. Is it some kind of trick or stunt of Wallace the Amazing, are they being duped, is there some shenanigan, some act, some magic that they don't yet follow, that he has been conducting from the stage? So perhaps they don't *tell* him that the DNA is a confusingly partial match, or they say outright that it's not. Or they say there was an irregularity, they have to run more tests, either to stall for time or because they actually believe it. But whatever they are saying, or not saying, Wallace knows the reality of the DNA. In fact, *only* Wallace knows. And maybe that is why he is proceeding now without them—without their help, or knowledge, or backup.

So here we are at the bank. At this sleepy, slow-moving branch, far from downtown, tucked unobtrusively into Vegas's distant outskirts. And this is a Las Vegas bank, which means, at this financial moment, it is reeling from a mortgage crisis, its attention is on onerous and complex new government regulations, on its precarious finances, perhaps to the neglect of its other two main lines of business: millions in savings, from thousands of retirees, and the movements of mob money, parked here. We duck out of the parking lot sunshine into the cool, simple lobby furnished with beige couches and low white marble tables—relax, take a load off, feel at home. The tellers sport Hawaiian shirts and American flatland accents, and it is all so obviously and transparently white-bread, smiley, and innocuous, in the blandly designed interior, that it is clearly not. This is a bank if not itself steeped in the illicit then a smiling crossroads, a happy upbeat crucible, of such. I can see the red-tied, white-shirted bank officers, in their offices, in front of their screens. Watching over, intent on preserving, the façade.

Amanda is our star.

The air-conditioning hums, a relentless droning, chilly with waste, creating another environment, another planet, here in a hot Vegas strip mall.

"Amanda Charitable Children's Trust?" Stewartson inquires at the door of the on-duty Vice President, Specialty Client Services. Reason enough for this motley group—a child, a guardian, a lawyer or two apparently—to be here at the bank. For signatures. For formalities. For paperwork.

"Ah, yes," the VP smiles in recognition. "Come in. Paperwork, transfer documentation is all here, ready for signatures." As in—we do this all the time, it's pro forma, hardly worth our attention.

We follow him into a simple conference room. With a genial smile, he gestures Amanda to the seat of honor at the head of the conference table, then motions the rest of us to be seated all around.

"Oh dear, what happened to your finger, young lady?" he says, on seeing the bandage.

Amanda shrugs and smiles shyly.

"I hope you can still sign the papers," the bank officer says with a smile.

She nods earnestly—not knowing that he is merely making pleasantries.

"And who is the guardian as witness?"

"That's me," I say, producing the ID I knew he would ask for in a moment.

He looks at it. "Very good. So we should be all set," he says, "let me just go get the representative the trust sent over. Their trust officer got here early, thought the appointment was at nine, so their officer's been waiting in an empty office down the hall for you." Explaining as he strode out, so the Stewartsons could not ask him anything, did not quite follow, faces scowling in incomprehension, until he came back in with the trust officer, dressed in a dark stylish legal suit, battered leather attaché in hand, nodding, smiling professionally, taking a seat next to all of us. Stewartson's look lingered on her, a little more than appropriate or polite, for her unexpected attractiveness.

Mine lingered because (as you probably guessed) I already knew her. Dominique.

The trust officer. Perfect—the only person that Wallace the Amazing can trust. The only person he can send to represent his interests, who is unrecognized, who is unknown by anyone. Except by me, which Wallace doesn't know, if Dominique hasn't said anything. How has she found her way here? Not tailing us, but getting here *before* us? But I can think of a number of ways—hacking into online bank appointment calendars; keeping an electronic eye on the Stewartsons since their "maid" meeting—she is expert in just the kind of detective work I am, maybe even more so. And her presence here? It's like Wallace saying to the Stewartsons, *I'm following your every move.*

Dave Stewartson looks again at her. Is he remembering the deaf, babbling, Eastern European maid? He only half looks at her, dismissive—but on the other hand, he hasn't seen many people in the past twenty-four hours, and these two happen to look somewhat similar.

I can't tell if the Stewartsons are silently assessing, debating saying something, considering stopping everything, taking prisoners, pulling guns (guns they don't have for once, metal detector, bank rent-a-guards, etc.), but by all indications the transaction is proceeding. By all indications the money will be theirs soon. So they say nothing.

Sandi looks at me. A look that is unreadable, that tamps down and disguises any panicky suspicion on her part. Any suspicion is cloaked in silent inquiry: *What the fuck?* If that is even what her eyes are asking.

In measured response, I shake my head, perhaps imperceptibly. *I don't know . . . let's just proceed . . .*

Dominique. My mirror. We have lived the same life, of the same blind loyalty, for years. Alongside each other, unknown to each other, prisoners in adjoining cells, discovering each other's existence as if when the prison guard makes a small but consequential procedural error. And now she is here, across the table. Only I know who she is, of course—and she knows that only I know.

She is here, presumably, as Wallace's emissary, his representative. Since the Las Vegas police are now watching Wallace the Amazing and the case (his own fault for bringing them in) and since Wallace is so recognizable to begin with, there is no way that Wallace himself or his wife can come personally to the transaction. Clearly they are going through with it, paying the ransom, behind the back of, without the authority of, the police. Which they are uniquely able to do, because Wallace can send a proxy that no one knows. A loyal cipher.

And presumably this is also obvious to the Stewartsons—why it is this woman they've never seen, and not the parents. Because this is unapproved by the police. In fact, Wallace and his wife, Sasha, not being here is the best evidence that they are actually going through with the deal.

As she sits, I see Dominique look at Amanda's hand, and frown, stiffen a little. And then she looks, briefly, only a blink, at my own curled fists. I can't tell of course what she's thinking, what she knows, or whether it is the innocent brief glancing look that anyone would make in assessment. I expect her to look up, briefly, at me, but she doesn't.

Amanda, understandably, looks confused. Papers, officials, what kind of a release, what kind of ending, is this?

"Where are my parents?"

"This lady is taking care of it," I assure her. "She works for them. It'll be fine." I try to soothe her. She looks suspiciously at Dominique. *Works for my parents? I've never seen her before in my life.*

The atmosphere around the conference room table feels charged; the Stewartsons are narrow-eyed, alert, as if sitting down to a poker game in a saloon, ready to rise and start shooting at any under-the-breath comment or sidelong glance. But the bank VP is oblivious to it. He is here to set up a charitable trust. How come he hasn't heard of Amanda, how come he hasn't read her last name on the documents, hasn't put two and two together? Probably because the documents are assembled by an underling, automatically, unthinking, and his or her boss here with us now has barely even looked at said documents, full of names and terms, all pro forma, and it would never occur to anyone that a transaction such as this has anything to do with a kidnapping or a Vegas stage show.

As soon as I saw Dominique, the questions began to spin, to dance above the documentation.

She has all the computer ability that I have, maybe more for all I know, so is she rigging something online to foil this, to fool the Stewartsons?

And does she think I'm allied with the enemy? Or simply, cleverly, helping to keep Amanda from harm?

"So once all the papers are signed and the funds are transferred, we just need to confirm that said funds have cleared," Dave Stewartson says pleasantly, nonchalantly, lawyerly—his first spoken professional advice as a counselor in the State of Nevada.

The bank officer and Dominique nod. Yes, of course. Pro forma.

The deep stack of paperwork is signed. My signature part of it, part of the record, proof of criminality for some future prosecution. (Or evidence of ignorance, which I would continue to have to feign.) I'm on the hook. While the Stewartsons remain hidden behind their shuffle of identities.

"And last thing, I just need each of you"—the bank officer gesturing to Amanda and me—"to enter your Social Security number and a new account pin on this computer keypad." He shifts the keyboard and screen around a little to face us. "Do you happen to know your Social Security number, honey?"

Yes, Amanda nods.

And here technology intersects with the human. Interfaces with the human, to make mistakes, to be fallible.

Because I always hit "Send" with my last finger. Instinct, unthinking, habit.

And focused on what I am doing, forgetting for a moment the necessity to hide it, feeling a moment of finality, of completion, of dropped guard, and joining a million previous keystrokes out of sheer habit, thinking of a hundred ever-changing codes in my online life, I type in a new code number, hit "Send"—unfolding my missing fingertip in the process.

I sense, out of the corner of my eye, that Sandi Stewartson has seen it.

I glance up at her. She is looking at me.

I am ready for all hell to break loose. Ready, fully expecting, to see her eyes widen in question and alarm, then narrow in realization of my lie, of where my loyalties lie. Ready for her to curtly, furiously, definitively stop the proceedings. After all this, all this careful effort, in my return to the familiar keyboard, my one true home, I have fucked up.

Has she seen it? How could she not?

Everyone's had the experience of hitting "Send," and wishing they could call it back.

Add me to that list.

My own unique version of it.

The tip sliced off that was a tip-off.

The tip of the iceberg.

But if Sandi did see it, she says nothing. Indicates nothing. Returns my look evenly, with no affect, nothing revealed behind her eyes.

Is she assuming—betting—that despite my deceit, the money, the deal, may still be going through? Is that a risk she's willing to take? Maybe so.

I can't really know what she's seen. Or hasn't.

I can't really know what she'll say to Dave, or keep to herself.

I can't really know what her silence means.

We wait silently in the conference room—Sandi, Dominique, Amanda, and I—sipping coffee, nervously breaking off pieces of blueberry muffins and edges of flaky croissants, while the bank VP and Dave check on the transfer of funds.

They return in a few minutes, and I catch Dave nodding curtly to Sandi. All of us thank the bank VP and the attractive trust officer, and we all exit the bank into the Las Vegas sun, nothing changed, everything changed.

Send—where technology becomes action, doesn't it? Where the cerebral becomes the tactile and consequential. Where the theoretical becomes the actual. Where there is no going back.

Outside in the sun-soaked parking lot, Dominique gestures to Amanda—a quick, authoritative little flick of her palm—to come with her to her sedan. I notice it is not her blue Camaro. The little bit of personality I saw in her driveway. Driving something more invisible for the occasion. And slowly, too slowly, I start to ask myself: Why? Amanda silently follows the well-dressed, official-looking woman her parents have sent to retrieve her.

Dave and Sandi Stewartson stand silently, observing them—watching until the trust officer's sedan pulls sedately out of the lot—before heading to their own car (a silver Nissan, rented for safety's sake at a discount facility last night), an energetic spring in their steps, car doors closing with a slap of exuberance, tinny little engine revving eagerly, backing the utterly forgettable sheet metal out and putting it into drive and aiming it toward a new life.

Not a glance my way from any of them.

There in the sunny parking lot, I don't exist for any of them.

A purposeful avoidance from all of them. A silence that speaks loudly.

Dominique's silence, her resolute looking away, because she doesn't know my role, where I stand, what my loyalties are or aren't, and her employer has no way to know either, and her best and only choice therefore is to cut me off. Why risk any interaction?

The Stewartsons' silence, to signal they are done with me. That there is no partnership. Never was. (They had brought me, their partner, in their rental car with Amanda. Amanda now returned. Partnership now dissolved.)

And Amanda's studiously averted eyes? Because she doesn't know where to look. Because what I've revealed, what she's experienced, what she's observed, is all too much for a fifteen-year-old to absorb, so all she can manage in the moment is to keep her eyes down and do what she is told.

I'm cast off. Instantly returned to the shadowy half existence that has constituted my adult life. Abandoned without a word in the sunbaked parking lot.

A purposeful message. That I don't exist. That I have never existed. A pedestrian left in a strip mall parking lot with no means of transportation. Not someone who's being handed five million. I can't even get a ride from them.

I can still see the Stewartsons' taillights. Heading quickly back to Big Eddie's? To dispose of Archer Wallace, in some way as efficient as it is unimaginable? Or leaving him chained to the bathroom fixtures, or the living room radiator, his body to be found by one of Eddie's henchmen weeks or months from now? Getting a head start, a quick jump, on their new life?

And I am left alone in the lot.

The late-morning sun beating down on the black macadam. The heat dancing up from the paved surface, malevolent and merciless. The birdless, natureless, eerie strip-mall silence.

Until Dominique pulls back into the lot.

Having circled around, I realize, to be sure the Stewartsons are gone.

She waves me over insistently.

"Get in."

I look once more down the road to be sure the Stewartsons are gone.

"Get in. Now."

And as I do, Dominique gestures to me to be silent in Amanda's presence, as she puts the big featureless sedan in gear.

She pulls out of the bank lot. I'm in the passenger seat; Amanda is in the back. Dominique looks at my hand. To Amanda in the backseat, "You can take off your bandage."

Amanda looks inquisitively at me. I nod that it's okay.

Amanda begins to work on the bandage. Eager. Relieved.

"I hacked into the database of the police lab, so I saw the DNA test results before anyone," she says. Smart, I'm thinking. And if I had not had the Stewartsons hovering around me, I could have done the same. Her voice gets lower, so Amanda, unwrapping her bandage in the back, can't hear. "I realized what you'd done for her, and I was furious."

I was confused. "Furious? But I . . . I *saved* her . . ."

"Not at you. At him. At Wallace. Because your sacrifice—it told me what you felt for her. How connected. So I knew he had somehow done to you what he did to me. Took the same advantage of your loyalty. Treated you just as badly. He used us. Used us both . . ."

"Wait. What are you saying?"

She pauses. Looks straight ahead, making sure not to look any-where else, not to see or gauge my reaction, not to let it burrow into her. "I'm talking about my role."

"Your role?"

She looks back in the mirror at Amanda, and says, very quietly, "Not just a bedmate."

Realization climbs up through me slowly. Like bile. Like poison.

And I see the perfect order of it. The perfect mirror of it. The perfect orderly mirror that I should have guessed at.

Her parallel life to mine—that has existed for years—is sud-denly more parallel.

The parallel slavery. The parallel loyalty. The parallel enforce-ment of that loyalty.

And the Amazing Wallace's MO, while perverted, is at least apparently consistent.

That just as I contributed the sperm, Dominique contributed the womb.

EIGHTEEN

I am instantly returned, tossed back to the moment—the vision—of Sasha being rushed to the hospital near the end of her pregnancy. I hadn't seen her enter or emerge from the hospital, of course, couldn't be there or risk being seen or even coming near, and afterward she was spirited away and holed up in Shangri-la as always, off-limits, and on the security cameras I caught only a glimpse of her leaving or arriving with her loose-fitting caftans and draped, layered clothing. Now I could fill in the blanks. Either her pregnancy had ended there at the hospital, the child stillborn, her fragile incompetent womb that had required so much care and attention beforehand (the female equivalent, the perfect match, to Wallace's own low-motility sperm and poor reproductive prospects). Or— those same loose-fitting caftans serving an opposite purpose—she had never been carrying a child at all, could not carry a child to term, and they had arranged beforehand for Dominique to be their surrogate. Either way, Wallace the Amazing had worked his magic. Because here was the baby they wanted, taking center stage exactly as needed, conveniently presenting itself at the right time, an identical product of my own sperm (with Sasha's own egg? or with Dominique's? I couldn't yet say which), the baby Sasha wanted and was ready for either way. A baby ready to step onstage from the wings, Sasha's husband saving the day, controlling the moment, anticipating the contingencies—just like his redundancy of me and Dominique, isn't it? Using us as redundancy one more time, so the stage act of their charmed lives can continue uninterrupted, the show can go on, and he is Amazing once more.

I am processing it, trying to see it, but with Amanda in the backseat, Dominique can't yet say more. And she is already moving on to a more urgent explanation, and I have to pay attention:

"Once Wallace decided to pay the ransom, and the Stewartsons decided to have the transfer done electronically, it put that money in play, made it suddenly digitally accessible, which you know as well as I do." She glances over at me, just for a moment, a look filled with emotion, but she is afraid of it, and I am afraid of it as she can see, and she looks back at the road. "The Stewartsons, or whoever they actually are, are going to head into a bank, and transfer the money to a new account, to keep it away from you and Wallace and everyone else." She looks at me once more. *Did you really think differently? Did you really think they'd cut you in?* "But when they try, there won't be any there. It's already transferring to another account at another bank. My bank. My name. The transfer took place a few minutes after they checked it. It'll take them at least fifteen minutes to figure out what happened. Which gives us a fifteen-minute head start."

Us. It's the word I hear clearest. The word I catch most, linger on.

Us, I am thinking, looking back at Amanda.

"We *made* him, we made Wallace the Amazing, and look at how he treated us, look what he did to us."

We made him, yes, but look what else we made in the process. A girl. A daughter.

We are taking our daughter, and leaving. Starting over.

She doesn't say it, she can't say it aloud with Amanda behind us, who is pulling her knees up in the backseat, curling herself in to comfort, to still her anxiety, squinting into the desert sun streaming in the window, but that is what is happening. I can feel that that is what Dominique is doing, where she is going, that that is why I am suddenly in the passenger seat: *Get in. Get in now. Us.*

And the startling possibility now occurs to me: Does Wallace even know Dominique is here? Has she launched all this without his knowledge, staying one step ahead of him, rearranged meeting times and locations? He probably doesn't even know this is happening. Was this bank meeting all hers to begin with?

Either way, now everyone will be after us. The Amazing, the Stewartsons, the Las Vegas police. And because it is a kidnapping, probably even the FBI. Everyone.

Yet amid this knowledge, this coursing current of anxiety, I can't suppress the thought:

We are a family. Parents in the front seat, our girl behind us.

A family with the open road ahead of us? A new start, a new life? Reclaiming our past? Creating our future?

We are a family.

A family for only a minute or so.

The briefest family ever.

"So what did you think when you saw the DNA results?" I ask Dominique. "I guess Wallace wanted to act before it became public." And not wait for all the questions, the swirl of motive and confusion, that those test results would cause. Unless, as I guessed, it was Dominique who was acting so quickly—and I hope her answer, or its evasiveness, will provide me a clue about that.

Dominique looks at me. "What do you mean?"

"The DNA results from the lab. Showing that I'm the father."

Her brow wrinkles. "What are you talking about?"

So she hasn't yet guessed. The DNA results *she* is talking about must only concern the fact, the reassuring fact, that the fingertip is not Amanda's. But I'm a little confused, thrown off—wouldn't a lab's processed DNA results note the partial match, no matter what?

If Dominique had intercepted the results, wouldn't she at least have been wondering about that?

"It was my sperm," I tell her—unconcerned right now about how much Amanda, in the backseat, hears or understands or believes. "Wallace asked, and I said yes. I'm the donor." It feels strange . . . my first admission to the world, my first assertion aloud, of my fatherhood.

Her wrinkled brow seems to suddenly smooth into understanding. She smiles sadly, wistfully. Shakes her head slowly—somehow mournful. And says it slowly, as if to a child, as if knowing the resistance, the incomprehension, it will be met with: "The DNA testing showed exactly what the world expected it to."

"What the world expected?"

"That Wallace the Amazing is the father."

"But how could it show that?"

A pause. A beat. "Because he is."

I am about to ask, want to ask, *But how could YOU know that?*

But I don't have to. Dominique looks at me. Smiling sadly.

And I realize that she knows it in the clearest, most fundamental way she could.

For the most obvious reason.

Because she is Amanda's mother.

Not merely a womb. Not just a surrogate.

The simplest possible explanation—usually the best.

And sometimes also the worst.

And my depositing semen for him? Watching Amanda grow? Seeing myself in her? Was that all my imagination? My faith? My delusion? The deposit of semen. The container. The sterile process. A kind of religious ceremony. Creating a holy moment and memory for myself. Enforcing my loyalty. My commitment. Including saving her finger. Protecting her.

But she *looks* like me. Our eyes. Our noses. Our hands. Our fingertips to momentarily fool the Stewartsons.

• • •

Had I only deluded myself?

Was it only the story I was telling myself? That Wallace the Amazing, the shaman, was helping me tell myself?

I'm the king of data. But here the data was interpretive. I am the one saying she looks like me. Was it just my interpretation of our looks? Could they be interpreted any other way? I needed data, and didn't have it. I was suddenly like any audience member—willing to be led by my own delusions.

I stared in the rearview mirror again. Drank in Amanda's features. Tried to examine them coldly, analytically, observe them without the rush of connection that I had always felt whenever I had a fleeting chance to see them. We identify one another differently, after all. Half a family swears that a girl is the spitting image of her mother, the other family members swear she's the very image of her father, others think they are seeing the reincarnation of a grandmother or a great aunt. Proof of how differently we can see one another. How differently we can see the world. Was it simply a delusion?

I thought again about the past. Further back than my mother's funeral. To my father's car crash. A father I didn't remember. Knew only through the small handful of prominently displayed photos, which my mother never discussed. His near-complete, pre-Internet absence. My missing, fractured history.

Dominique was watching me, silently, because she realized, a few moments ahead of me, what I was about to know.

Did Amanda seem to look like me, only because I so thoroughly deluded myself?

Or did Amanda look like me, because she was my sister?

And if she was my sister, then I knew—*you* know—who was my father.

I looked down at my missing fingertip. My sleight of hand.

Sleight of hand—primitive, elementary, a childlike skill, compared to Wallace's sleight of mind. His sleight of memory. Practiced on me, as if I were a silent stage assistant sawed in half. Folded into a box to disappear and never be seen again. Sleight of mind, sleight of memory, in which I was apparently an early practice subject. An early experiment—and an early, and encouraging, success.

His first success. His greatest success.

As soon as I can get to a computer, I will be back online, looking once again for news of my father's funeral, but there will be nothing. Because it was too early for the Internet? That was always the assumption I made when I had looked before. And yet with everything else, in my ability to search, to dig down digitally, to make connections, I have always found *something*, some wispy string of evidence, of a thing's existence, yet even in local newspapers of the time, there had been literally nothing, my research skills had hit a brick wall, and now I see: the only thing more shocking than what you can discover on the Internet is what you don't find there. The truly shocking thing can be absence. No story at all—that can be the biggest story of all.

• • •

And when I think through this absence, this *missingness*—the missingness of my own father, merely a photo on a table, merely vague imagery to a two-year-old, only an aura—and my lifelong fascination with and commitment to Wallace, it begins circling me. I start to see the possibility, the attraction, the allure, the "magic"—a magic so primal, so simple after all.

Like that locked trunk of my father's effects in our attic. The locked trunk that my mother and I had so violently argued over on the eve of my leaving home. I now know exactly what it contains. Nothing. Emptiness. *Absence. Missingness.* Those are its only contents. It is as false as my dead father's photo. The trunk that has separated my mother and me would now separate us even more. The trunk that contains only separation.

And my sperm "contribution"? To help explain to me how and why this girl would grow to look so much like me. Dominique's maternal loyalty was instinctive. Formed at birth, shall we say. My own loyalty had to be nurtured. Concocted. Cultivated. Grown in a test tube.

Wallace the Amazing, my father. Amazing once again—and amazing as never before.

• • •

Dominique's fluent, masterly transfer of the money? No surprise to me at all. The banks use the same encryption systems as the credit card companies that I hack and where I have IT contacts, because the credit card companies are owned by the banks, in fact they *are* banks, and they hire the same circle of firms to encrypt and encode and protect, and Dominique has her contacts and relationships inside those firms just as I have mine. Call it the oligarchic flaw: there's only a handful of credit card companies, interfacing with only a handful of banks, and only a handful of information technology firms serving them both. So as a hacker, you don't need to achieve mastery more than once. Like a club—once you're in, you're in.

And whatever I know how to do at the screen and keyboard, someone out there knows more than me—and someone, in turn, knows more than them. And that someone could easily be Dominique. Cyberspace is the Wild West; most have just arrived here comparatively wide-eyed, but a few of us have been riding out here a long time. We know the topography. We know what's buried in the sand.

We are today's superheroes, Dominique and I. Replacing yesteryear's bright-tighted superheroes with equal though less showy superpowers and abilities. The power to see into people's innermost thoughts. The power to see into their pasts.

Meek, silent, hunched over screens, even arthritic and sclerotic and paralytic in our chairs, we are superheroes with no uniforms, no magic belts, no swelling chests. More like the craven villains of superhero-comics tradition, crouched in the shadows, denizens of the dark.

Have the villains finally triumphed?

• • •

We are a family . . . yes and no. A family I am not truly a part of. Dominique and Amanda have each other, and yet even here, where I have invested my emotions, my defensive efforts, my fingertip, I am still an outsider. A bystander. Even at the core of this story, at this moment, I still don't exist. The questionable, indistinct, foggy half standing of the half brother.

And yet, I am strapped into responsibility. I am a bystander, but I am a participant. Dominique now has her daughter, and the transfer of the money clearly indicates she has a plan. A plan to run? To hide? To start over? And did she know or plan that I'd be with her? Do I fit into the plan? Is that what she is silently assessing, computing, as she drives the three of us straight into the desert, her silence as featureless, as broad and weighty, as the desert itself.

As for me, I have a plan now too—unformed but unquestioned, vague yet utterly focused. To confront my mother. To know what happened. Or do I want anything to do with her anymore? Do I want to leave it as I have always believed it, inhabit the lie I've become accustomed to? I already have the sense of the truth, after all. Its rough edges, its outline. Do I really want any more of it? Let sleeping dogs lie. Let lying dogs sleep.

Dominique and Amanda; my mother and me. It's a parallel trick, I realize. A trick repeated across a generation, as Wallace the Amazing repeats them, perfects them, from the stage night after night. Shrewd Paternity 2.0. The upgrade—road-tested, refined. Part of his stage act. Those two words—*stage* and *act*—come at me anew with all their force.

A trick repeated: Sire the child. Make a devil's pact with each mother—that in exchange for each's silence, she gets support, security. The illicitness is part of what binds them to him, the fact that no one can know. Does that make the bond more powerful? For my mother? For Dominique? The fact that they're in on the act? It's hard to know.

The fury courses through me. A fury at my father. Like some Oedipal drama in the Vegas desert, the full brunt of my fury delayed, amplified, by my blindness to events.

But of course, the fury is trumped—redoubled—by my realization about my mother. She had lied to me. My whole visit was a lie. She pretended not to know I was alive, to be shocked to see me at her door, to have been as fooled as I was. Yet clearly, she had been acting. She must have known of my existence, it had been some arrangement she had agreed to, and she was always ready with her stage performance, should I for some reason show up on her doorstep, should I somehow discover that she was still alive. What kind of mother makes a pact to not see her child? To send him away? Because she thinks it's better for him, that he'll have a richer more rewarding life? Or because the father made a persuasive, powerful case. Backed up with money, in the form of my monthly salary. Making good on his promise to her. Or because somehow, she had no choice?

• • •

I thought again about her fake funeral. Colored now, more believable now, because she knew. Had maybe even helped stage it. Of course she had. Why hadn't that occurred to me before? How could it have really been pulled off without her complicity? A funeral as fake, as staged for me alone, as my masturbating into a container. A similar veil of holiness, of purpose, of sanctimony and import, all the better to fool me. And where was my mother during her funeral—watching from a distance? No wonder it was all friends of hers that I never even knew. Hired friends, actors, who spoke to me in passing about how close they were to her, what a fine lady she had been. And in my distance from her current life, and in my distress, they knew I would accept it. And I did.

She was the master magician's dutiful stage assistant. Willingly sawed in half. Smiling from the confines of her box. From more than a thousand miles away, she was still his stage assistant. Why?

I had spent my adulthood without a father or a mother. And now, in days, I suddenly had both, and yet I was without either, as profoundly alone as ever. More alone with them than without them.

My mother, alive. My father, alive. Both rejecting me, and both believing in me and supporting me. What a strange and twisted family spin.

And when I had left from my emotional visit to my mother, my emotional reunion, did she call Wallace immediately? Tell him who had just been to see her? Warn him that I had been there, and knew of his elaborate lie to me? Reassure him that she had revealed nothing? That she was keeping the "pact," whatever it was composed of, whatever the agreement. In which case, he would know I knew, would clearly assume I was on the side of the kidnappers, seeking revenge, or would know at least that he couldn't trust me, wouldn't yet know how I felt, what stir and mix of emotions would have been unleashed in me by the discovery.

Or did she not say a word to Wallace after my surprise visit? Did she keep her mouth shut, seeing I still had no idea about who my father was, still ascribing fatherhood to the vague hero in the faded photo by the wing chair? (Did she always keep the photo there, just in case of my visit? Or was the photo to remind her of her pact? Of her commitment to deceit?)

Her weeping behind the bathroom door. Expertly faked to make the emotions of the visit even more convincing? Or a leaking out of authentic feeling, a sudden spill of regret, trying to hide it from me—hide her true emotions, hide the true story, to keep her pact with Wallace?

My mother, who went from victim to accomplice so instantly.

Who went from angel to corrupt succubus, she-devil of deception.

And here is Dominique—fucked by Wallace, to give him Amanda.

And here is my mother—fucked by Wallace, to give him me. I can imagine her trying to explain it to me: "We were just kids, Chas. I didn't know what to do. I had no money. And he did. He proposed this solution."

The simple, stunning parallel occurred to me:

Here, for years, I'd thought I was a father.

And it turned out that I was, instead, a son.

The son of a father I never suspected.

A father and a mother, both suddenly alive—and I couldn't decide which I was angrier at.

. . .

What am I doing in this car? I might be here only practically and legally: to meet the needs and terms for executing the funds transfer at this next bank, because I am still the guardian. Dominique taking me with her—is it intuitive, or planned? Out of authentic choice, or merely legal need? And what is my role after that? I don't know what Dominique has in mind yet. And things are happening fast.

And suddenly, more clearly.

"I'm taking her away," says Dominique. "I have the money. I have my daughter. I have the excuse I have waited for, for years. He will think the money went to the kidnappers, and to you, his disloyal, disgruntled employee, disgruntled enough to kidnap his daughter—the daughter you thought was your own—disgruntled enough to team with professionals, to out-scam a scam artist."

It's perfect for her, I realize. A perfect cover. A perfect getaway.

"He's never really cared about Amanda. He only cares how it looks, only cares about appearances. And I can't take the pain of watching from afar any more."

A pain I thoroughly understand.

"Why are you telling me?" I ask her. "Why are you revealing all this to me?"

"Because I know you won't derail it at this point. And I want you to know. You at least deserve to know. Because no one knows the feelings, the frustrations, the motivations, as well as you. You deserve at least that much."

It is an ingenious plan. With one major flaw. A flaw that, with her inexperience of actual motherhood, she seems to have overlooked.

What about Amanda? What about what she *wants?*

I glance in the mirror to the backseat. Amanda is pretending to look out the window, but I know she has been listening—listening closely—her eyes narrowed with focus and attention.

"Amanda is going with me. She has to. I'm her mother." As if Dominique could read my thoughts.

Yes, she is her mother. But this wasn't about Amanda's interests, and it should have been. It is clearly about Dominique.

And for some combination of reasons unclear to me at that moment—a surfacing resentment at being left out of the equation, a new (half) brotherly sense of protectiveness, or just some antagonistic impulse toward the neatness of her plan—I say aloud, so Amanda can hear: "She's going to try to escape you as soon as she can. She doesn't care about DNA or justice. She knows Shangri-la and her sister, Alison, and the father and mother who raised her. She has a life, and you are not part of it." Nor am I. "You can take the money. But you can't take Amanda. At some level, you must know that."

I think of Shangri-la. Its pink sandstone turrets. Her sheltered, protected, comfortable, and envied life there. *The house wins.* A truism of Vegas. *The house always wins.*

"I guess it's all a question of whether Amanda wants to continue living a lie," I say, "or to finally discover the truth, and to see, along with me, how that feels."

Dominique is silent.

Amanda, listening, is silent too.

We pull in quickly to the second bank—Western Loan and Trust—the transfer point of the funds, in another strip mall baking in the Nevada desert, maybe fifteen or twenty miles northwest of the First Desert branch, and I am still vague on exactly why I'm here. I sense it has to do with Dominique's sleek, slippery, hasty, and presumably untraceable movement of funds—but her purpose and my presence, beyond my "guardianship," become clearer as we turn into the bright, sun-drenched, largely empty lot.

"While I make this transfer, I can give you your cut. There's ten million total. What do you think your cut should be?"

Suddenly, I get it. Give me my money, my share, and we walk away from one another. We can each start over. Give me my money, so that she and Amanda can get away from me. Sever all ties. No attachment. No regret. No second thoughts. No guilt.

"I want to be fair," she says. "Name your figure. But you have about fifteen seconds. We can't be hanging around here. We have to keep moving. If you can't come up with a reasonable figure, I'll come up with it for you."

For me, it has nothing to do with the money. And Dominique knows it. And that's what makes this so insulting, so painful.

"I'm assuming your original deal was five million. That's what the Stewartsons would have offered you, fifty-fifty, knowing they'd never share a dime of it with you. They could afford to be fair, since it was only in the abstract. Whereas I am going in there to get you actual money. To transfer to you, in seconds, no shenanigans, straight up. Name your price."

What would you say? One million—10 percent, like a commission, a finder's fee? Two million? It's all fair, because none of it's fair, because it's not what I want.

What I want is in the backseat. And has nothing to do with money. Love, affection, connection, family. Precisely the things that money can't buy.

She looks at me impatiently. I remain silent.

She gets out of the car. "Then I'll decide," she says irritably, frustrated, barely audibly, under her breath.

She opens Amanda's door, and opens mine. It looks as if indeed we are needed again for paperwork. This slick and slippery and fluent transfer of funds still requires Amanda. And me, apparently. Or else she just wants to keep an eye on us. Doesn't want me grabbing Amanda and making off with her. Disappearing cleverly into the little strip mall, or sprinting desperately out into the surrounding desert. Amanda and I follow her in from the hot sun into the cool lobby, air-conditioning whirring with white noise—an insolent, mocking whisper.

We sit down in a small office with another bank officer, this one an overweight, slow-moving woman with a sweet smile. "We have the paperwork all set for you, Ms. Nuland." (*New land.* Terra incognito. Good one, Dominique.) "Thanks for calling ahead to arrange this, makes it so much easier, for you and for us. You just begin with these signatures here."

And watching Dominique and the bank officer hunch over the paperwork, I am not even vaguely aware of any other presence, until I see shadows crossing the desk . . .

Sandi leans toward me. Wiggles her pinky finger at me. Says nothing.

So she did see it.

The tip-off.

The tip of the iceberg.

Dave is leaning in now too, on the other side of me, whispering in my ear: "We checked the transfer. The money cleared. So your loyalty to Amanda, Chas, your fingertip, your self-sacrifice—we thought it wouldn't matter. But just to be sure, we doubled around after exiting First Desert. Saw you get in the car with the 'trust officer.' And the *way* you got in, Chas. Clearly you knew her. A prior acquaintanceship, a relationship of some sort. Meaning, you were possibly *in* on it with her somehow. So we followed you. Thinking maybe it was just your chance for a fresh start. With your daughter, or kid sister, or whatever the hell she is to you. A partial DNA match, after all."

So they accessed the same lab results that Dominique did. Probably an easy hack for them.

"Your excuse, your opportunity, to take Amanda. So go ahead, we figured. Let the authorities come after *you*. But when we saw you pulling into *this* bank branch, then we knew. Nothing so purely idealistic. Cash. Wired funds. A trick that was one trick ahead of us."

Tailing us. Old-fashioned detective work. The other kind. The simple kind. As I said: sometimes simpler is better.

Stewartson stands up from his whispering to me.

Amanda, Dominique, the plump bank officer, looking on.

Waiting for the result of all the whispering.

No one knowing exactly what would happen now.

The bank officer's voice quavers, as she stares up at Stewartson, hovering over her. "Maybe I shouldn't finalize that transfer," she offers, preemptively cooperative, as in, *Please spare me.*

"Maybe not," Stewartson says.

NINETEEN

"Now this is a cozy little grouping, isn't it?" The Stewartsons are looking at us, and at their handiwork. They've secured my wrists to Dominique's with plastic police ties, faced us away from each other, our four wrists bound together behind us. They've shoved us down into a kneeling position. Amanda crouches next to us, untouched, but confused, bewildered—terrified of the Stewartsons and their brutality, but unsure what to do, who to turn to, who to trust, what her connection is to her new mother and new half brother on their knees a couple of hundred yards into the off-road scrub and empty desert. Once Dominique and I were on our knees, I saw Amanda take a tentative step toward Sandi—and saw Sandi push her away. "I'm glad we could organize this family reunion. We should charge a little family-counseling fee. A finder's fee for bringing you together. Ten million or so? But oh, I guess you don't have it." He is slipping the extra police ties into his pockets, double-checking to see that he has all three of our cell phones. "I guess you can't get at it right now, because of your financial mismanagement. Because you were a little too smart, and moved the money too far ahead of you. And when Wallace's consigliere here"—gesturing to

Dominique—"doesn't show up with his daughter, Wallace will have the Vegas police out in force to retrieve you."

It was nearly a lawyer's summation from Dave Stewartson. And I had to hand it to him, that was the sum of it.

"One option is to leave you out here in the desert, to give ourselves a little head start. That's what you're thinking we'll do. And you're right."

He doesn't verbalize other, darker options. He doesn't have to.

The midday sun beats down on us. The Stewartsons turn to head back to their idling Nissan. But Dave turns back. Has something more to say. He looks at me. Shakes his big square head. I look again at his oddly chiseled features, their off-kilter angles. "Thing is, Chas, it was never about the money."

And I already feel the sense, the force, the logic of what is coming before he even says it. I already feel how it is going to fit together, before I even hear it. Because originally, they had wanted to *expose* Wallace. To bring him down. So isn't the financial motive really only secondary? To give a little meat and meaning to the exposure? It had only become more important, come to think of it—the right sum, the right deal between us—*after* I suggested the kidnapping.

"The money was just a consolation we were letting you sell us, because we figured we could get close to Wallace that way. We figured the kidnapping would draw him close, put us eye to eye with him. And we assumed you were the only behind-the-scenes operative, Chas"—looking at Dominique—"never thought there'd be two."

They hadn't imagined or conceived it, any more than I had.

"It was simple all along. We wanted to get him, have him, alone."

To kill him? No—you could assassinate him anywhere. Pros like the Stewartsons could engineer it easily. To get him alone—so they could whisk him away? Without anyone knowing? That would be the reason, the need, to get him alone. So no one else would know. To take him away. To where? To whom? To face retribution? To face justice?

"Who *are* you?" I ask them.

They stare silently. Debating how much to say. Dave shrugs. "Contractors."

And of course, when I thought about it, they had always worked for someone else. They were the type. Like Dominique. Like me. Were we all so alike after all? And yet here—pissed off, offended, frustrated by something in their shadowy careers—I figured they were striking off on their own. Like me in my rage, when I found out the truth about Wallace. Like Dominique, with this plan of hers. Were Dave and Sandi Stewartson disgruntled employees from some previous venture I knew nothing about? Part of that past I had helped erase and couldn't find much of to begin with? Part of those long-ago events in South America, as I'd imagined? Jesus, were we all really on the same mission after all? Nursing a grudge, discovering the depth of his falseness, all working for Wallace's downfall and yet at cross-purposes, tripping each other up?

"Contractors. Who do you work for?"

Dave shakes his head. "Can't tell you that."

And as I thought about it—thought about *their* past, their skill set, their style, who they really were, how this had all begun, it didn't take much insight to imagine who their employer had been.

A huge employer. Huge enough to have the Stewartsons invisibly on their payroll.

The hugest.

• • •

And suddenly the world expands, far beyond a Vegas act and my silent profession and clean little condo and routinized existence, beyond its interruption by the Stewartsons and a seamy, twisty little case of kidnapping and extortion; it expands suddenly into an enormous realm I know nothing about—never even think about beyond a glancing headline or one-minute story on the evening news. An amorphous ocean of geopolitics, national security, national interests, threats and counterthreats, secret operations. A realm where a detective's dogged efforts hit a brick wall—or perhaps a razor-wire fence. A realm where there will be no answers, only multiplication of questions. I feel it.

Because their employer, I suddenly realize, was the US government.

Whose case against Wallace fell apart? After they had invested so many years, so much energy? No matter. They were going to get him. And if they had to leave the justice system to achieve justice, they would.

They had *faith* that they would.

And I realize that this was not just a case of identity theft. Wallace had done something bigger. Something more elaborate. Somewhere in the past. Somewhere in South America.

Something more elaborate than what he had done to me? Some deal more sinister and draconian than the one he had struck with my mother? But he had proved to me, over these past few days, that he had the skills, the cold calculation, the will, the discipline, to pull that off. I began to feel the detective's dread of stumbling onto something deeper, of being pulled, lured from the edge into the swirling water . . .

Stewartson looks at me, reads my mind perfectly, confirms. "Yes, Chas. Bigger than what was done to you," he says darkly. "Makes yours look tame."

And once they had discovered it, stumbled into it, now they were doing what the federal government always did, using a time-tested tactic that usually worked for prosecutors, DA's, the criminal justice system:

Attempting to convict on a lesser charge. Fraud. Identity theft. To get him into the criminal justice system, where they can engineer the outcome, apply the justice, that they *really* want.

So "Dave and Sandi Stewartson"—even in their previous incarnation as Stewart Davidson and Sheila Barton—are not who they had seem to be, any more than Wallace is. Even their "identity"—my sense of the unrepentant thieves and seedy opportunists behind their fake names—has morphed again into a new identity: They are zealots, patriots, idealists, vigilantes. Uncompromising. True believers. The faithful. Even when America, perhaps, abandoned them in their effort.

And they had worked tirelessly, behind the scenes, unknown, thanklessly, for a paycheck and little else. Unacknowledged. In the shadows.

Gee—who does that remind you of?

How could I not have seen it? How could I not have seen myself reflected in that mirror?

But mirrors had been misleading me.

As if Stewartson could further read my mind, could know how far I could get on my own, and what he would have to fill in to get me the rest of the way:

"The case fell apart," he says, as if we have just been discussing it. "So sensitive, so potentially explosive, the federal government didn't want it discussed in open court . . ." He looks at me, the anger still alive in him. "He was working with someone. Someone he was very close to, whom we knew he would trust. But someone he ultimately had something on. Some point of leverage and control over this key witness of ours, who suddenly refused to testify . . ."

And suddenly the abstractly geopolitical goes personal. Comes back from the amorphous world stage to an inadvertent detective tied up in desert scrub at the side of a Vegas highway. Because I had a hunch who that someone was. And a sense that the balance of control and power had gotten cemented with a child.

A hunch that I was born not in a nameless and unnotable American town, but in South America, in the middle of this case—maybe the deus ex machina—the very reason for it.

Pulled from the curtains, to center stage.

"We started as federal agents. The highest ideals. And have ended up as criminals, kidnappers, *failed* kidnappers, who now need to go on the run." He shakes his head. "He's done it again, Wallace. He's pulled it off." He straightens, brushes the dust of his trousers, squints out at the desert and at his rented Nissan waiting for him at the side of the highway. "But that's how important it was. How important to at least try."

With Dominique and Amanda now so long overdue (and probably assuming that I have taken them somewhere), Wallace has likely called the Las Vegas police, who are undoubtedly on their way. Or he has somehow realized what Dominique is truly up to. Or else the timorous, overweight Western Loan and Trust branch officer, seeing the Stewartsons forcefully hustle us out of the branch, has stopped cowering and notified the authorities.

Whatever the reason, we can hear the sirens. Several now. Baying into the desert with high-pitched excitement.

It will be just us here with Amanda. The Stewartsons will be gone. Our wrists will still be tied. I can't imagine what the police will make of the picture.

But then the picture changes.

For the worse.

Amanda stands up.

Amanda takes off.

Turns on her heels, and heads out across the desert into the midday sun.

First walks, then breaks into a trot, then breaks into a run, as if afraid, expecting, that one of us—that any of us—will follow.

But no one does, of course. Dominique and I are tied together. We could never catch her.

And the Stewartsons simply watch her go.

The ten million has been delivered, after all. Who gets it, what the allocation is, where the money is exactly, that is all up in the air now. Dominique has stopped the Stewartsons from getting it. The Stewartsons have now stopped Dominique from getting it. But the ransom has been delivered, so Amanda is free to go. No longer a hostage. Released.

She has no further value to the Stewartsons. They just admitted they were never concerned with the money anyway—and even less with her. And now they are more preoccupied with the approaching sirens.

Dominique and I watch powerlessly as she goes.

Her biological mother. Her protective half brother.

"Amanda! Amanda!" I call out to her. Does she even hear me over the approaching sirens, over the wash of highway noise? Or is she ignoring me? Refusing to look behind her. Refusing to see, to deal with, any more of it.

Look what she's just learned about her past. Look what she's overheard about her father. Look what she's at the center of. *I'm your mother, Amanda. Your mother, and your rescuer, but now I am intercepting the ransom money and you have to come with me. I'm your half brother, Amanda. Your half brother, and your kidnapper.* She doesn't know what to think, doesn't know who to trust anymore, needs the room to think it through, to figure it out. A fifteen-year-old whose world has turned upside down. Who can blame the impulse for escape?

Come back here, Amanda. Right now, young lady. For your own protection. For your own good. You'll be in danger out there. But we don't say it. Because we recognize the absurdity. The danger is *us*. She is heading to safety. Away from us all.

And I, at least, have seen how determined she is. How smart. How strong-willed. And I know that words, argument, persuasion, will never work on her. And we are unable and unwilling to physically, forcibly, hold her anyway. That would only add a wrong to the wrongs we have already amassed.

She hears the sirens as well as we do. She knows this would be her rescue. That the police would save her from all of us, return her to Wallace and Sasha, her mother and father. So heading off into the desert is to escape that rescue, that safety, that return. Why? What is she thinking? Something about me? About Dominique? What has gotten under her fifteen-year-old skin, that she wants to avoid the reunion, be somewhere, anywhere, else? Maybe the impulses of any fifteen-year-old, writ large, amplified by circumstance, made suddenly and necessarily actionable.

Amanda heads off into the desert. A shrinking figure, soon a black dot, disappearing against the endless scrub and distant peaks. I cut off my fingertip for her, and now—just as cleanly, almost as physically—she has cut herself off from me.

The sirens draw closer, their tones broadening, deepening, as if sniffing prey.

Sandi and Dave Stewartson check our plastic ties once more. Then hustle to their rented Nissan and pull away, smooth, unobtrusive, onto the untrafficked boulevard. Disappearing sleekly. Pros.

Our hands tied. Our fates tied. Bound like this, we'd never get very far. We are stuck here, to be found by the Las Vegas police, here at the edge of the desert, only a mile or so from the bank branch.

We will look, at first, of course, like victims. We *are* victims. But when the police interview the bank clerks, the bank officers, the story will get more complex. And probably they already have descriptions from Wallace the Amazing. And no matter what, we will be held. If there is no Amanda, we will undoubtedly be held.

Bound to each other. And not able to see each other. The metaphor is all I think of, as three squad cars pull up.

TWENTY

The Las Vegas police holding cells are clean, modern, germ-free, and suspect-free, for that matter, except for Dominique and me, in adjacent cells, our plastic ties now cut. The cells are painted in cheerful tones, obviously the conclusion of a report from expensive industrial psychology consultants.

We wait silently, in a silence so total it is perhaps disconcerting to the two guards observing us. But our work has always been done in silence. Nothing feels more natural to us—even in cells next to each other. We have always been in adjacent cells, after all. We know, without discussing it, who we are waiting for.

In the afternoon, he arrives. Strides off the TV screen and into the holding cell area with the same forthright gait, the same self-contained aura of disconnection and indifference. Daddy—coming to get the misbehaving children. To rescue us? Or to teach us a lesson? Daddies do both.

He stops outside the holding cells, stares first at Dominique.

The accompanying detectives observe, can report, only the continuing silence.

He shifts his focus to stare at me. Equal time.

His daughter's captors. His mutinous employees.

It is the third time I have seen him face-to-face. The third and, I sense, last time. It has been twenty years since we looked at each other across the coffee shop table on the morning he hired me. There was also, of course, that frantic predawn moment when I freed him from the clutches of Big Eddie a few years ago, but that was rushed and desperate and in the dark, and did not even include a good look for either of us.

Both times were before I knew he was my father.

There are no lines around his eyes. He is as lean as ever. Anodyne. Artificial. His body, his physical presence, seems to have made little concession to time or reality.

"Do you know these people?" the detective asks him.

"No," he says. Our nonexistence, our orphan status, our aloneness, confirmed. By the one person who could resurrect us. Who could bring us into the land of the living. *No.* With that one syllable, consigned once more to our strange, faceless existence.

And really, how could he say yes? How could I expect it? Because that would mean investigating the connection, the link between us, and finding absolutely none at first, none at all, and that would only stir more interest, deeper digging, until the truth is revealed. He must think, somewhere in him, that if he refuses to recognize us—says he doesn't know us—that the show can go on. The consummate showman, or the consummate fool. The consummate illusionist . . . or delusionist.

"They haven't found Amanda yet," Wallace informs us, assuming (correctly) that it's the first information that either of us would want—and making it appear to all observers that it's what preoccupies him most. "No trace of her. Do you two have any idea where she is?" Asked with the naïveté and forthrightness of a desperate dad—imploring the criminals directly.

"She took off across the desert." I know he knows that already, of course, but I say it so that he hears it from me, from an eyewitness. And in truth, to hear myself say something live, actual, to him.

"You think she's going to turn up?" he asks us—generally, not directed at either of us specifically. It is almost merely rumination.

Dominique shrugs. I am silent. He looks at us.

His unspoken question: *What did you tell her? How much?*

And our unspoken answer: *Enough. Enough that she took off across a desert. Enough that she wanted to disappear.*

If he were to say to the guards, "I'd like to speak to these two privately," well, that would risk revealing a previous relationship among us all, which the Vegas police would feel compelled to explore further, and they might stumble into the whole truth of our cozy connection.

But he surprises his police and guard entourage, if not us, with his next statement.

"I don't want to press charges." Wallace looks at us. Altruistic, superhuman, always surprising. "However these two were involved or not"—a dismissive flutter of hand like a magic wand—"I forgive them."

"But your daughter hasn't been located," blusters the detective standing next to Wallace—KITEGAWA, his nametag says, presumably here in special deference to Wallace—and he is on the verge of outright anger. "Your daughter is still missing."

"Yes. But these two didn't take her."

The detective: "How do you know that?"

Wallace turns to the lead guard, smiles thinly, sardonically, tilts his head a little. *Are you kidding? How do you think I know? Because I am Wallace the Amazing. And I know.*

The detective appears sheepish. Looks uncomfortable. But then stands taller. "Well, look, sir, it doesn't really matter if you want to drop charges. The state will press charges in any case."

"Oh, they will?" And I can hear in his tempered response, a challenge. *We'll see about that.*

And for once, Wallace the Amazing is not the mind reader. I am. I can read his mind:

He can't do the show without us. He needs us. At least one of us. His redundancy system, his backup plan (in case one of us gets sick and dies, or is in a crash, or has a stroke) is now side by side in a Las Vegas holding cell. Unless there is a third, or a fourth data specialist. But if there were, Wallace wouldn't be here at all. He wouldn't need to be. He wouldn't be taking the risk of being seen with us. He needs us.

And without our jobs, jailed here—nonexistent, off-the-grid black holes for the LV police to begin to explore, unless he steps in and claims us—we need him. To get us out, his clout the only way—we need him.

So it's symbiotic. As symbiotic as ever. Which makes any assessment or judgment about love and true feeling a mere side consideration. Need is first. As simple as it is transactional. As defiant of any deeper subtext. He needs us. We need him.

The detective looks at us. "Anything to say for yourselves? In your own defense? To explain yourselves?"

Yes. I'm her half brother. This is her mother. But that startling revelation wouldn't change anything. Oh, it would create a little stir. It would be interesting. It would provide context and explanation. But we still kidnapped her. We still demanded ransom. We still stole her away from her life. Remaining undiscovered. Unknown. Ciphers inputting the data to the Amazing machine.

So we remain silent. Our customary silence, easy to maintain, and the detective, taking us for hardened professionals (yes, but of a certain kind), mildly disappointed but unsurprised, turns away.

But not before asking me: "What happened to your finger?"

The missing fingertip.

Proof forever that I am a kidnapper.

An extremely masochistic kidnapper.

A misinformed kidnapper.

An incompetent kidnapper.

But a kidnapper just the same.

TWENTY-ONE

Eventually, everyone comes to Vegas.

Everyone wants to see it at least once. Feel it once. Experience it once. Its institutionalized happiness. A city just for the fun of it. For the thrill of it. For the hell of it. See if it's really different. But most of all, see if it makes them *feel* any different. If it takes them outside their own personalities, their familiar selves, if only a little bit, if only for a little while. That's the secret of Vegas. Its unspoken, misunderstood appeal. Not to escape your own *life* for a little while, or for a little longer, or forever. No—it's to escape your own *self*— for a little while, for a little longer, maybe forever.

That's the secret of the Vegas vacation. Vacating your usual perceptions. Vacating your habits. Your previous point of view. For a little while, vacating your self.

And like twenty thousand people who stream in every day from across the country, a woman shows up among them. She is dressed plainly—print dress, flats, hair up, sunglasses up on her head, ready for the sunshine. Tall, thin, wrinkles on her neck and around her eyes, but former beauty still in evidence. Oversize purse. Roller bag. Moving with the crowd through the airport. Taking the bus into town. Dropping her bag at her hotel. But then, not walking along the strip, looking up at the hotels, watching the fountains, like the thousands of others who arrived with her. No, instead, hopping into a cab, and giving the driver directions he's rarely heard an out-of-town tourist ask for, if ever, in all his years here. A downtown address. The Las Vegas police station.

"Welcome to Vegas," I say to my mother, as she stares at me, silently, through the bars. "Everyone should see it once."

And while there are bars between us, that's the least of our prisons, and we both know it. The setting is as metaphoric as it is real, and that is what renders it surreal.

For a week now, I have imagined flying back there one more time, confronting her, asking—but not asking, of course, demanding to know—what was it exactly between her and Wallace the Amazing, why had she done this, what are the details of this deal with the devil? And if she understood what she was doing, if she understood the damage she had done, how could she do this to her child?

But of course, she didn't know. Or didn't know at the time. At the time she thought it was the right thing. Security for her son, a place, a career, a way to guarantee that he would not be merely an afterthought, an annoying byproduct, of the man she'd had a liaison with. A way to engage the man, make the boy a part of the man's life. But the man of course had concocted a way to make the boy a part of his life *and* keep him *away* from his life. To put him—me—into a permanent half-life. A ghost life.

She is silent. But the silence feels entirely familiar. Because there has always been silence. We are separated, but that feels familiar too, because we have always been separated. It is a prison, but that also feels familiar, because we have always been imprisoned—by the agreement, by the "arrangement," the floating, unwritten, unsigned document, the human codicil between her and Wallace, delivered and agreed to amid circumstances still opaque to me.

"That locked trunk that we fought over when I left for college," I say to her quietly. "It's empty, isn't it? A big argument over the contents, that big padlock on it for all my years growing up, and it's always been empty." Nothing in there. Nothing but whatever I chose to imagine, to create a father out of the one who died in an accident. Nothing but a further note of Wallace the Amazing's psychological mastery.

Her silent downward glance confirms the trunk's emptiness. An emptiness real and metaphoric. *What were you thinking?* I want to scream. But I know what she was thinking. And she knows I know.

"Say the word, and I will bring him down," she says to me now, looking up, eyes narrowed, her prey vivid in her mind. "I can do it. DNA shows that he is your father, that I am your mother, and I will tell the world how he abandoned us. Another celebrity with a buried past. By itself, it's nothing of course. *People* magazine stuff. But this celebrity has baggage he can't shrug off and discard. A past the world won't be able to brush off and ignore. His whole identity, swiped wholesale from someone else. A complete fake, onstage and off. A young woman, seduced and abandoned as almost a child herself. Say the word, Charles, and I can bring him down for you."

I look at her. I *don't* say the word. I shrug—unsure, undecided, defeated. I have the sense she knows I won't "say the word." That whatever my rage, resentment, fantasies of revenge, sense of justice, she knows it isn't in my personality to say the word.

And then her posture of action, of force, of "say the word," melts away in front of me; her eyes are suddenly soaking, and tears roll silently, plentifully down her cheeks. I instantly remember her weeping from behind the bathroom door. Grief, regret, suppressed and subverted—hiding no more.

My mother's small, rounded shoulders heave. Her head hangs, her tears flow, a pained whimper, the burden of all the silent years sluicing through her body. I can't reach for her, the bars are between us, and it occurs to me that's exactly what permits her to cry. Experiencing it alone. Safely separated from my sympathy or recrimination. All the suppressed feeling triggered by my presence, but taking responsibility for it alone. *I made a mistake. I'm so sorry. I've ruined so much for us. I've hidden the truth for a lifetime. Two lifetimes—my own, and my only son's.* All the things that could be said, but don't have to be said, they are so obvious to us both.

And then—absently wiping her eyes, straightening her spine, drawing a breath—she alters the picture a little, in a way that my imaginings, my scenarios, had not factored in. A way that displaces the midwestern matron, the quiet, safe, exceedingly private, shy woman who raised me. She drops the last (I hope the last, I assume the last) in these two weeks' series of bombshells, which have pockmarked and torn up the road ahead of me to where its route, even its direction, is unrecognizable.

"I was with him in the jungle," she says. Looks at me, gauges my reaction, lets me absorb it for a moment, prepare myself a little for the unexpected, dense path down which she is heading, before she continues. Smiling. "You were conceived in a hammock. Born on the banks of the Amazon. The only white child for a thousand miles."

The demure midwestern widow. There is turning out to be much more to her. My sense of being ambushed, my resentment and anger at being kept in the dark, is tempered by my sense of discovery—my innate, professional, detective curiosity.

She pauses for a moment. Furrows her brow. Thinking, it seems, how to express the next thought. And when she does, I see it is, and she means it as, a summation of Wallace's life, his philosophy, and his appeal for a conventional, impressionable young girl.

"He followed no rules." She smiles wistfully. "Saw no boundaries."

In the abstract, it sounds ridiculously romantic. Overstated. Except of course, the evidence is overwhelming. The case was consistent over years, over decades, over an entire lifetime. *No rules. No boundaries.* So he made his own. *No rules. No boundaries.* It was succinct. It was *explanatory*.

Yet he had forced me to live by the strictest set of rules. A tight little box. Organized into a life of unvarying routine, predictability, strictly enforced by my occupation. My only escapes imaginary, temporary, not real.

"What's his real name?"

She smiles softly. "Robert."

She said it so sweetly, so quietly, so full of ineffable and long-suppressed connection and emotion, it made the moment all the more painful.

Real name: Edward Lambent Corder. The name from my pains-taking research, now blinking its warning pixels in my anxious imagination.

I had expected to hear "Edward," of course. My question had been intended only as confirmation—not to probe whether my mother was finally being truthful, or still respecting some pact, or hiding in some further weave of secrecy. But suddenly, all those questions were opened. And the element of testing her that was hidden in my question, was front and center in her unexpected answer. Was she lying? (Why now?) Or was my Internet research somehow wrong? (Planted there expressly for me?) Or—and this only occurred to me at the moment, from the tonality of her answer—*does she not know?*

In the next moment, the human trumped the analytic; mother-hood triumphed. Because she must have seen my face fall a little, must have seen the falter, the stutter in my expression, the moment of disappointment, the involuntary blink.

"Not Edward," she says with a knowing smile, clearly aware of what I'd been thinking, what I had found in my Internet searching. "Robert."

In that simple moment, proving herself in a way that required no more research from me. That let me finally shut off the computer.

And in that same moment I realize something fundamental about identity. Something simple and profound and undetective-like. *It doesn't matter what his name is. It only matters who HE is. Who he is to her. And to me.*

"Robert," I repeat. A little crumb, an edge, a tincture of actuality.

She waits a beat. Looks around at the holding cell behind me, as if aware of it for the first time. As if aware of the world for the first time.

"The connection was all the more surprising and profound for both of us, considering how the deck was stacked against us to begin with."

"Meaning?"

"I wasn't just an innocent midwestern girl. Though I was certainly supposed to appear exactly that way to him."

I feel my heart accelerate. My stomach feeling queasy.

"What do you mean?"

"I had been hired to become his girlfriend. Recruited by the US government." With irony, with bitterness, muted but not extinguished by the years. "Summoned by my country."

I am simply looking at her, while she continues, explaining . . .

"To be on the inside. Become his lover. Report back . . ."

"Report back to who?"

"To the two federal agents who hired me. A man and a woman."

No question which man and woman that might be. My heart beats a little faster, the detective's thrill at the puzzle pieces—intractable, impossible shapes—finally shifting toward one another. But there is a problem of course. A problem of time. My mother was young then . . . she's now sixty . . .

"Federal agents?"

"Very young, good looking, both of them. Newbies. Confident. Freshly recruited themselves to blend in as college kids traveling the Amazon, so not much older than me. Bent on getting their man." And even as she continues, I am getting an inkling. *Las Vegas. City of new beginnings.* I feel a first, mild itch of comprehension. *Online photos that don't match the databases.* The puzzle starts to take shape. Only more so. Only deeper. "But they made a serious mistake, didn't they," my mother says, "a serious miscalculation, when they convinced an impressionable, beautiful nineteen-year-old to go to bed with him. To appear as if she had fallen under his sway. The problem being, I *did* fall under his sway. He was . . . so . . ." And here she searches the cell, the bars, the ceiling, for the word, and can't find it, and settles with a shrug for an inadequate substitute. "So *everything*, I guess, to a nineteen-year-old girl. They feared him, those two agents. But the fear they felt, that was part of his allure for me. I became his girlfriend, all right, just as they hoped, and then so much more than that. His muse. His confidante. His companion. But it was *my* deceit at first, Charles. I deceived him . . . I was the first deceiver."

Perhaps the first deceiver. But not the last. Now I understood why Vegas for the Stewartsons. Why here. And by extension, why me. Vegas. Gambling, prostitution, entertainment . . . and plastic surgery. Radical treatments. The latest techniques. Whatever, however much, you want. Pushing the envelope. The clinics will do anything. Combining it with vitamins, pharmaceuticals, the latest unapproved unlicensed breakthroughs in extending youth and strength. Ground zero for the shadowy, quasi-scientific, anti-aging industry.

The strange animal vigor of the Stewartsons. That odd, pasted-on, eternal look of theirs. The strange, eerie, indefinable angularity I saw in their faces. Taut skin, bulging eyes. Their appearance struck me only as odd, vaguely disconcerting. Part and parcel of their sense of menace and threat.

I am so naive—so disconnected, so closed off in my online existence—it had never even occurred to me. And in fairness, I always saw them only glancingly at first—tracking them from far behind, ambushed by them in my condo at night and Debbie's apartment at night as well, shades always cautiously drawn, tied up in darkness after a disorienting blow to the head, light purposely low, and then dark motel rooms and hideout, also kept cautiously dark. Never a single full-on, well-lit view, as I thought about it, until the bank meetings. As our furtive existence had worked so well for hiding my own fingertip, it had worked for hiding the freshness of their identities.

It went back to the very beginning, didn't it? No wonder I'd been confused by the online photos of the original Dave and the fake Dave. No wonder my original research was so flawed, why the data was so contradictory, made no sense. Because "Dave" and "Sandi" *were* different. Different, even, from their own previous selves. Had new, different faces. Photo cross-referencing doesn't work, with new, different faces. That indefinable, floating *otherness* emanating from their hands, in their eyes. You idiot—it *was* an otherness.

And simply assuming that the shriveled-up ghost I rescued from the motel bathroom was the real Dave—*living* with him, nursing him back to health—until he turned out to be Archer Wallace. Showing me once more, proving again, how wrong I could be. How fallible, how vulnerable, are my own assumptions and perceptions.

Being so certain that Amanda was my daughter. The obvious inheritance of my features, my aptitudes, even my gait. All calling out so loudly to the world. Yet Amanda is not my daughter—misconstruing that one too.

Shame, incompetence, frustration, humiliation, swirl around me, grim themes rising up thickly, threatening to smother me. I'd been locked in a room at a computer screen for twenty years. Yes, ironically, doing detective work. But not a real detective. No experience in real life, a lack of human interaction, a lack of common sense, no feel for people or the rhythm of the street or life as it's actually lived. In fact, the very opposite of a detective. Sheltered, cut off, isolated, and therefore, probably, the least qualified detective in the world. A detective who never detected anything amiss in the myth of his father, the absence of his mother, or in the odd features of his shadowy antagonistic partners.

The strength I felt in Dave Stewartson's grip. The athleticism in Sandi Stewartson pinning me down. The obsessive physicality, the relentless training that was no doubt a subculture, if not a mandate, of federal operatives like them. (And certainly their law enforcement network had helped direct them, back channel, to the sharpest shadowy "doctors" and "trainers.") A youth and fitness obsession that would let them continue their other obsession:

Pursuing the Amazing Wallace. Across America, across careers and occupations, across time itself. Were they trying to redeem themselves? They had screwed it up the first time, hiring an impressionable young girl as their insider—never predicting how hard, how fully, she would fall for him. Was this the crazy reach of their obsession? Trying to reorient, upend, time itself? No wonder they had been so brazen and confident standing up in the audience at that night's performance. Because they looked, they felt, completely, safely new.

The plastic surgery, the workouts, the gym—they had actually tried to cross time in pursuit of their man. My God—*that* was sticking to the case, *that* was dedication. They had false identities, but they were real detectives. I was merely a pale, ghostly, imitation.

And time was, in a sense, collapsing around me as well, becoming newly fluid . . . an unwanted jungle birth revealed for the first time . . . twenty years in front of a computer screen reduced to a blink of stunned rage . . . a plane trip into the fracturing past . . . and the Stewartsons' surgeries now amplifying that collapse . . .

Ceasing to exist—quite a trick, Dave and Sandi. Erasing your former life, creating an alternate identity, right down to faces and muscles and rejuvenated vitality. I felt, in my years of behind-the-scenes dutiful silence and shadow, that *I* had ceased to exist. But I was apparently a rank amateur. The Stewartsons, once again, were the pros.

Oddly, obliquely, the Stewartsons had a lesson for me here: When it comes to ceasing to exist, the only way to fully accomplish the job, is to forge a new existence. Wasn't that now the next step for me?

And inspired perhaps by the thoroughness of Dave and Sandi's deception, a startling question suddenly occurs to me:

"Did you ever tell Robert . . . about the agents? About who you really were? What you were really doing there?"

She pauses. Shakes her head. "I never said a word." She looks at me, eyes imploring. "But come on—what's a naive nineteen-year-old midwestern girl doing in the middle of the South American jungle? It's ridiculous. It's transparent. He must have known."

Yes, agreed. The idea of Wallace not knowing, being fooled, seemed so remote. "Maybe you weren't fooling him at all. Maybe his eyes were wide open. And if the deception failed, then there was no deception." And he fell for you, Mother, honestly, fully, naturally.

"Maybe," she concedes. But clearly doesn't believe it. Or at least, still doesn't know.

Like mother, like son.

A legacy of deceit.

The fact that I was actually *conceived* in deceit.

And went on to live a life confined by, defined by, deceit. Practiced a profession of deceit. It's too much to take in. So I push it away, retreat from it, by pressing on with my detective questions . . .

"Why did they recruit *you* for this? What were they afraid of with this guy?"

"What were they afraid of?" She smiles a little here. She has obviously thought about it. "Well, they weren't about to tell a nineteen-year-old girl what they were afraid of. They weren't about to entrust me with that . . ."

And here it is again—the brick wall, the bottomless pool, the sudden amorphous expansion, a lone detective against the shape-shifting and unknowable. The resolutely unsolvable—tantalizing and taunting forever. Reminding the naive, earnest detective of lesson one: the limits of detection. I could even imagine a scenario in which the government itself did not know. Had no full clear record of its investigation or intent. Had lost its original purpose in paperwork, in bureaucracy, as if intentionally, so there could never *be* an answer. It reverberated, didn't it, with the dark, always lurking, existential risk of all detective work: the unsolved murder, the cold case, the crime still in the files. The fruitless search for motive. The immense, teleological, itch-you-raw theme, of not knowing. Of never knowing.

"So all you have is my guess"—she shrugs—"and my guess is: everything. They were afraid of everything. A government's paranoia and suspicion. They didn't know what to be afraid of first. The cult of it. Mind control. He was on friendly terms with local rebel factions. Shared jungle with them. That's probably why the Feds first got involved. Plus there were drugs coming from that region, some unstudied, uncategorized hallucinogens grown in the jungle flora, then smuggled north. So, a cult, rebels, civil war, drugs. In the eyes of the state, a perfect storm, I guess. All personified, I suppose, in a powerful, charismatic young man outside his country. Outside its laws and institutions. Outside its norms. But what were the specific reasons for pursuing him? The official excuse or version? They wouldn't tell me. I'll never know. I only had my little job. Which I obviously blew."

The government. Drawn to the power. Both believing it and doubting it. Loving it and despising it. It occurred to me: just like a Vegas audience.

The government. Finding the magic riveting. Attention-getting. And wondering, I'll bet, *How can we use it? How can we profit from it?* Just like Big Eddie.

But the real point being, that was all only her guess. A guess from when she was nineteen. We'd never know for sure.

I look at her. On the one hand, a collaborator, recruited to deceive. And then practiced enough in deceit to deceive her son with a fake father. With a fake past. But then again, pushed into it to begin with. Only nineteen. Barely older than Amanda.

"But this isn't about Robert," I say—stumbling, choking a little on the name. On its unfamiliarity. "This is about you and me."

I am spending the first honest moments with my mother. We both know it. As we both know we are bound by a lie, an enormous, stupefying, silently kept, wildly successful lie. In which we are complicit. For my part, unwittingly until now, but still, implicated, a participant. The amazing lie of the Amazing Wallace.

I am feeling, not fully consciously but in my bones, the profound tie of mother and son. It is inescapable, a golden braid, a reassuring wrap that binds you tight perhaps in support but perhaps a noose, with strands—thousands of strands twisted together inextricably—that you cannot completely escape. It shapes you so profoundly you can't get perspective enough to see it, but as you grow, you catch glimpses of the connection, of its shape and form that have shaped and formed you so thoroughly. The little perspective you *can* get, is only in realizing it, only comes from experiencing the tie more profoundly.

"When were you going to tell me this? Any of this?"

"I wasn't going to. Ever. But to pile deceit on deceit after your visit . . . when you were so clearly pained, and hurting, and confused." Her eyes moisten again, with fresh tears. I picture her once more, crying quietly behind the bathroom door on my unexpected trip home, trying to hide the truth from me.

She shakes her head. She couldn't bear it. She came to Vegas.

The moist denseness of the Amazonian jungle versus the aridity of the Las Vegas desert. Climatological opposites that stir up, inspire metaphor. The thickness, the intrigue, the teeming life, the rampant biology, versus the simplicity, the sterility, the bright cloudless predictability. Lushness, sap dripping, flora and fauna variegate and profligate and intermingled and indiscriminate, an essence and aroma of fecundity, growth, reproduction, birth, beginnings. Compared with this spare, stark, sand and dust—a place teeming with nothing. With only the barest, sparest elements—sand, rock, wind, air, incidental struggling flora only a reminder of the spareness surrounding it; a reminder of the struggle. Was this a contrast, a natural opposition, that I was exaggerating in my own mind, to bring a theme to it? Certainly I was trying to bring meaning to their time in the Amazon together. Had he learned something there, some secret with which he could fertilize the desert? Was there something genuinely instructive, revealing, in these opposites?

I have a little flash of insight: they are the two extreme settings of religious experience. The jungle, where man confronts the primitive, the untamed. And the desert, where prophets seek, confront, reckon with God. Seeking nature, inhabiting Eden, looking for the heart and richness of life. Versus seeking God, reckoning with the eternal, with the meaning of life. Cults set themselves up in both. From the tribes of Abraham to those of Joseph Smith, the desert is a holy place. From ancient times, the birth and cradle of civilization. The jungle has hosted the rise of the species—and the desert has been its place of reckoning.

And another little observation: a corollary of my "religious" insight. Another embarrassing little commonality of mother and son: Her relationship with Wallace centered on worship. On idolatry. On being swept up. On believing. Just like her naive, foolish son's has. Like mother, like son—once again. We had both experienced, a generation apart, our own bit of religious conversion, being "born again" to a knowing almighty.

And wasn't it, in a way, another stage show? Like Wallace's Vegas act, like my mother's funeral, like my deposit of semen, another show? This show staged amateurishly by two hopeful, naive producers working for the government, and starring a young and even more naive midwestern girl. The stage show of my mother's love for my father. And just like Wallace's act, a scam.

And where exactly did the show go wrong? The plan for my mother to supply *information* (just like me, an information purveyor—once again, like mother like son, another unsuspected repetition, another echo). Information for a paranoid/nervous, dutiful/anxious government; information to protect their citizenry, information they collect and store but cannot sift or analyze; information for its own sake; information simply so that they have it.

I realize with a sinking feeling the precise moment it probably went wrong—with *me*. It went wrong at the moment my mother got pregnant. A simple, overly cooperative and dutiful midwestern girl, suddenly had connection, had meaning to her life. It was no longer an exercise. No longer a game. Her loyalty inevitably shifted at some level, from her shadowy employers to the charismatic father of her child. In effect, *I* was the reason that the Stewartsons had failed in their mission.

Irony? Inevitability? Circularity? Connection? Any and all of the above?

And the prospect of a child both tied them to each other and pulled them apart, drove a wedge between them. She could sense his fear that it would slow him down, hold him back, compromise his extraordinary, singular life. So did they make some kind of arrangement, reach some dark understanding?

An inauspicious beginning for any kid.

For this kid.

Abruptly my mother stands.

"Your bond's been paid." She smiles. "Your mother has come to the police station and bailed you out." Like it's a shoplifting charge or a speeding ticket or disorderly conduct or underage drinking in the park. "You're free to leave." Looking. "With me, or without me."

She had waited to tell me—left me behind bars long enough to tell me the story. Maybe she felt safer that way. Felt that I might leap for her and strangle her if there was no barrier between us. Or now maybe she is willing to remove the bars, and willing for me to strangle her, because she has at last told the story—her version of it, anyway—and at least now I know.

To put a true sense of release into my release.

She reiterates her offer. It has about it the gently warning tone of one last chance. "I can tell them everything—bring him down." She alone has the power to do it, I realize. But toward what end? What would it achieve now? Getting even . . . why? . . . for what? We have shared loss. And perhaps because of that, my fury has subsided.

The guards materialize as if on cue. Buttons are pushed. Locks are clicked. Steel shifts, adjusts audibly.

"You're free to go," says one of the guards.

Free to go? Oh, I wouldn't say that.

And though she has made the joke about a mother coming to bail out her son, I know, by the weight of the charges, that my release has little to do with my mother's sudden, near-magical materialization, and everything to do with Wallace's local influence. His contacts. His popularity. His persuasiveness. He has somehow managed to get any kidnapping charges dismissed. Perhaps by convincing the police that we must have been victims of the Stewartsons. That the e-mail and threats all came from them. That we—whoever we were—were merely being used. Perhaps he pointed the police to the Internet, where they found no criminal record from either of us—in fact little record at all—yet a long trail of criminal behavior and shifting identity and identity theft from these "Stewartsons." They were the real culprits and masterminds; we were clearly pawns. He must have convinced them of something along these lines, because as I walk past Dominique's holding cell—I've been so absorbed by my mother's presence, by her story, I haven't even thought about Dominique—I see her cell is already empty.

He needs us back at our posts—and he knows we will go there, that we have no choice, that this is the unspoken, implicit cell-block deal we have struck with him for our release. This is Las Vegas, and he is an entertainer. And periodically, in certain cultural places, at certain cultural times, entertainment trumps law. Entertainment trumps everything.

We are destined—Dominique and I—to continue sharing his life.

Sharing his world.

Sharing his magic.

Delivering it daily, nightly.

Sharing, as it turns out, his pain and loss as well.

Because Amanda is gone.

Disappeared, of her own volition. Sightings occasionally. A trail of her movement, enough to indicate that she is on her own, and that Dominique and I have nothing to do with, are no longer responsible for, her absence. But no communication. Nothing definitive. Elusive. Somewhere out there. Starting over.

A new name? A new identity? (That's all I can assume, since I could never find her with all my online intelligence.)

Reimagining herself. Remaking herself.

Just like her dad.

Was she somewhere, somehow, still in Vegas?

Or anywhere but?

That clever fifteen-year-old. Brave, self-possessed, quick witted. Whom I had grown in just days, in just hours, to love and admire.

An absence, a punishment, the three of us are fated to share. Her father, her half brother, her biological mother.

Amanda, gone.

I see her still, striding out across the desert away from me, just as her dad strode out across the desert away from Eddie's thugs. Yes. Same blood. Same DNA. Same step, same stride, nonchalant yet purposeful. An eerie behavioral echo. Like father, like daughter.

I stride too. Out of lockup. Out into the dry desert air, the breeze steady, low, a hum, as if dutifully sweeping away the recent past.

But it cannot so easily sweep away mine.

Because my mother is beside me—and I don't quite know what to do with her, as she doesn't quite know what to do with me. There is an anxious, tentative, ill-defined sensation hanging between us. Here in the desert—mythic land of whole civilizations' beginnings and endings, of fresh starts and inviolate finalities, is this a start for us, or an end? Is our destiny before us, or pushing us from behind?

Like mother, like son.

TWENTY-TWO

The lights drop low. The audience hushes. There is a pause of silence—eerie, anticipatory.

"Connection. It is all connection. More than we know. More than we understand. And as you all know from the news reports of the kidnappers' capture, I have been the beneficiary of those connections."

Going to his knees. Crouching as if in worship of a god, this man who is his own god, so it is more startling, more moving, more convincing, more compelling, than any tent show, this god-man going to his knees in recognition if not of God than of some higher force at least. And yet this god-fearing audience accepts it. Doesn't question it. Going to his knees in gratitude, prayerfully.

"You know from the news reports, my daughter's been found. You all had a role in bringing her back to me. My daughter is okay, thank God. I have my family back. We are back together, and we can go on. Thanks to all of you."

The audience erupts. Chaos. A happy bedlam. A rush of affection, of bonding, of love, chaotic and massive and inimitable, idealized and immense and unique and unprecedented and lofty and transformational.

A useful lie. Let the world think Amanda is recovering quietly, privately, at home. No visitors, please. A bit of magic so easy for a magician to manage. A bit of absence so simple for a lord of identities—present and absent—to master. Let the dream continue. Who's ever going to know?

I have circled Debbie's house for hours. No lights. No car. No sign. And I can tell without even looking in the windows, without ever letting myself in to see, that it is empty. She is gone. It was too much for her, too strange, too frightening, too confusing, too dark, too troubled, too wrong. So she has backed away. Has silently (yet loudly, the painful fact pounding and pulsing in my ears) disappeared. I was once the ghostly one, unknown, unknowable. Now she is the ghost. As if to turn the tables on me, show me how it feels. An uncanny echo of Amanda receding across the landscape, a repetition humming in my soul, she has "deserted" me. And I am clearly not invited to turn to my array of detective tricks to find her. And what would be the point? Her silence is deafening. Her message is clear.

The camera goes close on Wallace the Amazing, and I can see the considerable mist in his eyes. I have watched him for more than twenty years now, and I could not say if those tears were real or not. Probably he couldn't either. And anyway, what does "real tears" mean exactly? This is Vegas.

I deliver the next night's digital packet.

It's a family business.

TWENTY-THREE

The lights drop low. *The audience hushes. There is a pause of silence—eerie, anticipatory.*

I step onto the stage one more time, to conclude the magic act that you—faithful, or skeptical, but rapt audience member—have been so closely observing.

The Vegas act in which I have conjured up a secret assistant, and his past, and his story.

You feel a little dizzy? Well, that's a sign of good magic. An engaging show always makes heads spin a little.

And throughout I have called myself Wallace the Amazing because, as you remember (perhaps with this little bit of prompting), I hadn't yet decided—and still haven't—what readership, what audience, this account will have. Whether for public consumption, or a private, personal record, meant only for distant posterity. (Remember now? I'm sure you do. When I wrote, as if nonchalantly, *I don't know, let's call him Wallace the Amazing.* Weren't you a little suspicious right there? Didn't something seem a little off?)

And the unenviable, tormented Chas? Did he seem real to you? Did all this seem like exactly the document "he" promised? I hope so. I assume so.

But now the show is over, and it is time to pull the curtain closed. (Or open?) Time to head offstage. (Or onstage, for my final bow?)

Time to let you come forward in the emptying theater. To inspect the proscenium, glance into the wings, catch a glimpse "behind the scenes" before you too exit.

Time now, not just to read, but to *ponder* this entire document, left (unwisely, impulsively) in the possession of the Las Vegas police. (Meaning, of course, the entire document up to these words, up to but not including this last chapter that you're now reading, which has obviously come later.)

The manuscript dropped off, I'm told, by a bent-over, ghostly looking specimen, barely noticed, a mere shell of personhood, emaciated, hauntingly pale, but eyes alive, leaving it at the front desk, exiting without a word, never announcing himself, they said. But the desk sergeant remembers the wraith smiling wryly at the sign-in log and carefully signing it—mysteriously, defiantly, and I would argue insanely—with the name Archer Wallace.

I informed the police captain that I have dealt with these charlatans my whole life. How my purposely scant early biography (part of my persona, part of my act) seems to encourage a steady trickle of these daft souls—some of them con artists and operators, but some who seem to truly believe it of themselves—who periodically come forward, claiming to be me, angling for some part of my fortune and success. I've dealt with them all my professional years. This assortment of nuts that I've consolidated into one person, one personality, for the purposes of this account.

But this particular nut must have had access to my home, and access to my personal effects, to my "magic" (which, you presume, isn't really magic). Someone clearly intent on bringing it all down. This person, it would seem only logical to assume, if he was able to break into my home that night to take Amanda, was probably the same one who had broken in earlier (these nuts are persistent, fixated, monomaniacal) and had taken the manuscript—a manuscript that I was, as you can readily understand, too embarrassed to report stolen. And having read it, he (whoever he actually is) was clearly inspired to execute the deed in reality—to actually kidnap Amanda—turning my fantasy of father/daughter drama, my literary experiment in heightened horror, my speculative staging of an idea for my act, into reality. Using my telling as a template to actually kidnap her, in order to shake me down, just as my manuscript suggests—and then, even signing the police logbook as "Archer Wallace." A nice little annoying flourish. Touché.

Turning my own vivid imagination against me. Delivering to the police the evidence of my planning and my complicity. A perfect trap, he must have thought.

Alerted to the theft (which the police assumed had just occurred), I stopped into the police station to reclaim the manuscript. I'm fortunate to have so many friends on the Las Vegas police force that they would call me immediately. I have informed them—have had to admit, guiltily, sheepishly—that, yes, these pages are mine.

Embarrassing? Of course. I'm sure the police have read at least some of it. Though likely not much of it, categorizing it right away as private, personal, a magic act prop they do not fully understand, and a story related by an obviously fictional narrator. And in any case, they have not seen this final chapter that you are now reading, which was not yet attached, because it was not yet written—I hadn't yet gotten to it. But now, obviously—newly motivated to finish—now, finally, I have.

A confessional document? Yes, of a kind (we'll get to that shortly)—but here, in the last chapter, the magic is revealed. The story is transformed. Inspiring the oohs and aahs that a Vegas audience, that any audience, wants.

The first job of a magician is to know his audience, of course, and I know you very well: You feel I am trying to take away Chas's past. To erase him. Yet another theft of identity from Wallace the Amazing. That would be in my nature, you say. That might even be the deal I struck with Chas, yes? Erasing him once more, in order to give him his old job back.

But isn't that what you think simply because you have lived with the earnest, brooding, troubled, pitiable "Chas" for a couple of hundred pages? That's how magic works. Create a convincing universe, inhabit it, populate it, *command* it to come alive, make it indubitable. That's just the practice of magic. Just a signpost of mastery. And the surprise, the real magic, is that Chas never existed. Well, that's not fair—exists, yes, but only in the pages of this document, this elaborately detailed, but severely angled "explanation" of my act and life.

You feel I am trying to take him away, don't you? Delete him with one last trick? Make him disappear from the stage? Cast away his entire existence? But can an existence be so tenuous to begin with, that I can erase it within one document? Erase it by merely altering its final moments, its final breaths? Ask yourself: is an existence that fragile really an existence at all?

And be practical. Be skeptical. Does it seem at all realistic that I could find this perfectly qualified kid and then so elaborately arrange, with a funeral, with obituaries, with other tricks, his isolation from normal life, in order to serve me for over twenty years, for both of our working lifetimes?

Or isn't it far more likely that I have created him as a way to protect myself, by telling my own story under the cover of this poor, made-up, hard-working drone.

Admit it—hasn't the whole story strained credulity for you? Lying fathers, lying mothers, a concocted funeral, all the rest of it— but that's what makes audiences gasp. What makes you pay attention. I always push the edge of the envelope.

Doesn't it all feel suspiciously biblical? Progeny and off- spring, loyalty, disloyalty, half brothers and half sisters and tangled relationships, and at their center a dominant, domineering male figure, godlike. Omniscient, as it turns out. Set in the desert. All a story? All meant to bring down this false god?

But if biblical in themes, the opposite in scope. Just a strange, sordid, sorrowful little tale of heartland America. Unwanted teenage pregnancy. Dad shirking his fatherly duties to seek his fortune. Mom wanting to secure a better life for her out-of-wedlock child. They strike a deal. *I'll keep your son a secret, as long as you stand by him,* she says. How American—to strike a deal.

And now *you* must be the detective. You must say whether I have conjured this entirely. Made up this life, this career, recorded it safely from the angled point of view of a tormented employee, in order to *have it both ways*, and this is the important point—to tell my tale, reveal the secrets of Wallace the Amazing, and yet protect those secrets for a little while longer. In order, yes, to ultimately finish off this false prophet, this larger-than-reality personality, this Amazing Wallace—but only when the right time comes. Meaning, a time of *my* choosing. When *I* want. To amaze you one final time, and then escape, exit in a flutter of curtain and cape.

You must conclude your investigation. (You see? Staying with my manuscript's "detective" theme.) You must make the judgment.

It's a simple question, in the end. (Meaning, simple to pose. Not simple to answer.)

Have I created the detective?

Or has the detective—dutifully writing this himself—"created" me?

(Revealed me, "conjured" me, brought me fully and believably to life?)

Or, as you probably suspect, are both my "creations?" The unknown detective and the celebrated mentalist? Are we really one and the same? Two figures carrying forward the same story? Certainly it fits with the theme of identity, doesn't it? Its fluidity, its mutability, its unpredictability. Is the creation of "Chas" alongside me, a way I can safely reveal my own stage tricks and techniques—as well as my own loneliness and isolation, my own thoughts, my own actual past, that "Chas" has so diligently unearthed?

Or—even simpler—is this document just a way to tell the story of my son? The son who for practical and professional reasons I cannot be close to? Who I cannot spend even a moment with? Who I cannot risk revealing? Who I cannot speak to directly, who I can never hug or even touch? So telling his story like this is the best I can do. Is the only way to be close to him. The only way to show him that I know who he is, that I understand his suffering, that I thoroughly comprehend his life. That I have understood it, and shared in it, and absorbed it, more than he knows.

So is this document a way to record the truth, to create a record, that nevertheless admits nothing? That lets the show continue.

Until *I* say it stops. Not someone else. *My* decision. *Me.*

(And do you hear in my tone just now anger and arrogance? Or confidence and clarity, an unwavering sense of mission and self?)

And however much you may now feel upended or ambushed in your view of this account—however unmoored you now feel in comprehending what you've read—you can certainly understand (you've noticed throughout, I hope) how I inhabit this strange space, dance on this strange edge between the seen and the unseen. Between the worldly and comprehensible, and the otherworldly and inexplicable. It's not a place anyone else inhabits, so I must inhabit and negotiate it alone, and that is why I both hide and reveal myself here, in this document, continuing to balance on that edge, poised between the knowable and the unknowable. Between what is comprehensible in ordinary life, and what is not—which, after all, is part of ordinary life as well.

The clues were there for you, after all, right from the opening curtain (to which we now return, full circle, to create an artful, reverberating ending):

It's the strangest job you've ever heard of. Remember? My opening line? My compelling entrance?

Yes, the strangest job you've never heard of. *Because it doesn't exist.*

Because the act of revelation—of a long tortuous look behind the curtain—is only a further act of magic, to convince and persuade you.

And credit card purchase records, Internet research, old-fashioned detective work—that's how you *would* do such a nightly trick of telepathy. How anyone *could* do it. Anyone smart enough, skilled enough, careful enough. Logical explanation, for you who seem to insist on logic. Ye of little faith . . .

It's how you *would* do it . . .

If you were *not* a shaman.

If you did not have years of training, from jungle to desert.

If you were not a mind reader.

If you could not conjure worlds, shape perceptions, as I have shaped yours . . .

If you still clung to previous identities—like Edward, or Robert—identities that were merely intermediate, part of the tale, but are now irrelevant, small, conventional, meaningless way stations when only one identity has come to matter.

That of . . .

Wallace the Amazing

TWENTY-FOUR

That is the trick I'm offering to Wallace the Amazing.

That is the escape.

That is the compromise.

And I will convince the white-haired, withered, real Archer Wallace to drop off this document at the Las Vegas police station—which he will do gladly, eagerly, since it will expose and reveal Wallace the Amazing at last. Archer Wallace, who a landscaping crew heard screaming for help, finding him chained to a radiator in an unoccupied house whose yard they maintain.

He will be dropping it off, of course, without this final chapter.

And without the previous chapter.

Which I will deliver separately, at the same time, to Wallace the Amazing. The chapter you just read, the chapter that erases my existence, the one that imputes all powers to him, the one that proposes it is all merely one more ingeniously disguised, well-executed performance of his own.

I will deliver it to him, as I deliver him everything. Once more doing the work for him, behind the scenes, delivering the materials he needs to maintain the illusion, to "do the show."

Is it blackmail? Yes, since the document—except for that last chapter—will already be at the police station. Hopefully, he'll have little choice but to add that chapter to it, to go with my proposed version of events. And why not—that chapter will solve the "problem" of my confession. Will erase it. The police will easily believe that the document was stolen from his desk in Shangri-la. That it was one more "trick" he was working on.

(After all, didn't you? For a moment, anyway? Magic needs to be magical only for an instant. It's the opposite of a "trick"—it's the brief moment when you think it's *not* a trick. When you experience the impossible, the irrational, and momentarily believe it.)

The truth as blackmail. An odd concept, in a way—the truth as a lever of criminality. But a long, illustrious history, after all. *Do what I want, or I'll reveal the truth.* Since time immemorial, the truth has been unwelcome.

Simply blackmail? One final instance of blackmail in a story filled with it? The longest blackmail note in the world?

But I hope he doesn't see it as blackmail.

I hope he sees it for what it really is: A plea.

To let me go.

To release me.

To let me start my own life, out of the shadows.

To release me from my servitude, by erasing my existence the rest of the way, leaving his magic and his myth intact.

Will he let me? Will he do it?

Or is this effort too little, too late?

Is it too transparent? Too Vegas? Too much of a trick?

Will he do it for his son?

Knowing in his heart, I am certain, why I want it, why I need it:

To search for Amanda. My sister. His daughter.

And to find Debbie.

Debbie, who is outside all of this mess. Debbie, who represents the future. Who is my chance to go forward. To connect truly, authentically, to rejoin the wider world, and no longer be tied only to the weighty, twisted bonds of the past.

I'll find them. I'll find them both.

Because I am—because I can finally *be*—a detective.

Will he do it?

Will it work?

One more trick from him?

One last trick from me?

One last moment of our strange dance of antagonism and collaboration, of love and hate?

Will he accept this solution?

Will he let me go?

We shall see.

Yours truly,

Charles "Chas" Stanton

About the Author

Jonathan Stone writes his books on the commuter train between his home in Connecticut and his advertising job in midtown Manhattan, where he has honed his writing skills by creating smart and classic campaigns for high-level brands such as Mercedes-Benz, Microsoft, and Mitsubishi. Stone's first mystery-thriller series, the Julian Palmer books, won critical acclaim and was hailed as "stunning" and "risk-taking" in starred reviews by *Publishers Weekly*. He earned glowing praise for his novel *The Cold Truth* from the *New York Times*, who called it "bone-chilling." He is also the recipient of a Claymore Award for best unpublished crime novel and a graduate of Yale University, where he was a Scholar of the House in fiction writing. He is also the author of *The Teller, Moving Day, The Heat of Lies, Breakthrough,* and *Parting Shot.*